Melinda West:

MONSTER GUNSLINGER

"A full-throttle action-packed western-adventure with fantastical goodness poured throughout."
—B. L. Blankenship, author of *Josey Wales Rides Again*

"Join team Melinda! Melinda West: Monster Gunslinger is as woman and as western as it gets, no shame in being a lass with some smooth on a rifle. A bounty hunter too. Kicky horsie, boot crunchilicious, and with a soul stealer on the fantastical spectrum."
—Eugen Bacon, World Fantasy Finalist and award-winning author of *Danged Black Thing*, *Mage of Fools* and *Chasing Whispers*

"I relished every genre-blending minute of this story—strap in for a bumpy and exhilarating ride."
—Jerry Roth, author of *Throwing Shadows: A Dark Collection* and *Bottom Feeders*

"Haunting, chilling, and entertaining…The story felt like a natural blend of The Witcher, the cult classic video game Darkwatch, and a mind-bending Lovecraftian story. The twists and turns in the narrative and the powerful draw of the protagonist will have readers enthralled with this brand-new saga that introduces a hero worthy of the reader's attention."
—Anthony Avina, author of *Identity* and owner of Cosmic Writing Studios

Melinda West:

Monster Gunslinger

by
KC Grifant

Edited by MJ Pankey

Cover illustration and design by Luke Spooner
https://carrionhouse.com/

First Edition: February, 2023

ISBN (paperback): 978-1-957537-37-5
ISBN (Kindle ebook): 978-1-957537-36-8
Library of Congress Control Number: 2023931688

BRIGIDS GATE PRESS
Bucyrus, Kansas
www.brigidsgatepress.com

Printed in the United States of America

To my family, especially my parents, Vivian and Jason for believing in this book and encouraging me.

Part One:

West Ridge

CHAPTER ONE

Melinda never missed, not in her 29 years on this earth. But then again, she never dealt with giant, flying scorpions before.

She aimed at the two shapes above a cactus several hundred feet away, fired, and watched as one of the bodies dropped.

Aside from being bigger than any insect on this earth ought to be, the scorpions' six back legs were webbed, giving them the oh-so-handy ability to become airborne. A calf-sized one flew through the air with its green-tipped tail poised directly toward her head.

She slid behind a toppled boulder, dust whipping up and stinging her eyes, as the scorpion soared past, pincers outstretched. Its back legs brushed the tip of her wide-brimmed hat, caught a draft, and swept back toward her like a giant leaf in the wind.

Four sets of white eyes alongside its orange head fixed on Melinda as it came back around. She sucked in a breath and fired her pistol again, praying the wind wouldn't shift.

The bullet tore through the insect's shell, ripping open its soft insides. Its chitin shattered like it was made of fine china. Bright green goo splattered on the cacti and rocks around her.

"These bugs ain't joking," Lance huffed as he crouched next to Melinda, his brown hat askew. The grooves along his mouth deepened as he rooted in his knapsack for a weapon, the blondish stubble on his chin dark with dust. "Never seen this many air scorpions before in one place except in pictures. Looks like their guts'll sting something awful."

"Poisonous, no doubt. Aunt Beatrice would sure love a sample. Bullets?"

"Almost out." He hoisted his rifle.

"Bombs?" she asked.

"Just the one," Lance said as they both peered over the edge of the hill at the sharp drop leading to the mine. Hundreds of the orange and beige insects scuttled out of the mine entrance, agitated, it seemed, by Melinda and Lance's presence. The gash in the side of the hill was flanked by a steep rise in the earth around it, creating a bowl into which the scorpions poured.

One of the creatures lifted its webbed legs to catch a gust of wind blowing toward them. Before it could take flight, Lance's shot rang out, exploding the bug into green goo. The rest of the scorpions in the pile chittered and clanked their pincers. Though they'd seen plenty of odd creatures in their line of work, this sound was one Melinda was sure would haunt her dreams.

"Shouldn't have used them all up in Old Rivers." Melinda tucked an escaped dark strand of hair back into her hat as Lance passed her the tacky bomb, one of Abel's inventions.

"It did a pretty good number on those fire cattle though. Splattered their guts like fireworks. Want me to toss?"

"Who has better aim?"

Lance chuckled and handed her the air-pressured blaster, in the shape of a clunky gun. She set about the tedious process of loading it with the tacky bomb, a trap of hammered metal housing a custom explosive.

Hooves thundered behind them. The local sheriff who had summoned them, named Gatsum or Garry or something like that, Melinda couldn't remember which, scrambled off his horse. He stared aghast at the mine, his badge flashing like a beacon in the morning sun.

"What do we do?" the sheriff shouted, his eyes wide as his mustang's spots. He peered at the pit. "Lordy help us. We got to evacuate. We're ruined. I told that goddamned Carson not to blow a hole into this godforsaken land. Couldn't wait for his hermit of an uncle to die so he could start mining. Dammit, Carson."

"Easy, partner," Lance said. "We've dealt with bigger bads than this, believe it or not. Any bug can be squashed, and we're the ones to do it."

"What do they want?" The sheriff wiped his forehead before replacing his hat.

"Sometimes critters get it in their heads to look for greener pastures," Lance said. "So, they wander out from the Edge."

"We don't know much about that here," the sheriff sniffed. Melinda understood. Some folks didn't want to say the Edge out loud from superstition; they did the best they could to ignore the no-man's land of monsters nestled in the northern mountains. Even so, plenty of creatures swarmed out from the Edge, taking up residence in the pockets of hills or lakes, or wherever they could find food.

But never this far south.

"First time we've seen critters this big way out in the dustlands," Melinda said. "You got any idea why they ventured so far? Or how?"

"Something disturbed them, maybe," Lance mused.

"Don't matter none. We'll teach them," the sheriff huffed. He reached toward his saddle and yanked out a mallet nearly the size of the horse's leg.

"Mighty fine-looking hammer, but wouldn't do that," Lance said. "Their blood's got a sting."

The sheriff moaned. "They're coming out!"

Melinda turned her sights back on the pit of squirming scorpions, more of which poured out of the entrance. She breathed, the tiny muscles around her eyes relaxed. She fired the blaster, sending the tacky bomb soaring through the air. It stuck along the top of the wooden frame of the mining entrance.

Melinda pulled out her rifle and steadied, putting the explosive in her sights. The mix of Abel's unique concoction of compressed gunpowder cake and one of his experimental potions would make the tacky bomb consume everything—natural or unnatural—in its path. *So long, suckers. You picked the wrong place to nest.*

"Hurry," the sheriff said as a fresh wave of scorpions crawled out of the mining entrance. A few lifted themselves up as the wind picked up again. "What are you waiting for!"

"One thing," Melinda said. "Got our payment?"

"You gotta—they're about to swarm—"

"Let's see it," she said without moving.

"What in the lord's name is she waiting for?" the sheriff shouted. "I'll do it myself."

Lance spat out a small glob of tobacco. "Most people can't make that shot there. Surprised if I could."

"Your money's right here, goddammit." The sheriff pulled out the envelope wrapped in twine. Melinda waited until she heard Lance rip it open and the sound of his satisfied breath.

She took the shot.

The pit went up in a fireball, as lovely a one as she had ever seen, painting the early desert sky reds and oranges against the crystal-hard blue. The trio clapped their hands to their ears as the explosion shook the ground and the wooden frame around the cave entrance crashed down.

"Make all your clients sweat like this?" The sheriff demanded, taking out a handkerchief to wipe his forehead under his hat.

"We try not to take jobs without payment up front," Lance said, tucking the envelope inside his duster. "Keeps us from making any … business mistakes."

"Some folks'll try to stiff us after a job," she added.

The sheriff turned red, and she tried not to laugh, the adrenaline from the explosion still racing through her veins.

"Who's gonna clean this up?" The sheriff surveyed the shattered bugs and green gore that stretched out below them. A few bodies in the pile of guts twitched.

Lance scooped a tiny bit of scorpion blood from a severed pincer into a vial. The sheriff knelt to examine it.

"Don't touch it." Lance capped the vial. "In our experience, things like these can have a nasty bite, even after death."

Melinda set to wiping down the guns as Lance and the sheriff exchanged idle chatter. Lance liked to make friends wherever they went, and a moment later, the two men shared a flask.

While they talked, something caught Melinda's eye at the entrance of the mine among the bug guts and fluttering legs. A little flash, like a piece of gold. She grabbed a gunpowder stick and a handful of bullets from their bag.

"Be right back," she said and started to climb the few feet down to the pit.

Lance glanced over. "See something?"

"Maybe nothing."

Lance resumed his talk with the sheriff, but Melinda knew he'd have one ear and eye on her should anything arise. That was what made them good at what they did, and good together: they never let their guard down and always had each other's backs. It was why Abel loaned them his one-of-a-kind devices and trusted them to bring back samples to study.

She unhooked one of those custom devices now, a magnetic heat tracker infused with the blood of a rare goldheart homing bird. Magnets, clustered in tiny blobs on the glass, indicated the bodies around her and were packaged neatly into an old pocket watch case. It showed two blobs behind her for Lance and the sheriff, and one smaller blob directly ahead. The material behind the glass—cracked from when Lance had dropped it during an encounter with a mutant cougar—flashed from gray to white.

"Never seen that before," Melinda muttered to herself.

Something was still in the mine.

She shoved aside the flaps of her duster to climb down the last rock. Her boots crunched on the orange chitin, squishing the arachnoid body segments underfoot. A sharp, almost curdled-milk smell along with metallic dirt made her lip curl, and she fought back a mix of awe, repulsion, and the tiniest smidge of regret. Why couldn't the Edge creatures stay in their lands, leave humans alone? In a lot of ways, the Edge creatures were like other animals; trying to make a home, reproduce, survive.

Doesn't mean I got to feel sorry for ant swarms when they flood the stock, or a hornet nest set on attacking, she reminded herself as she wiped her boot against a rock to get a smudge of green goo off. *If it's me or them, it's no contest.*

Something flashed again a few feet ahead, in a small opening between fallen wood and boulders of the caved-in entrance. She squeezed into the space, straightened in the tunnel, and made her way closer to the spark's source. It was a smooth bit of stone, silver as the moon and the size of a fingernail, partially embedded in the otherwise gray bands of rock.

"I don't know what you are," she said as she pulled out a thin rod of iron from her belt pack. "But if you're setting off Abel's watch you might be valuable. C'mon." She used the rod to pry at the stone. No way to tell how big it was, but she could surely chip some off.

A few rats scuttled in the darkness, their blue florescent noses flashing as they chattered to each other in a language too high-pitched for Melinda to make out. A striped centipede the size of a pig slivered above her and she jumped, waiting until it was safely out of reach. Both Edge species were harmless, but who knew what else had found its way into this cave.

"Hurry up now." Another jab and the stone nugget came out easily onto her hand, about the size of an acorn. As soon as it touched her hand, a wave of vertigo hit, and her fingers went numb. A sound—shuffles, or whispers—tickled the edge of her hearing. She pulled off the handkerchief from her neck and wrapped it around the stone. The sounds faded.

A hiss and clicking to her left made her freeze. Out of the corner of her eye the tracker flashed. She turned her head an inch.

Six white eyes stared back at her in the gloom, shining with the bit of sunlight that found its way in the tunnel.

The shadow of a scorpion twice as large as Melinda rose on its back legs.

Melinda readied to jump at the first sign of its tail stinger or pincer moving. But the giant scorpion held still, hissing all the while, and in a moment she saw why.

Along its stomach, dozens of translucent eggs were piled onto one another, just barely lit by their own pale green phosphorescence and covered by a single membrane stretching across its belly. More tiny tails than she cared to count flicked in the eggs.

"Find something, love?" Lance called down.

"Nothing a boom stick can't handle," she said back steadily. "I got it."

She planted the gunpowder stick in the dust and lit the fuse, all too aware of the six eyes fixed on her. The momma scorpion's grasper clicked warningly.

"See ya," Melinda said and slowly backed out.

She hurried past the piles of carcasses again and ducked behind an outcropping as half the mine blew open. Once rock and dust stopped raining down, she scanned the remains of the entrance. The momma scorpion was obliterated. A tiny pang nagged at her, but momma or not, Edge monsters couldn't just settle where they pleased.

A plume of red smoke rose from the broken mine entrance, hanging in the air for a second before fading. Maybe something in the scorpion's toxin reacted with the gunpowder. She checked her tracker to be sure. It wasn't showing the blob anymore, but it still flashed white. Must be busted. She tapped it and made a mental note to have Abel take a look.

"Damn!" The sheriff hollered as Melinda climbed back up.

"All set," she said.

"You gonna charge me for that too?" he asked.

"You want more of those creatures coming?" Lance tapped the side of his head. "Mellie and me have a sense better than a bloodhound for the strange. Half the time you're only seeing the first wave."

"First wave?" The sheriff paled.

"Consider that a complimentary add-on. We do a thorough job." Lance handed the flask back to the sheriff. "I'd say tell your friends, but you have the honor of being our last gig."

He and Melinda tipped their hats and started toward their horses, tied half a mile off. She brushed her hands off on her duster, trying to shake off the feeling that something was behind her. Normally she didn't mind whatever creatures they encountered, but the sight of that scorpion belly with all those eggs left her stomach doing flip flops.

"That momma scorpion was a big one," she said. "And something else. It was like a monster shindig in there. Like they were drawn to the cave, somehow."

"Doesn't matter much now anyway," Lance said, chipper than a jaybird. "Seeing as how we're officially retired."

She fished in her pocket to pull out her handkerchief. "There was something else down there. Some kinda stone. Rare maybe." She pulled back the cloth to show Lance the rock, whose silver and purplish milky opaqueness looked like frozen clouds at twilight.

He squinted at it. "Looks a little like moonstone, little like amethyst. I've never seen one like that before."

"Might be toxin on it. Gives off a weird feel if you touch it. You think they'd like it back home?"

"Sure. Abel and Beatrice love anything odd." He considered, a little grin tugging his mouth upwards. "Wage ten pieces when we get there they moved in together by now."

She shook her head. "They're about as happy a spinster and bachelor as I've ever seen. Can't wait for some of their home cooking." Her stomach nearly rumbled at the thought. *One more day of dried jerky, and then a real meal*, she told herself.

Pepper strained her white-and-black speckled neck for the furthest grass she could reach while Mud lifted his head in greeting. Melinda patted his dappled brown nose.

"Tell you what, let's wager double or nothing," she said while they saddled up.

He finished packing the payment into one of the saddlebags. "Double then. Call me a sucker for love."

"Seeing as how I won the last half a dozen wagers, a sucker for losing, more like it."

He laughed as they set off at a trot. "Mellie, what'd we do without each other?"

"You'd be just fine. Me, on the other hand, would probably end up a recluse."

He groaned.

"It's true," she said. "People expect a certain thing. This gunslingin', monster-hunting life is something most people wouldn't ever understand."

Lance tapped the bag of cash below his left leg. "Hard to believe we're finally cashing out."

"So we can be dull old ranchers?"

"Sure as a gun, I won't miss being covered in bug entrails."

"Psht!" she laughed. "You're gonna miss this roamer's life just as soon as we set roots."

"And you're gonna wonder why we didn't retire sooner." His grin broadened and she couldn't help but smile too.

Their plan had worked well, rounding out a 300-mile loop to offer their services, helping towns and settlements take care of more ... unusual problems. Plenty of the villages spoke languages she'd never heard of, or dialects she could barely make out. One thing was always unmistakable though, and that was the word for monsters, whether uttered with fear and fascination, hatred or grief. *Monstruo. Belua. Guaiwu. Enee.*

They'd seen more in the last year than most saw in a lifetime.

"It's been fun at times, especially when we do good work and a town's grateful," Lance said, and she nodded. They had saved a few lives, at least, during their adventures. "But it'll be nice to start something new too." His eyes locked with hers, and her gut stirred like it did when they had first met.

"You are too charming for your own good, Lance Putnam."

"Well, thank you, Miss Melinda West."

They nudged their horses to pick up the pace, and she tried to shake the uneasy feeling of the scorpions and the mine. It happened every time they took out a nest or infestation. Thoughts of the critters would haunt her for a night or two, then come back mixed in with other dreams like leftover coleslaw. Something about the composition of the Edge creatures, she figured, left more impressions in her mind and dreams then she'd like to admit.

No need to think about it anymore—they were done, she reminded herself. A heaviness seemed to slide away at the thought of never having to exterminate again, even though they had a knack for it and there were still plenty of critters left.

A part of her whispered she could never really be done. There were always more monsters.

Someone else can handle it now, Melinda thought. They'd done enough. Someone else could deal with the dreams, someone who didn't hesitate or feel those annoying itches of guilt like mosquito welts. Guilt at not having done enough to save people. Guilt at the swell of anger she felt when they wiped out an infestation—anger at the monsters, mostly, for putting them all in this situation to start with.

She squashed down the feelings like ants underfoot and turned her focus outwards. She watched the sunlight on the rolling hills covered in scrawny trees, Lance's cigarette smoke plume up into the hard blue sky, and a hawk's wide circles overhead, until her breath came easier. She'd have other, more mundane thoughts to focus on soon enough.

Like how quickly she could eat some of Aunt Beatrice's world-famous chili.

CHAPTER TWO

The town of Five Peaks stretched out across the small valley, its birch windmill rising from between a double set of wide streets lined with storefronts, homes and parlors. Log houses and farms filled out the rest of the valley, cut through by a modest stream. The sight of the familiar buildings sent a wave of relief through Melinda.

She inhaled as they dismounted next to a horse post, breathing in the smell of freshly sawed wood and livestock mixed with pine. It wasn't anything special. But it was home.

"Could eat a whole cow, but first, the bank," she said, stretching her legs. Expert riders that they were, things still got sore after a full day of riding.

"I'll stable these two, then meet you at Abel's." Lance unhooked the two bags on Mud. He crammed the envelope from the sheriff into one of the drawstring bags and passed both to her.

"Oof," Melinda said, taking the first one. "Mighty fine sacks of cash we racked up."

Lance wrapped her up in a hug despite the dirt. His cheeks were still smudged from the morning's fight, and she was sure she looked just as filthy.

"Well, I just about never seen you so peachy keen," she said.

"We finally got enough for our little house, some space for Peps and Mud."

"They'd be happy anywhere. Got to say, I'm looking forward to sleeping in a real bed rather than rolling up camp and cotton every day." She heaved the bags onto her shoulders. "Get those horses some grub. See you at Abel's."

The bank was quiet at this hour, readying up to close. The teller nearest her barely glanced up as she approached.

"Evening sir, how can I help you today?"

Melinda cleared her throat. The teller looked up and blinked.

"Sorry, ma'am." He flushed deeper than a beet. "The hat ... your height ... I didn't look."

"No harm done." She set the two sacks on the counter, dust and the odor of dirty leather puffing up. "Depositing these please."

As she waited for the teller to count the various bank notes, cash, and coins, she ignored the few sidelong glances from other tellers, who maybe wondered if she was a bounty hunter. They'd only been gone a year, but there were more new faces than she expected.

The wooden door creaked behind her and a voice as familiar as her own duster rang out. "Melinda West! So, it's true, you are back!"

A woman twice her age in a pea-green shawl, with a messy dark bun beneath a simple, low-brimmed hat, rushed toward her and swept her up in a hug, not even minding the dirt.

"News travels faster than a stung cat," Melinda said, the warm feeling of home hitting her tenfold. "Howdy to you too, Aunt Beatrice."

The woman who had all but raised her as a teen looked a little more stooped, a little grayer, since Melinda last saw her, but her cloud of ink and soup spice smell brought Melinda right back to when she had first made her way to Five Peaks after her momma had passed on. Aunt B had taken her in like her own daughter, doing everything from teaching her how to use herbs in the wild, to trying to matchmake her with any eligible bachelor in a fifty-mile radius.

"As soon as I heard someone spotted the two of you, I had to come and see my girl," Beatrice said and turned to the teller. "Tom, I hope you're caring for her and Lance. They're the most trustworthy folks you can find."

Before Melinda could chime in, Beatrice pushed her back to scrutinize her. "Goodness, no matter how many years go by I will never *not* be surprised at how tall you are." Her nose wrinkled. "You need a dunk in the hogwash, but I can't tell you how good it is to see you. Is Lance here? Ah, never mind, I'm sure he's at Abel's. I wish I had known so I could've fixed you up something proper."

"Don't fret, Aunt B." Melinda tried to keep up with Beatrice's gunfire of words. "You don't have to go to the trouble."

Beatrice tsked. "I made a promise to your momma long ago, what would her ghost say to see I wasn't having my niece properly fed? Never seen you looking so flea-bitten and weary. But also happy. Are you happy, Mellie? Ah, we'll have plenty of time to talk tonight. Lucky for you, I have enough leftover chili and can pull together some other bites. I'll see you soon."

Chili! Melinda's stomach rumbled at the thought. "Thanks, Aunt B."

Beatrice rushed out after one more hug. Melinda watched the last of the sun's rays slip below the mountains as the teller finished. He handed her a note of the total and she blinked to make sure she had read it right.

Enough for a good-sized house and a ranch, and then some.

We really did it, she thought. Hard to believe her days of tracking were over now. For what felt like the first time in a long while, her shoulder muscles unknotted.

"That's all of it, Miss West," said the teller, whose demeanor had become considerably warmer since counting her notes. "If you would like us to advise you on any investments, you let us know anytime."

She thanked him and headed out onto Second Street, taking in the familiar sights. There were small changes here and there—a newly painted wooden post, a chopped down tree—but mostly things looked the same. She recognized the Miller and Weber kids, so much taller now, crouched under a porch, trying to coax out a rooster. There was Miss Patti, who kept no partner and said she preferred it that way, throwing out a tin of dirty water on her front porch and giving a friendly wave. Next to hers was John and Jack's place—Jack with his albino skin that would just about blind you in sunlight. Folks who weren't always welcome elsewhere seemed to find their way to Five Peaks. The first families who settled there some fifty years ago had made it a place where any decent folk could find a home, no matter what they looked like or where they came from.

As Melinda passed the ever-bustling piano bar, she paused at a knot of trees between buildings. She smiled to herself as her gaze fell on two crooked trunks. A lot of things had happened behind those trees, not the least of which was spotting Lance for the first time three summers ago, swinging in a makeshift hammock and carving a wooden talisman with a look of concentration so intense it had nearly made her laugh. It had reminded her of a schoolkid mulling over a test. The first thing she had noticed were his eyes, dark blue like the sky before a storm. His arms weren't half bad either. But what caught her most was Lance's voice. Easy, like the feeling of swinging in that hammock, warm like a favorite blanket. Something about it made her like him instantly. The next time she passed his hammock, he had tossed her a little wooden figure he had whittled.

"It's supposed to be you," Lance had said, pointing to the wooden figure.

"It's the ugliest thing I've ever seen," she had said, and he laughed. The head piece swung open, crookedly, to hold tobacco. Melinda still had it, a charm that tucked into whatever pocket or satchel she wore.

A few doors past Lance's hammock spot sat Abel Yao's place, his windows lit above the store that Beatrice helped run. Melinda didn't dare show up to Beatrice's supper without washing up first, so she slipped in the back entrance of the store, using a key that hid in a carved-out pinecone that sat vigilant above the door frame.

She headed into the back storage room, lit with a few lanterns and housing plenty of odd animal parts and minerals, some of which were ones Lance and Melinda had sent back on their travels. Beatrice and Abel studied and cataloged all the strange items in their leather-bound books lining the wall, sometimes extracting poisons or samples for new weapons and medicines. Fun for them, useful for Melinda and Lance.

Footsteps and Lance's muted laugh floated down from above along with the smell of soup and pie. Melinda's stomach growled. When she walked through the storage room, she saw the kettle was already steaming next to the basin in the adjacent washroom, with Lance's hat and duster hanging under the base of the stairs.

Grateful, she filled the basin with hot water. It had been too long since they had had a proper wash, not since a few weeks back when they had sprung for a real room. Beatrice had laid out a cotton shirt and linen pants, along with raw eggs for her hair and a bottle of vinegar infused with rosemary. Melinda grimaced as a piece of orange chitin tumbled into the basin from her hair and scrubbed harder until the water ran clear instead of gray.

She had just finished getting presentable when she heard a rustling in the storage room. She grabbed her gun and peeked cautiously around the corner.

Abel paused at the back door, absorbed in a book in one hand, key in another.

She smiled at the sight of him. He looked the same, with his patched horsehair jacket, long dark hair clasped back, and faraway gaze. Though Lance was closer to Abel than she was, Abel had treated her just as warmly, taking both of them under his wing and teaching them about everything he knew, though it was an impossible task. The man was a jack of all trades, his know-how ranging from custom weapon building to horse wrangling, though some things were off limits—he'd never talk about his past dabblings in magic or politics. Between Abel's tutelage and Aunt Beatrice's encyclopedic knowledge of animals and plants, Melinda and Lance had had enough lessons to last them a lifetime.

She cleared her throat to get his attention. He lowered his book, a thick, musty-looking text titled *The Histories of Old Isles and Alternate Visions.*

"My dear, dear girl!" Abel's eyes focused and burst into a smile. She was immediately swept up in a hug by the older, sun-creased man, his lean form stronger than she remembered, and inhaled the familiar smell of beeswax, gunpowder and tea.

"Must've been good reading," she said.

"Didn't even realize you were here. Still in fight mode, huh?" He gestured toward her lowered gun.

"You know me too well."

"I'd hope I'd know you both good enough by now," Abel laughed. "But tell me, how did the traps work out? And the flingers? And Plymouth? Tell me everything. What worked, what didn't, let's hear it."

"All aces, Abel, like usual. Though, the tracker's broken."

"What do you mean?" A flicker passed over Abel's face so quickly Melinda thought she had imagined it.

"I know you wouldn't be chatting down there while your food's getting cold up here!" Beatrice called from the top of the steps.

"We'll do a full inventory in the morning," Abel said as they hurried up the staircase.

Lance sat at the wooden table, midway through a soup, stripped down to his sleeveless cotton shirt and wool pants, and looking fresher than she had seen him in weeks.

Beatrice stood over him in an embroidered apron, a magnifying glass trained on a patch of orange scales at the back of his shoulder, a scar from a run-in with glow-in-the-dark reptiles in Agave Lake. Behind the table, a small fireplace kept a pair of cauldrons warm. Lance sprang up to give Abel a big bear hug, nearly picking him off the floor. Melinda chuckled.

"Looking a little gray, old man." Lance smiled in the wide way he did when they were home.

"Feels like just yesterday I was teaching you both to wrangle." Abel clapped Lance on the back, beaming at him like a proud papa before setting out to pour glasses of golden brandy.

"I'm so hungry I could eat a saddle bag," Melinda said and started shoveling the chili into her mouth as fast as possible. It was everything she remembered and more. The bite was spicy and hot, full of beans, meat and some herbal concoction that gave it its lingering kick.

"Gets old chewing on peppermint leaves," Melinda added between slurps. "This is the best thing I've had in a long time, Aunt B."

"You still eat like a starving wolf," Beatrice said. One of her eyeballs magnified in the curved glass's reflection as she resumed her exam of Lance's orange scales. "Doesn't look like it will spread. And it doesn't hurt?"

"Not in the slightest." Lance tapped the patch of skin. "Just another scar."

Those they had plenty of. Their scars ranged from bite marks on her thigh from a close brush with a half-rodent, half-porcupine, to a sprinkle of dots on Lance's neck from a gel centipede's venomous spikes. They had invisible scars too, from their close calls: dealing with psychic-empowered creatures and coming to terms with losing a few people they hadn't been able to save in time. But Melinda quickly walled those thoughts off and focused on her food. No need to pick at old scabs, invisible or otherwise. What was past was past.

"Try this salve, anyway." Beatrice slid a green jar toward him. "How about you, Mellie?"

"Nothing too bad, just a little numb here." She showed Beatrice her two fingers where the mine stone touched. "Reminds me, got a rock to show you."

"I don't see anything unusual." Beatrice pushed back her flyaway strands and let go of Melinda's hand. "Something else I don't see—a ring. Am I ever going get to plan a wedding around here?" she asked with all the subtly of a shot to the nose.

Melinda shrugged. "In due time."

Lance munched innocently on a chicken wing.

Beatrice clapped and looked all too hopeful. "Kids?"

Melinda rolled her eyes, trying not to feel too irritable. Beatrice liked to act like having children was the be-all, end-all, but it wasn't. "Dunno."

Beatrice clicked her tongue in annoyance.

Lance flashed his dimple. "You know us, B. No rush. No worries."

"Speaking of," Melinda said. "You shacking up with anyone, Aunt B?"

Beatrice laughed, picking at her lace sleeve. "Oh no, I'm quite sure I'll live the end of my days as a spinster."

Melinda shot Lance a look and mouthed, *you lost the bet.* He shook his head, pretending to be baffled. She rolled her eyes and downed the glass of brandy. Sweet and warm, it immediately loosened the last of the tightness in her back and she sighed in content.

"Now that you're not fixing for high riding anymore, what's your plan?" Abel asked.

"Ranch mostly," Lance said. "Maybe pick up a trade."

"I remember when you came into town, a fresh-faced cowpoke after your pa died." Abel rolled a glass in his hands. "And you, Mellie, a sullen gal taller than a snake on stilts. You barely spoke a word but were the best sharpshooter I'd ever seen. I'm not getting any younger. If one of you—better yet both— wanted to follow in my steps, well, I'd be more than happy."

"Ain't no one bright enough like you to put those guns and contraptions together. We're good at using them but that's about it," Melinda said. Truthfully, learning to make custom guns and weapons was something she had no patience for, and Lance neither. She preferred to be handed the finished product and be well on her way.

"That's not quite what I'm saying."

Lance straightened. "What *are* you saying, Abel?"

He spread his hands wide. "You can have all this. The store and the live-in space. Do what you will with it. I'm planning to write your names in my will if you'll have it. I know it's small."

Melinda stared at him in shock while Beatrice beamed.

"You're too generous, Abel. We just saved enough for our own land," Lance protested, holding up his hands. "And you got plenty of years left."

"See what I'm saying here is what I always tell you, Lance. Think bigger. Think of what's ahead. A house, farm, and store. Why, the two of you could be running the town together. And Billy's thinking of heading south this spring, so you'd be a shoo-in as the next sheriff. Either one of you."

Beatrice nodded in agreement and ladled a second serving into Melinda's bowl.

Melinda shook her head. "Awfully kind Abel, but dealing with neighbors complaining over who took whose cow and whether another building can go up? I'll stick with the ranch."

"You, Lance?"

Lance chuckled. "We'll see. How about a toast? To hanging up our hats."

"To home," Melinda added, warm from the brandy and food and the four of them sitting there, together after so long.

"Poor, tired dears," Beatrice said. "We got your room all set up, and I'll come over in the morning with some fresh bread and other things. I know a few other folks who'd love to see you."

Melinda stifled a groan. Beatrice's friends couldn't get enough of their adventures, and Lance loved to indulge them. Of course, he skipped over the gruesome parts, the fire cattle that munched on people's guts, or the dreambugs that nearly consumed a whole town. Something caught her eye before she could reply. A smear of red collected at the window between the half-closed, patched-up curtains. She blinked a few times. Too much brandy, probably, making the moonlight blur. But something about it knotted her stomach in ropes. A little part of her nagged again: *you can never be done*. She shook her head, trying to clear it.

"It all sounds so romantic," Beatrice continued, getting that look in her eye like she was a kid playing pretend. "Roaming on new lands, meeting new people."

"Nothing much romantic about flea-bitten camping and critter glop on you half the time," Lance said, standing. He picked up a guitar in the corner and started strumming. "But no one I'd rather have by my side. Always watching each other's backs, that's the key to it."

"You hear that?" Melinda said. A low hiss sounded, just under their conversation, like a rattler echoing through a cave. Between the curtains, the red glowed like a harvest moon, as if the town were on fire.

A knock at the window. Everyone stood, except for Melinda who stayed frozen, eyes locked on the glass. Two long black pointers tapped insistently, and her heart sank right down to her toes. *Never be done, never be done …*

"What in the world?" Beatrice said.

Abel's brow creased, his voice sharp. "What kind of stone did you say you found?" His hand went to his chest, where the herbal bag he always wore rested. His "good luck" charm as he called it.

"It was silver. Flashing." Melinda tightened her grip around a fork and wished she hadn't left her gun downstairs with her duster.

"Eyestone," Beatrice gasped. At the window, two legs moved forward to reveal another pair, all attached to a round, insect-like body. At first, she thought the scorpions had followed them somehow, but this was a spider.

"What's an eyestone?" Lance asked and turned the guitar like a bat.

Abel said in a panic, "Mellie, where is it? Give me the st—"

Before she could respond, the arachnid slammed into the window like a cannonball. Shards of glass flew into the room. Everyone hollered and went for a weapon as the bug shot inside.

Larger than her fist, the spider was glossy as obsidian, with a pile of red eyes like beans on its head.

Beatrice threw her kitchen knife, nicking the spider in the leg as it ran across the room. It scurried under the table while Abel and Lance flung open the gun cabinet. Lance passed Melinda an axe and grabbed a pistol for himself.

Abel pointed his six-shooter at the table. "Stand back."

Melinda's head swam, but she hoisted the axe. She whirled around as something ran behind her. Smoke the color of fire flitted through the air.

"Where'd it go?" Beatrice was saying, her voice faraway like she was underwater. Melinda tried to focus but couldn't tear her gaze away from the red cloud.

Two more spiders emerged from the direction of the stovetop, and one along the wall in the corner of Melinda's eye, all swarming around Abel.

"Mellie, you get any of them?" Lance shot her a quick glance. "What's wrong—" He cut off as he slammed the pistol into a fast-approaching spider, taking a leg off. The leg dissolved into a black puff and the rest of the spider ran behind a curtain.

Abel shot at the one under the table and Beatrice dodged another that dropped from the ceiling. Six at least, maybe more. And yet, Melinda still couldn't pull herself away from the red cloud that was moving from the window toward her. Like it was *drawn* to her.

"Don't let them touch you! Whatever you do!" Abel shouted as he and Lance had cornered three of them in the kitchen.

Beatrice whacked a spider next to Melinda with the butt of Abel's shotgun, her hair in disarray.

The sounds of the room faded away. Melinda tried to call to the others, but her throat was coated in molasses. All she could do was watch the red cloud undulate, and then condense. Growing into a shape. It couldn't be—but it looked like the outline of a person. The stench of wet dirt and fungus filled her nose as the cloud moved toward the table. Nearing her.

For an instant she saw him through the red.

A man.

But she knew he wasn't a man.

For one, his feet didn't touch the floor. His face was white as a ghost. A thin mustache curled over a sharp, cruel mouth below even sharper cheekbones. Human eyes pierced her, pulling her into their darkness.

"*Who are you?*" Melinda tried to say. It was hard to move and looking at him was like looking at a heat mirage—blurry and disorienting. The man in the cloud smiled and snapped his fingers silently.

All the windows and the door blasted open, sending everyone tumbling back. The candles went out and lanterns burst.

A beat of silence and Melinda shook off the haze. She blinked in the darkness, waiting for her eyes to adjust.

"I'll get the fireplace." Beatrice's voice rang out, breathless.

"Y'all OK?" Lance called.

"So far," Melinda managed, rubbing the back of her head.

"One just went down. Two, injured, ran off through the window. There's one left." Abel's voice, strained, floated through the darkness.

A shiver trickled over Melinda's waist, cold as river water. The fireplace came to life a second later. She found herself staring at the ceiling, head pounding like she had been thrown from a horse. As she started to sit up, she bit back a muffled scream at what she saw.

The last spider perched next to her, arching its legs toward her heart.

CHAPTER THREE

Melinda couldn't breathe as the spider climbed onto her chest and opened its mouth, ready to strike. It paused, as if waiting.

But for what?

"No!" Abel shouted and dove forward. In one quick motion, he swept the spider away from her, taking it with him as he tumbled into the table.

"Did it bite you?" Beatrice rushed over and helped her up. The spider scuttled away from Abel and bolted back out the busted window.

"Not me. Abel. Is he—" Melinda couldn't bring herself to finish. The words choked in her throat as she spotted his slumped form on the floor.

Lance shook Abel and turned him over.

"Breathing. But something's wrong," Lance said, his voice hoarse.

Trying to keep it together, Melinda thought as her own panic reared up at seeing Abel so limp, so lifeless. Beatrice splashed some whisky around Abel's mouth. His gray eyes, half open, stayed blank.

"The spider must've gotten him. But I don't see a bite mark," Lance said and gave him another shake, firmer this time. "Wake up, dammit."

"He's not dead," Beatrice said, sounding like she was fighting back tears. "Oh, thank heavens. But he's not right either. Help me get him up."

Together, the three of them dragged Abel to his bed, gently setting him down on the cowhides and scratchy wool.

"He said something before he went out … sounded like kill stone," Lance said. "He convulsed for a second, then it felt like, I don't know, I can't explain it. Something went off in him."

Melinda put a hand on his shoulder to stop the flow of nervous words, and they fell silent, watching Beatrice do a quick exam, peering at Abel's pupils and feeling at his wrist.

"Some kind of soul poison, I'd wager." Beatrice leaned back and fought back a sob. "Oh, dear Abel."

"Why? *How?*" Lance pounded his fist into the side table, sending Abel's pipe clattering.

"That stone you brought back. Eyestone. Where is it?" Beatrice said.

"My duster pocket downstairs," Melinda replied. "Why?"

"It counters any masking spells." Beatrice's eyes settled on Abel's charm bag around his neck. "Abel wore that as a cloaking to keep creatures at bay. The eyestone nullified it."

Another beat of silence as a wave of horror washed over Melinda. "It's my fault," she said. "I brought it here."

"It's not your fault, love," Lance said, but the rock of guilt that had hardened in Melinda's gut didn't budge. "We had no way of knowing what it would do. But why are creatures after him?"

Beatrice didn't answer but stood instead. "I need to take care of that stone and I'll check the books to see what can be done. Don't take your eyes off him."

Beatrice hustled downstairs, and Lance collapsed in the chair in the corner of the room.

He buried his face in his hands.

"He's got a dead man's look, Mellie."

"We aren't gonna let him die," Melinda said. She perched on the edge of the bed to clasp Abel's hand. It was long and bony, and faster than a blink when it came to showing off a new weapon or fixing one of his inventions.

Clammy now.

Beatrice emerged a few minutes later with a leather-bound book and a glass jar. A green-backed beetle skittered against the glass.

"Dreambug. Last time I got bit by some of those I couldn't sleep for weeks." Melinda fought back a shudder remembering the sleepless nights, waking up in cold sweats. "How's that gonna help Abel?"

"I'll explain." Beatrice opened her book. "It's worse than I thought. Soul sucker. Breed of creatures that can drain the essence right out of you. They were targeting Abel." She pressed her fingers to her eyes and spoke, barely audible.

"What aren't you saying?" Melinda said.

Dawning fell over Lance's face as he noticed the same hesitation in Beatrice. "B?" he prompted.

"He thought something like this might happen." Beatrice's voice was nearly a whisper.

Lance drew in a sharp breath. "What do you mean?"

"There's something he never told you kids. When he was held against his will working on the railroads, he would have done anything to get out." Beatrice patted at her eyes and pulled up a chair to grasp Abel's limp hand. "Those railroads nearly killed him you know, like they did his brothers."

Melinda nodded. They had heard the stories Abel told, factually and briefly, before changing the subject.

"What he never told you was he found a way to escape, but it cost him. He met someone out there that had a spell. It was his way out, you see. It infused his soul with a power, let him break free. Nearly killed him, but he survived. Like a scar, the spell had lasting effects. It helped him to have the vision ... he has now. You may not have noticed but—"

"How he seems to read your mind," Melinda said quietly. "How he can be such a good peacemaker. How he knows how to put parts together."

"Well that last part is all him through and through," Beatrice laughed, wiping her eyes and giving Abel's motionless hand a squeeze. "But power like that comes at a terrible price. It changes you. His soul burned too bright ever since. Eventually, he figured out a concoction to keep it hidden, but before that, his soul was like a beacon, attracting the attention of ..."

"Monsters," Melinda finished.

"Wait a minute," Lance cut in. Melinda hadn't seen him this angry in, well, ever. "Why the hell is this the first we're hearing about this?"

"He had put all that behind him. He trained you both so well, and it seemed like everything was quieting down. But this..." Beatrice broke off, her voice catching.

Lance stood and hovered over Abel. "How do we fix it?"

Beatrice creased the book open to an entry. "Soul suckers collect pieces of souls to deliver back to a hive or master. They can't hold a soul for long—they usually deposit them into some sort of vessel, like an egg or other container."

"What are the souls used for?" Melinda asked.

Beatrice looked grim. "Lots of things. Mostly having to do with unnatural power. Bring back whatever is holding his soul and we can restore him. Make sure the vessel stays intact or we'll lose him." She lifted the jar with the dreambug and looked at Melinda with a hint of regret. "It won't be easy to track, but this will help you follow the spider's trail."

The dreambug flashed green, sending a flood of memories back to Melinda of getting jabbed by dozens of their pincers when a swarm had attacked. She spent days in a feverish haze after, the details of which she could not recall, but the memory of it made her break out in a sweat, even now, months later. She tried to draw some air back into her lungs. Funny how the smallest critters could do the most damage.

"I'll do it." Lance plopped in the chair and stuck his arm out on the table. "They just about killed you before."

"That was dozens. I can handle one." *Plus, all this is my fault.* He shook his head and she scowled. "I told you a hundred times, don't treat me like I'm broken."

"I'm not. You've been through a lot. You were in a damn near coma. You already look like you've seen a ghost. And your nightmares—"

"You have them just as much as me. I'll be fine."

Lance shook his head again. "No deal."

"Too bad." Melinda held out her hand for the jar. "Aunt B?"

"Her chances of having a less severe reaction and getting the vision is better since she's been bit before," Beatrice admitted to Lance. "It's a far bigger risk for you."

"Settled, then. Abel doesn't have much time, I'd reckon?" Melinda grabbed the jar before Lance could argue, though she could see him grinding his jaw, about to come up with another protest.

"He probably has a few days at most. If that," Beatrice all but whispered. Lance closed his mouth, rubbing his temples.

"So, we got a whole lot of nothing in terms of options." Melinda unscrewed the jar. The beetle, bright as a scarab and lit only by the fireplace's light, ran frantically around the bottom of the glass. She stuck her hand in and held her breath.

The beetle unsheathed its pincers and plunged them into the back of her palm. Pain seared up her wrist. The sensation of the swarm pricking her arms and legs came back to her, but she bit her lip, letting the controlled pain ground her.

"That should be enough." Beatrice used a cloth to grasp the back of the beetle, which had gone from green to black, and pried it off.

"You all right?" Lance asked, peering at her face.

Melinda shook off her hand. "Stings like a rattler—"

Darkness descended mid-sentence. She stood in a sage-colored mist. Floated in fact, her legs somewhere far below her. Billows of white dust congealed like week-old milk into figures, whispering in hushed tones. The shadows roamed past in another world or realm, one she didn't care to spend any more time seeing than she had to.

She turned, looking for a sign.

Abel, Melinda thought. *Where's Abel? And that damned soul-suckin' spider?*

A mine stood in front of her, Abel's charm bag hanging from a nail in the wooden frame's entrance. A dreambug the size of a horse barreled out and opened a mouthful of pincers. Melinda ducked and the giant dreambug disappeared in a burst of emerald shards. When Melinda straightened, she teetered on the precipice of a glass cliff. A figure below her three times the size of any man looked up. His face, white as a maggot, was shrouded in shadow, but she could make out one feature.

His mouth, grinning.

"Melinda!"

The hard floor and Lance's firm grip materialized around her. A pins-and-needles tingle ran along her body and her stomach tossed like she had drank sour milk.

"I'm fine," Melinda said, shooing them away in case Beatrice's chili decided to make an appearance.

"Your eyes." Lance's voice was tighter than a drum. "They're green like the bug's."

"It'll only last a few hours, at most. What do you see?" Beatrice asked. Melinda watched in fascination as her words turned into tiny prisms in the air.

She looked around with her new vision. Lance's quiet despair spiraled out like an unspooling thread the color of grass. More rainbow droplets surrounded Beatrice's head, exploding in miniature fireworks as she murmured her worries to herself.

There. A small cloud, the same shade of red that she had first seen at the window before the spider attacked, hung suspended over the bed. Over Abel. The spider's trail.

And something else—tiny flickers ran along Abel, like molten sparks from a blacksmith's fire. They were hypnotic, something she wanted to touch and couldn't pull her gaze from.

Traces of his soul.

Focus on the trail, Melinda told herself, and scanned the room. Behind them, a few crimson motes floated out the bedroom door.

She moved to the shattered window the spiders had escaped through and peeled back the curtain. Sure as day, a ruby glow wound to the end of main street and up toward the five sharp peaks that gave the town its name.

"I got it. The trail," Melinda said. Her words floated, the color of a mountain river at dawn. "North. Direct up the range."

"It's too steep," Beatrice said, chewing on her lip. "And snowy."

"Pep and Mud are tougher than a sow's snout," Lance said, craning out the window. His green threads of distress flickered out, eaten by the darkness. "There's enough moonlight. We'll take it slow. Let's roll it up and get riding."

"Be careful," Beatrice said. Golden blurs followed her hands as she readied a cotton sack of breads and dried meats. "Take whatever you need. Oh, and this." She unlocked the cabinet, pulling out a shotgun overlaid with all manner of wire and a red tube. "Abel's latest, Malgun. It's got a kickback and works about half the time, but when it does, oh, it's something to see. This'll take care of those devilish soul suckers, but mind you, he's only made the one missile for it so far, a powerful mix of flammable components and serum from a xoetic welldeep lizard. What else you need?"

"We have our forty-fours," Lance said. "Rifle. Boom sticks."

Beatrice nodded. "I'll get you ammo, oh, take extra just in case. And take Abel's charm, to hide you from the soul suckers so you can get the jump on them." She left the room, tangles of gold twinkling in her path.

In the breath of silence, Melinda reached over to touch Lance's cheek.

A silver mist curled around his face, glowing and warm. She savored it, pushing away the whispers and topsy-turvy feeling in her gut.

He glanced back at Abel's room, the strings of worry swayed like weeping willow branches around him.

"Don't worry," she said. "We'll get through it. Always do."

You OK?" Lance cupped her hand against his face, and warmth moved down her arm.

She flexed her hand that had been pierced. "Won't be good for a while. Last time it took a day and a half to get feeling right again. But a small price to pay."

"That's not what I mean."

They moved back to the bedroom and her chest twisted at the sight of Abel, feeling the same hollow pit gaping as when her momma had left this earth after a brush with a monster infection. The supernatural goo left behind by a luminescent moonslug had sank deep into her mother's freckled skin, spreading its lavender flecks up her arms and neck. No matter what medicines Melinda had tried, she had watched as her mother's cheery face caved in on itself and became unrecognizable, her laughter replaced by moans. It had been the stuff of nightmares. Worse yet, the infection had dragged on and on, day in and day out, until finally, the silence Melinda had both feared and wished for arrived. She'd never forget that morning: coming into the room and spotting her mother's hands first, motionless and curled over the blanket, grasping a wilting bluebell stalk she had pulled from the vase next to her. Everything had been silent, still.

She wouldn't let the same stillness take Abel.

"He's not gonna die," Melinda said now.

"Damn straight. We can handle one little spider." Lance touched Abel's shoulder. His protective worry flowed in cascades of emerald bits, fine as dandelion seeds, over Abel. "We'll be back before you know it."

They headed out to get ready under the moonlight.

CHAPTER FOUR

The pre-dawn air cooled her lungs as they set off toward the cluster of northern peaks, following the particles that hung suspended like an arrow in Melinda's newfound eyesight.

Normally she'd half-doze on Pepper whenever they rode this early, but she was too knotted up to sleep. Abel's sack of charms lay nestled inside her pocket next to Lance's wooden figurine. Melinda wasn't the superstitious or sentimental type, but the weight of the charm bag and carved wood piece Lance had given her gave her some peace of mind, kept the tide in her from breaking free. She couldn't put the image of the figure in the red cloud out of her mind. She tried to remember the face—*his* face—but it was no use. Details blurred like a rapidly dissolving dream. A hallucination, Beatrice had told her, when she mentioned the mystery man.

"Still got the trail?" Lance asked a few hours later as the sun rolled up behind piles of clouds.

"For now, but fading." Her vision had all but returned to normal, save for a few of the hovering red motes trailing up the pass. "I'll need another sting soon to see the trail again." She grimaced down at the netted jar that swung from Pepper's saddle. Inside, the dreambug ran in circles and knocked its pincers against the glass.

"What kind of spider heads up into the snow?" Lance mused as their horses fell in a single file line along the steepening path. "Doesn't make sense."

"Maybe to meet its maker." An image of the momma scorpion came back to Melinda, and she shifted uneasily in her saddle. She tapped her two fingers together, which had started tingling again like they had when she touched the eyestone in the mine. At least they had Abel's Malgun. Judging by the gadgetry and its weight, she suspected not much would withstand its blast.

Melinda pulled to a stop at a fork. The cold pricked beneath her layers of cotton and wool, and wide-brimmed hat. She spotted the red speck at last and nudged Pepper over a narrow pass to continue upwards, receiving a snort in protest.

"C'mon, you've done fancier footwork than this," she said to her. The wind kicked up, the sky sagged in billows of gray and white. Behind her, Lance's tobacco paper crackled as crows squawked overhead.

Lance stayed quieter than normal as he smoked. Melinda glanced back to see him pulling up the collar of his gray duster, the mist curling around his shoulders and meeting his plume of smoke above his hat. His face hung grimmer than she had ever seen it, and she tried not to think of Abel still in the bed, Aunt B's mouth twisted with grief.

Melinda turned back around—and bit back a shout when she spotted what was in the trees.

Winged figures larger than crows nestled in the fir branches. Their tails like snakes whipped against the sky.

And at the ends of their tails flashed sharp barbs.

"Dragats!" Lance said as they slowed their pace. "Looks like they're tracking something. Must've marked a good one by the size of the flock."

A dozen took off from the branches and fanned out above them, soaring blurs in the mist.

"Let's skedaddle," Melinda said as both horses shifted. They had read enough of Beatrice and Abel's book collection to know basic facts about most Edge critters. Dragats marked their prey with a scent before the group attacked. "They won't bother us. We ain't marked—"

Before she could finish the thought, the hovering dragats swooped toward them.

"Here they come!" Lance shouted.

Melinda ducked, the barbs of their tails snapping at her hat and nearly knocking her off Pepper.

Lance fired a shot in the sky. A dragat folded and dropped faster than a stone. Half a dozen soared up to join the others in a vortex, preparing for another ambush. More gathered on branches, watching.

"Didn't scare 'em off." Melinda mentally crossed off their options. "Too many to shoot."

"Retreat?" Lance said as both horses sidestepped and whinnied. Only about another minute or two before one broke into a panicked gallop, despite being well-trained.

"Too narrow. They'll run. Can't risk one of them tripping." To her right, the trail dropped off sharply into the snowy mist. To their left, dense firs and boulders prevented any kind of animal from getting through. The path straight ahead was their only choice.

"We must be marked," she continued. "Somehow—"

A dragat swept toward her and flicked its tongue from a stunted beak. Melinda wound her hands around Pepper's mane and held on as the horse reared in panic.

"Watch out!" Lance shouted.

Pepper scraped the saddle against a trunk, knocking off bags and very nearly Melinda. Half their wares flew over the side of the cliff.

Including the dreambug.

"Damn it!" she cried as she reined Pepper in. "Calm down, girl!" The dragats dove again toward Melinda. She braced but they fled past her, down after the fallen bags.

Lance leaned over the ice-encrusted edge as more snowflakes swirled down. "Flock is as gone as a drunk man from church," he said over the howl of the wind. "Something about the dreambug drew them."

"Damn." Melinda squinted, urging back some of the vision, but it was gone. "Now what?"

"Nowhere to go but up." Lance tried to sound easy, though a line of worry ran across his brow.

They continued upwards, the horses losing steam while they stomped through the snow mounds. At least they reached the summit, the incline leveling out to endless white around them. The sun, a smudged-out, dim glow behind the clouds began to sink. And the red trail was nowhere to be seen.

Melinda pressed her eyes shut and tried to will back anything that would give her a sense of the red trail: the whispers, the visions, the feeling of the world spinning. She felt a little stirring, the start of a prickle. Then—

Nothing.

"I'm sorry." She met Lance's eyes and his face fell beneath his snowflake-speckled hat.

"No worries, love," he said. "The dreambug got us this far. We'll figure the rest out on our own, we always do. We'll track the old-fashioned way if we have to."

"We got nothing to go on." She spread her hands out to the snow around them, punctuated occasionally by the fir trees. "No tracks, no dragats, even. Feels like the end of the world up here."

Lance looped Mud around in a wide circle and paused at one of the paths pointing down the northmost side of the cliff. "Here."

Melinda pulled up alongside him. Miles below, dots of light glowed feebly from behind gusts of snow.

"That's got to be High Hawk." Lance straightened. "We can hole up for the night at least, replace our provisions and look for a fresh trail in the morning. Maybe the snow will clear."

"We can warm up at least," Melinda said and something in her uplifted. "I'd bet we'll find our bearings there."

"Vision back?"

"No. Just a feeling."

They kicked the horses toward High Hawk.

CHAPTER FIVE

Melinda had never been to High Hawk, though its reputation preceded itself as having the best games on this side of the northern range.

Melinda understood why as they descended and the buildings came into view. Dozens of gambling halls and dining establishments lined the street behind crowds spilling out for fresh air. Buildings three times bigger than any in Five Peaks rose around them, built in pristine white wood or red bricks, with painted blue shutters and a variety of signs: MINGS TAVERN, RENDEZVOUS, SAWDUST SALOON, LA SOULE, HORSE HEAD PUB. The horses picked up the pace, their footing surer and their necks tossing, eager for a bite.

"You know much about this place?" Melinda said as they fell in line behind jostling horses and carriages. Feathered hats and thickly embroidered dresses brushed alongside the carriages, and laughter rang out in the twilight.

"Gold vein and start of the railroad," Lance said, licking off a tobacco roll. "High Hawk was built the same time as Five Peaks, believe it or not. That must be the showpiece." He pointed down the street where CANDELARIAS GAMBLING HALL glowed between two candlesticks the size of fledgling trees. Would-be patrons stood in a line twice that of the other buildings.

Melinda and Lance hopped off, flagging down the attendant for pails of grain for the horses. A sheriff started to pass, then stopped, pulling back next to Melinda to take in their snow-covered clothes.

"Help you with something?" the sheriff asked her. About their age, she noted, but with a well-practiced, stern look. A hairline scar bisected his otherwise smooth black face from his temple to cheek.

"You greet all your out-of-towners face to face?" Melinda said. Sometimes people reacted to them badly—Melinda for her height or not wearing a dress, Lance for being half firstcomer tribe-born, which some more discerning folks detected in the shape of his nose or cheekbones. But she'd found most people didn't care too much about where one was from or what they looked like when there were monsters to contend with. Nevertheless, they'd had enough strangers greeting them with suspicion that she always kept an eye out for trouble. They were always outsiders it seemed, no matter where they went.

"Sheriff William Mathings." He tipped his hat. "No offense ma'am, but ya'll don't look like the high-betting type. Where are you lovely folk from, if you don't mind my asking?"

"Five Peaks. Lance Putnam and Melinda West, pleased to meet you. We got plenty of funds," Lance said and pointed to the small sack hanging from Mud's saddle. "Gold, silver. Enough for a fair run of faro or blackjack and then some, don't you worry. We did, however, hear of a strange infestation of arachnids making its way around these parts. Seen anything like it?"

Mathings shook his head. "We're not afraid of a few insects here."

Lance gave his easy smile. "Made our profession taking down the hard-to-exterminate. If you see a problem, we'd be happy to oblige in between games. First wipe is free of charge."

"Hope your hands are full of aces." Mathings took them in one more time and tipped his hat again before moving on.

Melinda's neck suddenly prickled, like someone was staring her down.

Lance finished unsaddling the horses and glanced at her. "See something?"

She cocked her head. Anyone else might've brushed off the feeling, but they had been through enough to know when to follow their guts.

"Can't shake the sense of eyes on me," she said finally. "Not sure about it yet. Let's get a bite and maybe I can figure it out."

They had turned to one of the small pub entrances when her fingers gave a twinge.

"Wait." She turned a circle and stopped to face the long line to Candelaria's Gambling Hall. "Something's in there. Maybe the spider. Not sure what to do about that crowd though."

"Got it." Lance strode toward the front of the line.

She hung back as Lance worked his magic, moseying up to the two burly men in fine leather vests at the entrance. Their gruff faces eased up a minute later as Lance started to chat with them and finally passed them a few coins.

Melinda tried not to roll her eyes. How folks could be so easily persuaded to change their tune she had no idea. Coins made sense, but half the time Lance's words alone seemed enough to sway a person. Coins—and weapons—could be controlled, people not so much. She saw after a while that it wasn't so much the words but how you said them, and Lance had a knack. Beatrice always said he could've sold a rain barrel to a fish. Melinda started to smile, until an image of Beatrice crouched over Abel's bed made her chest knot up. In front of the hall's door, Lance tilted his chin under the candlelight, signaling her, and she headed over.

"Have fun," was all one of the gruff men said and lifted the rope for them to enter.

"Don't you get tired of pretending to be someone's friend all the time?" she asked Lance as they pushed open the door.

"Pretending don't get you too far. If you really wanna hear someone's story, that's the difference. Everyone's a little oyster, ready for cracking. And if you *have* to lie ..." Lance grinned. "A little truth makes it go down that much easier."

The saloon's smells, sights, and commotion hit her like a wall. Not one, but four stages at the opposite end of the enormous hall showcased dancers as colorful as peacocks. A boxing ring next to it prompted a mix of groans and cheers from the crowd.

"Monte? Fan Tan? Poker? Craps? Faro?" a velvet-vested man said. He swept his arm out toward the tables covered with ornate dressings, and the patrons with more well-crafted hats and sparkling jewels than Melinda had ever seen. Over the smell of sweat swirled sweet tobacco, a rich mix of floral fragrant oils and wisps of fried meat smoke.

"Take your pick, you won't find fairer games, finer food, or more heavenly singing." The man directed them toward a bar of polished redwood that stretched along an entire side of the hall. Half a dozen barkeeps worked in a frenzy, passing out sloshing drinks as fast as they could pour them. "But first, we're gonna need you to skin yourselves."

They lined up to check in their firearms and hats. Melinda reluctantly set down her six shooter, knife, and Malgun. The attendant tapped his quill against the counter, frowning at Malgun before writing down 'other' next to their names, while another attendant slotted guns on shelves.

"Woo-wee." Lance gave a low whistle as they turned to survey the scene. "Look at the floor."

Marble shone beneath their snow-caked, muddy boots. Another attendant mopped behind them with a scowl.

"Too bad we're not here under better circumstances," Lance said as they made their way past the fanning of cards and flash of brass roulette tables.

"Can't shake the feeling that something's here. Maybe the soul sucker." Melinda's gaze drifted up the diamond-patterned wallpaper that ended at wrought iron and glass chandeliers.

"We could start with her." He pointed. Next to them, a portrait in a gold frame showed a woman in her fifties with "Candelaria Hernández" written beneath.

"Must be the proprietress. In the flesh," Lance said and nodded toward a woman in a tall wheelchair near one of the stages, possibly the only person in the place without a drink in hand.

"Hard to miss."

Candelaria's laugh boomed and a silver chain above her low-cut white dress shook with the movement as she maneuvered over to a faro table. The proprietress had forgone a slim cigarette holder that most of the other women carried; instead, she held a cigar, looking to all the world like she was having the finest time. Her dark eyes, however, were somber and calculating, scanning the tables.

"Ready to crack that 'oyster'?" Melinda murmured as they moved to open spots at a table near Candelaria. Melinda slid next to a woman with coin-sized diamond earrings who was waving away a kiss from a top-hatted man.

"I run the best tables as far as the north winds reach." Candelaria's voice reached the nearby tables, easily commanding attention. She pointed her cigar beyond the stages where, next to a full-sized stuffed bear, a red carpet ran upstairs to the second floor. "Hotel rooms are still available for anyone looking to try their luck in money or love."

The top-hatted man tapped the table, huffed, and laughed as a two of spades flipped. Onstage behind them, a woman, skinny as a newborn calf, erupted into song. Her voice sent her whole body trembling and her blond curls shaking against her black bodice. The red blush smeared up her cheekbones beneath darkened eyelids couldn't make up for her paleness.

"Miss Lil sure is something!" The top-hatted man exclaimed.

"She's one of my sweetest girls." Candelaria turned to their table. "She's come a long way. You want an autograph for a small fee, just head on out back after the show."

"We're antsy to try our hand. Here's hoping we don't spring a leak in our pockets." Lance plopped their bags of coins on the table and tipped his head toward Candelaria. "Don't think we've ever seen such a lovely establishment, and proprietress to match, in all of our travels."

"Fancy yourself a lucky man, stranger?" Candelaria leaned forward in her chair, her considerable bosom flashing.

"Less times than I'd like. But enough." Lance rested one elbow on the table in a casual flex.

Parlor tricks, Melinda thought, but they worked more often than not.

"Where are you all from?" The man she thought of as Top Hat chimed in while the dealer set out the next round.

"Five Peaks, just north."

"That odd town?" Candelaria laughed. "Well, I get about one visitor from there every other year. Something peculiar about a place that don't do enough gambling, if you ask me. Here, you have all the best food, the best entertainment. Everything."

"We're quite fond of the place, believe it or not," Lance said, and Melinda wondered if anyone else caught the small pause, as the vision of Abel in bed likely crossed his mind. "Found ourselves in the way of some extra cash. Want to see if we can make it sing before we settle in."

"You've come to the right place," Top Hat said and leaned to whisper something to the diamonded woman. She laughed and gave him a playful shove.

"Me and Mellie, we take care of unusual problems," Lance continued, locking eyes with Candelaria. "You ever find yourself in the unfortunate circumstance of having some strange critters you can't deal with, Miss, well, then you be sure to call us."

Top Hat laughed.

"Miss Candelaria don't need anyone's help. Hell, you know what put her in the wheelchair there?"

He leaned in confidentially when the proprietress turned away to greet a customer. "They say it happened when she was a kid. She held off an entire flock of vermin in front of the school, and not the natural kind. A band of Edge fire cattle made it all the way down here, believe it or not. But you know their teeth?" He held his hands two feet apart. "Mouths like sharks. Took a clean bite out of her. But she held them off long enough for the other kids to escape. Yes sir, don't let the pretty face fool you. She's tougher than a poked hornet's nest."

The diamonded woman rose an eyebrow. "I heard she led away a swarm of sand mammoths and had to dive off a cliff at Salmon River ..."

Candelaria wheeled back to their table next to Lance. He said something in a Southern language. Top Hat chuckled and chimed in; his accent clumsy even to Melinda's untrained ear. The group erupted in laughter. Lance leaned closer, whispering something else to Candelaria.

Melinda resisted drumming her fingers on the table. They didn't have time for this.

Patience, she told herself, checking her cards. A decent hand.

The diamond-clad woman sighed loudly and turned to Melinda. "Old Candelaria flirts with everyone," she whispered. "I don't normally have a leaky mouth, but rumor is she's had at least three husbands. Honey, how long you been with your man?"

"Three years, just about."

The woman leaned close enough to waft off an orange-scented oil. "Don't it bother you to see him flirting that way? I could never."

"The way I figure, if he sees something he likes, he's welcome to it. I don't have chains 'round him, and he don't 'round me." Melinda didn't add that it was business, evidenced by Lance's hard-working dimple. When it was just the two of them his whole face folded in a full smile, the dimple buried in creases.

The dealer pointed to Melinda and pushed her the pile of winnings. She turned her attention back to the stage, hoping the diamonded woman would get the hint.

"I died one hundred times," Lil wailed from onstage. *"Tripping on the devil's kindness ... Tempted by the dark ..."*

While she listened, Melinda's gaze drifted to Lil's wide belt. It was studded with gemstones, probably worth more than all the money on their table. A metal canister the size of a small mug swung from the belt. Small, dirty.

Melinda's vision swam as red flecks appeared around the canister. The vision vanished a second later.

"That's sweet. You know there are little things you can do. Wear your hair just so, or put some powder on your face," the woman next to her rambled on about tips or other nonsense that Melinda couldn't care less about on a slow day. She glanced over at Lance, who was admiring a ring Candelaria handed to him, and stood.

She threaded through the crowd as the song drew to an end, trying to get closer to glimpse Lil's belt. Lance sidled up next to her a few minutes later.

"Having fun with your new lady friend?"

"Just blending in, love," he said. "And learning a few interesting facts. Two exits in the back. Staircase outside is another entry point. What's cooking?"

She nodded toward the stage. "Canister. Something off about it. Maybe the spider or soul's in it."

A long moment went by. "Strange," Lance said finally. "You think she's the one who sent the spiders?"

"Dunno."

"But why go after Abel?"

Melinda shrugged as the singer finished her song and bowed before heading off the stage. "Scorned lover? Spellcaster? Don't much matter. Get the guns and meet me round back."

Outside the rear exit, Melinda hovered near a lilac bush, keeping an eye on the outhouses.

"Excuse me," a voice said behind her. A uniformed man, about her height and holding a stack of wiping papers, sized her up when she turned.

"Looking for something?" he asked.

She paused, taking stock. One colt at his waist, and roughed knuckles. He'd been in fights before, probably had a move or two. She could handle herself if it had to go that far. Nothing else nearby but a pile of firewood—could come in handy if she needed a makeshift weapon.

"Fan, eh?" he said, taking a slightly kinder tone. "You want an autograph or have a special request for Miss Lil, it'll be two bits at least."

"Just offering my services," Melinda said. The outhouse door banged open and Lil hurried out, not back into the venue but up the outdoor stairs behind the building.

Melinda caught the whiff of something acidic. Darkbellas.

Girl was using. Melinda had met a person or two who got hooked on it; most didn't live too long.

"Miss Lil!" Melinda called, thinking fast. "Your friend sent me."

Lil glanced back, brushing a blonde curl out of her face, her dark-rimmed eyes suspicious. "What are you—"

"Your friend wanted me to bring this." Melinda tapped her pocket. "Something new for you."

"Right. Yes. Don't worry about it, Bill," Lil said to the attendant after a look of eagerness pinched her face. "Come on up then, lady, what are you waiting for?"

Melinda hurried onto the second floor and into a hallway lined with numbered doors. Lil headed into the last one without so much as a glance behind her until they were both inside.

Lil stood by the window and dragged on a cigarette in her gold holder. She expelled a cloud of olive green, acrid darkbella smoke. One sleeve fell off her shoulder as her glare melted from tension to a dreamy openness. "So, what do you have for me?"

"Doesn't make much sense," Melinda muttered. This was the mastermind behind the soul-sucking spiders? Seemed like Lil could barely take care of herself. But it didn't matter much now.

Melinda pulled the switch knife from her waistband she had hidden from the check-in attendants. "Give the canister here and no one needs to know what kind of devilish thing you're caught up in. I'm guessing Miss Candelaria down there wouldn't be too keen on anything that threatened her nice establishment."

Lil stared at her, wide-eyed, then started to smile. "I think you're a mirage." She rose her hands in a surrender and swayed, grinning up at the ceiling.

"Damn addict. Hand over the canister. Now." Melinda stepped forward, knife raised in case Lil was about to try

45

something. Doubtful, but the feeling of something wrong raged like winds on the plains as she started to close her hand around the canister.

The door banged open. Melinda swung around.

A woman stood framed in the doorway, dark as Lil was pale, an enormous hat perched on her black puff of hair.

And with a gun pointed directly at Melinda.

CHAPTER SIX

"So that's what's been on my trail. Gotta give you credit," said the woman, holding a small, engraved two-shot pocket pistol. A red-checked shirt peeked out from under a beaded, fringed jacket. "Nothing like a decoy to bring out the vermin." The woman laughed, a chuckle that grated.

Melinda raised her hands and the knife.

"Decoy? Who are you?" Lil rubbed her eyes, looking between the two women. "Am I dreaming?"

"Eloise Jackson," the woman said, nearly proud. "And I'll be asking the questions."

Eloise's relaxed but steady grip on the pocket pistol meant she was probably a decent shot. Melinda quickly assessed: the woman also stood in an easy, but guarded, stance, like someone who knew how to handle herself in a hand-to-hand fight.

Lil's gaze flitted back and forth between the two, landing on Melinda. "Did you sell me rotten bella?"

"Get back!" Melinda shouted, but in one fluid movement, Eloise was behind Lil.

One of Eloise's hands pointed a gun at Lil's head. The other hand wrapped around Lil in a chokehold, flashing a tattoo of a bird on her forearm. She stood in a strong, stable stance, her knees pressing behind Lil's.

Lil stifled a scream while Eloise tapped the pocket pistol against her temple. "Uh-uh."

Melinda lowered the knife. "No need to hurt your decoy. She ain't part of this. And I know when I'm licked."

She slid the knife across the floor toward Eloise, careful not to let her gaze flick to the side to give any hint that she suspected backup. She just had to keep talking long enough to buy Lance time.

"Quite a getup," Melinda said, nodding to the leather and beaded fringe on Eloise's jacket. "You heading to the rodeo?"

"I spent enough time being invisible in my life. Now, I'm going down in the history books."

Eloise's arm shifted slightly and Melinda tensed, readying for her to move. But Eloise was careful, keeping her gun trained on Lil as she used her other hand to unstrap the metal canister tied to Lil's belt.

Lil looked down in surprise.

"Nothing like an addict to not see the nose under them," Eloise added before she roughly shoved Lil toward Melinda.

"Get out," Melinda said to Lil, sidestepping and turning so her body was between the two. "Now."

"Awfully philanthropic of you," Eloise said while Lil climbed clumsily out of the window. "Seeing as how this is where you fold 'em."

Melinda kept her face motionless as a figure appeared in the doorway.

"You back off nice and slow now, miss," Lance said, his .45 aimed at the back of Eloise's head. Melinda breathed a sigh of relief to see Malgun hoisted on his shoulder. "Gonna be needing our friend's soul back. Right now. And your weapons down." His voice was friendly enough, but his eyes were hard.

"Should've known there were two of you," Eloise said, setting down the pocket pistol on a dresser next to a jade-carved tiger. "Oooh, he's cute though." She winked at Melinda.

Melinda picked up her knife. Something wasn't right. Eloise didn't look as concerned as someone ought to with lead pointed at their skull. In fact, she was still smirking.

Melinda's tensed when she heard the scuttling.

"Lance, Malgun, now!"

Lance tossed her the device. She didn't have time to load it as three spiders scuttled in the doorway behind him, moving unnaturally fast with their razor-thin legs. The three that escaped Abel's place, she guessed.

"Call them off." Melinda pointed Malgun at Eloise. "Or this'll take you to high heaven and b——"

The spiders sprang.

Melinda batted one out of the air with Malgun. It wasn't enough—the spider rebounded and scurried out of the room. Out of the corner of her eye, she spotted Lance using a side table to crush the second spider, which promptly disintegrated into black smoke. Eloise darted to the dresser but Melinda beat her to it, sweeping up the pocket pistol. She swung around in time to see Eloise grab a glass bottle on the desk and hurl it at Lance.

He ducked, but not quickly enough.

The bottle exploded and he stumbled back into the wall.

"Lance!" Melinda shouted as he grabbed his face, sliding to the floor. The third spider leapt from the ceiling onto his shoulder, exposing fangs.

Melinda raised the pocket pistol. One miscalculation and she'd blow a hole through her favorite person in the world.

But then again, she never missed.

She pulled the trigger just as the spider readied to bite. With the gun blast, the spider disappeared into a black puff. A peculiar wisp of light gray smoke lingered for a moment until Eloise whipped out a second canister from her pocket to capture it.

"Stop!" Melinda tossed the empty pocket pistol aside and pointed Malgun at Eloise, though everything in her wanted to run to Lance. "End of the line for you."

"I don't think so." Eloise looked up. "You've been outta aces for a while."

"Bluff," Melinda said, but a red cloud appeared faster than a twister, obscuring her view. Before she could get her bearings,

Eloise lunged through the mist. Melinda's arm shot up reflexively to block, but she was half a second too slow. Eloise's fist bounced off her temple. Melinda staggered back, lights exploding behind her eyes. The floor shifted, sending her slumping against the wall.

The throb in her head swelled, threatening to take over. Melinda gritted her teeth and forced her eyes open past the flashing pain.

A pale face with black hair and a thin mustache hovered in the red cloud, talking to Eloise in a low tone that sounded like rodents scuttling.

Something about his voice would have sent Melinda automatically reaching for her gun if she could move. It wasn't just his tone that set every one of her nerves on alert. It was also the fact that his shoulders blurred into the hovering crimson fog, and his feet had vanished entirely.

The man in the red cloud.

"... want to reap the benefits, you need to bring me the souls. Only one spider left ... can't fail."

A pause, then Eloise's voice, almost cocky. "I won't, Harston. Three days at most to get them there. What's special about this one anyway?"

Harston, Melinda thought through the heaviness settling into her eyes and ears. It seemed important to remember. She tried to stand but wasn't there yet. She strained to see Lance through the smoke. Still unmoving.

"Imagine a little candle, flickering with the wind, that's your soul. Now imagine a ten-foot-tall fire," Harston said. "That's what you're bringing to me, see? No more delays. You get your reward then, and more."

Melinda pulled herself up on her forearms before the floor rushed up to meet her face. She turned to see Harston smiling directly at her. It looked like the smile of a corpse, cheeks pinned up to mimic joy.

"What ... you want ..." Melinda managed.

"Shame there's no time to take a little taste," Harston said.

He was harder to see, maybe more translucent, or maybe it was Melinda's vision going. She could just make out Eloise's smirk as she tipped her hat and blew Lance's unconscious form a kiss.

"It's been fun," she said.

Melinda reached out for Lance, but a curtain was falling over her thoughts. The last thing she spotted through her tunneling vision were the two canisters swinging against Eloise's belt before she strode away.

CHAPTER SEVEN

Melinda stirred.

It was dark and quiet. Well, not completely quiet. The faint hum of music and drunk chatter floated up to her. Her mind stayed blank, peaceful for a minute before the memories of the last day, the last hour, slammed back into place one by one like soldiers reporting for duty.

Abel. Harston.

Lance.

Melinda shot up and winced. The back of her head had grown heavy and what felt like a bruise started to bloom along her forehead. Splinters seemed to be wedged behind her eyes. Given the stillness of the air, she guessed a little while had passed. Nearby, Lance groaned.

"You alive, I take it?" She tried to blink the world back into place.

"That'll leave a mark." Lance unfurled to a sitting position, touching his forehead before looking at the blood on his hand. He winced. "We were so close."

"Eloise had someone with her. The man I saw. Some sort of sorcerer or ghost, appearing out of thin air." Melinda racked her brain through the fog, trying to remember the conversation, hoping talking about it would bring some details back. "Name was Harston. Eloise said three days to get him something. Shoot, there was something else. Maybe it'll come back to me."

Before Lance could answer, footsteps pounded down the hallway. The door swung open, and two figures loomed in the sudden lamplight. Sheriff Mathings and another, even younger, lawmaker stepped in, looking fresh in a neatly trimmed mustache and beard, striped vest, and polished badge. Mathings moved his shotgun in a controlled arc around the destroyed room, before pointing it at them.

"Well, I had a feeling you two were trouble," Mathings said matter-of-factly while Melinda and Lance raised their hands from their sitting positions. "Wong, cuff them, would you please?"

"We can explain," Lance said, staggering to his feet with his hands still up. His words came slower than normal, shooting a stab of worry through Melinda. "There was a gal here, gunslinger, using some soul-sucking magic. You seem like a reasonable man. Please, you got to listen to us."

"That's enough, if you don't mind," Mathings said. "Miss Lil is missing, so we'll be bringing you in as the first order of business."

"You got some things to answer for," Wong chimed in.

"We aren't who you're looking for," Melinda said and assessed. Mathings kept the shotgun trained on them, while Wong moved behind Lance to cuff him. Malgun was just out of reach and no other weapon in sight. One look at Lance and she knew he didn't have it in him to try to get out of this mess right now, whether through fighting or words. She didn't either, as evidenced by her spinning head. Not much she could do anyway with the shotgun pointed at them.

"Locking us up with no proof?" she said, as Wong clasped iron cuffs around her wrists. "Isn't that overstepping?"

"Looks like a bull tore through here, I'd say that's proof enough." Mathings raised an eyebrow, a fold along his forehead burying half of his thin scar. "But if you don't feel like conversating now, you can cool off with a few nights in jail and we can try again."

"We don't have time for that," Lance burst. "You got a soul-sucking criminal on the loose."

"Watch your tone with the sheriff," Wong said, a firm hand on each of their shoulders to push them forward. Melinda looked over her shoulder to see Mathings pick up Malgun with interest.

"I'd appreciate you taking care with that," she said. He merely nodded, but she could see from his quick glance that he understood it was a weapon that needed gentle handling.

Ten minutes later and despite their protests, she and Lance were shoved into a jail cell barely bigger than an outhouse. Iron bars, no windows, just a few vents high above their head for a little bit of air and moonlight. Stone, Melinda saw, not adobe brick that they might've had a chance to dig out of.

Lance ran a hand through his hair in agitation and pounded a fist against the small wooden bench. Dried blood and gunpowder darkened his face, but his eyes were what really made Melinda worry – he looked more hopeless than she had ever seen him.

"The canister is probably miles away already." He slumped against the wall. "And Abel's getting worse by the second, no doubt."

She sat on the bench next to him, pulling out her handkerchief to blot at his forehead cut. At least it had stopped bleeding.

"We'll figure it out. Always do," she told him, though her words felt hollow even to herself. "A jail cell isn't gonna stop us."

For a second, she wanted nothing more than to curl against him, feel his arm casually swung over her, and take a long nap.

A gaze pricked her shoulder.

She turned to see a jail mate across from them, grinning at her with a face full of freckles. His body stench reached them from even a few feet away.

"You cross Ms. Candelaria, you ain't never getting' out." The man's voice hit a faint whine. "You cheat once, lie once, whatever it is, she goes sour on you. All I did was try to up my luck at some cards, and whaddya know, I'm in here for days. It ain't fair."

"We didn't do anything wrong," Lance said, and the man stiffened, staring at Lance in a way that Melinda knew wouldn't be good.

"I don't wanna share a pen with no halfer!" The man hollered. "Hell no! It's bad luck!"

Melinda rolled her eyes as the prisoner kept shaking his bars. Lance ignored him, shoulders slumped, undoubtedly thinking of Abel.

"Roy, you better cool it in there." Wong's warning floated over from a massive wooden desk down the hall. "No one needs to hear that kinda hateful talk."

Melinda stood and strained to see the desk better, hoping to spot Malgun. Piles of papers, plates, mugs, and other junk towered high enough that she could barely see Wong. He was peering into a handheld mirror and combing his neat mustache with the concentration of a surgeon. Behind him fluttered a thick layer of posters and notices tacked onto the wall.

She tapped the bars. "You have the whole history of High Hawk over there?"

Wong looked around like he was seeing the mess for the first time and scratched his chin. "Plenty to track. No thanks to you all adding to my workload."

"Hey." Melinda squinted, focusing on one of the fluttering notices that read WANTED - ARSENIC THEFT PETTY CRIME ASSAULT BATTERY DISORDERLY. Beneath it was drawn a smirking face and wide, beaded hat. "That was her, Eloise! That's who attacked us!"

Lance jumped up and joined her at the bars. "Mellie, you have a sharper eye than an eagle! That's the lead we need."

"Shush, all of you," Wong said crossly. "How's a man supposed to get any work done around here?"

"By work, you mean getting ready for the ladies," Roy cackled.

"Shut it, Roy."

Melinda could practically see Lance switch into his slick mode, his voice lifting and dimple flashing. "That's her, deputy, I'd swear it on my pop's grave. List is longer than a horse trough." He whistled. "Seems like no crime has escaped our friend Miss Jackson. If we'd find her, we'd find your missing Lil, and a big bag of cash besides. It'd be a shame to let that opportunity go up the spout."

Even Roy quieted at that, listening keenly. Wong looked over his shoulder and back at them.

"Bounty hunters have been looking for Eloise Jackson for months," he said. "Hard to believe you just happened to see her."

"She had a ..." Melinda racked her brain for the details. *Pocket pistol. Gaudy hat. And a—* "tattoo on her right wrist. Some kinda bird."

Wong unpinned the wanted poster and flipped it to the smaller text on the back. After scanning it, he stood up. "All of you stay quiet 'til I get back, now."

Wong banged through the front door and Melinda and Lance exchanged glances. No telling how long he'd be gone, but this could be their chance to skedaddle.

"Ever been in a jail cell before?" she asked.

Lance thought for a second. "Locked in an outhouse for a night after losing a bet. That'd be the closest."

"Figures. You always lose at bets." Melinda tested each of the bars.

"Lucky in love at least," he said, a hint of his mischievousness coming back. They inspected the cell, combing every inch to see if there was anything that would give, anything they could use.

"Shoot, what else do you know about this outlaw?" Roy said. "You can get me outta here too, maybe we could partner up, split that reward money?"

Melinda ignored him. "There's got to be something," she said to Lance.

"Place is tighter than a mechanic's watch," Lance said. The little bit of hope went out of his eyes, making her more determined.

"Well, I'm not giving—"

The front door swung open. Wong returned, this time with Mathings. Melinda stiffened, readying in case there was an opportunity to escape, until she saw Candelaria wheel in behind them; her piercing gaze marked them like an arrow. Mathings and Wong stood more squarely toward Candelaria like good soldiers, though Melinda saw the shift in Mathings, how he held himself a little more attentively.

"We can explain," Lance said.

"Not much to explain. Lil told us everything." Candelaria's eyes seemed to glisten. "She's like a daughter to me. If you hadn't been there to save her who knows what the outlaw would've done."

Melinda blinked, not sure she was hearing right. With an unsure look at Lance, she kept her mouth shut and he followed suit. No need to mention that they were the ones who got Lil into trouble in the first place, on account of Eloise needing a decoy and all. But Lil, in her darkbella haze, maybe didn't catch all the details of their close encounter.

"Glad you found her," was all Melinda said.

"Poor dear was in a fright at her friend's house. Could barely talk for a few hours," Candelaria said.

"Miss Lil's description of the outlaw fit it to the T," Mathings said, while Wong unlocked their cell door. "Already sent a telegram to Thousand Hills and Green Juniper. Last spotted there and caused a ruckus before vanishing. People say she's untraceable."

Lance and Melinda exchanged looks as they shuffled out of the cell, keeping their card faces on. So far, it seemed like the folks running this town didn't have a sense of the more unusual aspects of Eloise's criminal spree, but no need to get into all that.

"We have our ways of tracking," Lance said.

Had, Melinda thought, picturing the fallen dreambug. She nodded thanks to Wong as he opened a wooden cabinet and handed them back their hats and guns. She checked Malgun, making sure its missile was still strapped along its barrel, and took Eloise's *Wanted* poster from the wall too.

They trailed Candeleria and Mathings outside the propped-open door. Melinda took in a few long breaths of the cold night air, waiting for it to rejuvenate her. But she just felt tired, her head aching something fierce. What she wouldn't give for some of Aunt

B's chili and a pile of sheepskins to sink into right after, maybe a brandy or two first.

"Eloise stole something dear from us, so we aren't letting up anytime soon," Lance continued.

"Good." Candelaria's eyes hardened, all traces of the flippant hostess gone.

"I can help! The more the merrier, ain't that right?" Roy's shout, eager and muffled, drifted out the door.

"Roy, I *swear.*" Wong's voice floated in response.

"You track her down with whatever ways you have, and a few folks'll be mighty glad," Mathings said, sizing the two of them up.

"More than glad. Justice must be served. But first, this one needs a stitch or two. He's rugged, but not that rugged," Candelaria said, looking Lance up and down. Though Melinda didn't fancy herself the jealous type, a stab of annoyance cut through her cloud of fatigue. "You get yourself cleaned up and some substance. Hotel room and food on the house. We'll send the doctor over so you'll be tiptop shape before you go."

"That would be fine," Lance said.

"Can't keep running on nothing," Melinda agreed. Though she hated to admit it, exhaustion weighed her bones down, and the mention of a meal and sleep made her want to collapse in relief. The thought of Abel back home and Beatrice beside him flooded her with a cold wave of guilt. But Beatrice would've been the first to tell them that they wouldn't be good to anyone unless they were healed up and rested.

"We leave first thing. One problem," Melinda said, more to Lance than the others as she scanned the Wanted poster in her hand. "This doesn't give us any idea of where she might be headed. Trail's cold. Only thing I can think to do is go up to the last two towns where she was, ask around for some clues."

Lance's face fell. "Damn. That'll take too long, we're playing catch-up."

"How'd you track her this far, if you don't mind sharing?" Mathings asked. "Plenty of good bounty hunters have tried and failed. One's been tracking her for months, got close a few times, from what I understand." He rubbed his cheek alongside of the scar, looking pained for a minute. "If I had known an outlaw of her stature was in my town, I wouldn't have stopped until she was caught."

"Don't be so hard on yourself," Candelaria said. "There's no one else I'd rather have as sheriff."

Mathings ducked his head the slightest, masking his embarrassment.

"She's got someone helping her. Someone unnatural," Melinda said. "I had ... well, a vision to help us. But I lost it."

She watched the reaction—or lack of—in Mathings. Not shocked. Candelaria too. They must've seen a thing or two in their town, and seemed to be exchanging silent signals.

"Tell you what," Mathings said at last. "We have a bit of a mystic too, in fact. Lives on the outskirts of town. She doesn't normally take visitors, but she'll help you, maybe be able to get your vision back."

Lance perked up, but Melinda couldn't help but feel skeptical.

"If she don't take callers, why would she help us?" she asked.

"Everyone owes Miss Candelaria a favor," Mathings chuckled.

Candelaria smiled. "Mutual relationships build a better world. An escort will go with you. I'm sure Mathings has some good folks to recommend."

"Uh-uh." Melinda rubbed her temples. "We travel on our own. Way it's always been."

"Sweetie, you both look run ragged," Candelaria said. "One thing I learned early on in my life is to take help when it's offered."

"Just point us to your mystic. We'll take it from there," Melinda said.

"I'm afraid there's no arguing with Miss Candelaria," Mathings cut in. "I insist on meeting you at dawn and taking you there myself."

"Guess it can't hurt," Lance piped up.

"Fine." Truth be told, she was too tired to argue. "But you can't slow us down."

"Go now, eat and rest." Candelaria gestured grandly toward a nearby building that Melinda assumed was another establishment she owned. The smaller saloon emitted cheery banjo music. The wood and paint looked well-kept, with lit windows on the top floor. "Anything else you need, tell any of the barkeeps. And just know, you are always welcome in High Hawk."

CHAPTER EIGHT

After the doc patched up their wounds as best she could, Melinda and Lance enjoyed a spread of chops, buffalo beef, roasted deer, and grilled snake at a roped-off table next to the bar. Pie, mashed potatoes and plenty of blackberry liquor and whiskey ensured they were fuller than ticks.

But none of it was enough to ease the knot in Melinda's stomach. With past jobs, they were done in a day or two. Simple, clean. This was a different story. Trying to find someone they didn't know without a good way to track, while Abel's life depended on them, seemed like a losing hand.

She kept drinking, more than she should've, in part to chase away the worry about Abel that gnawed at her insides. She nudged Lance, who had stopped eating and was staring into space in the direction of the band onstage.

"Worried about you."

"Just tuckered. Getting too old for this." Lance picked at the bandage on his forehead above the decent-sized shiner.

"I told you, no calling yourself old until we're both sitting on a porch with bad backs, after a good fifty years at least."

He chuckled and motioned for more whiskey.

"Fancy Mathings has a crush on Miss Candelaria?" Melinda asked, downing the rest of her drink.

He considered. "Powerful woman like that and his boss besides? Probably wouldn't be the smartest move for him."

"Bet you ten pieces."

"You're on." Lance tapped his fingers as the band started the next song, *West of the Purple River.* "Nice to have a real room at least to rest up," he said, the whiskey putting some color back in his cheeks. "Shall we dance?"

"You're joking. I'm bone tired and you've looked better."

"All the more reason." Lance pulled her up. "Anything to make us feel normal for a breath or two."

Melinda relented, the buzz of liquor making her limbs loose. The band was decent, a little heavier on the fiddle than she preferred, but it had a good mix of strings and percussion, and a banjo to boot. They headed to the floor and hooked arms, boots clinking on the marble. She allowed herself a smile as they spun. She couldn't remember the last time they had shed off their cares, at least for a few minutes. Dancing was one of the things she was good at – anything physical really seemed to come naturally to her, as long as she didn't have to talk to anyone.

The music cast its spell and for a second, she forgot about Abel and Harston and Eloise. The only things that mattered were Lance's face, close and intense, lamplight glowing along his cheekbones; his arms firm and unwavering against her; the murmurs and laughs of drunken gamblers a chorus beneath the strumming.

The music swelled for its grand finale, as the fiddler played his heart out. Lance wavered. One too many drinks, Melinda assumed, until he lurched.

"Lance!" She grabbed his shoulders to steady him. "You must've taken a bigger hit to the head than—"

"Just too much thunder for one day." He straightened and ran a hand through his hair. "Sorry, Mellie. Call it a night?"

She hooked his arm. "That's the best idea I've heard all day. Let's get you to bed."

Candelaria hadn't spared an expense; an attendant led them upstairs to one of the immaculate guest rooms. Lance barely hit the pillow before he started snoring. Melinda took a little more time, setting her wooden figurine on the oak stand next to them—part of her bedtime ritual in hopes of keeping the nightmares away. She added Abel's satchel on the windowsill, sending Beatrice a silent thanks for giving it to them before turning down the lantern. Whatever supernatural powers they were dealing with, at least the pouch would keep them hidden enough so they could sneak up on Eloise, maybe get the jump on her before Harston appeared again or unleashed another spider.

When sleep finally took hold, nightmares came and went, more vivid than usual, probably from the dreambug's bite. Lance and Abel dissolving into skeletons. A momma scorpion chittering in a cave. Harston, with his pale cheeks and burning eyes, grinning at her as though she was a piece of steak on the table. Eloise's laughter. Her mother's hands, grasping the bluebell in her bed.

Melinda woke up in a start, the sheepskins sliding off her.

"What is it?" Lance mumbled, grasping her hand in his half-sleep.

"Dream. And dawn."

Lance hauled himself up, blinking bloodshot eyes. She started to ask if he wanted to wait but stopped herself. They didn't have the time and Abel didn't have long either. Whatever Lance was feeling, he could fight it off. Truth be told, she didn't feel so great either, with a whiskey headache shooting a drumbeat through her temples. After chugging coffee and shoveling down eggs with a few other bleary-eyed souls at the bar, they headed outside to meet Mathings.

"Late night?" Mathings said, sipping his canteen from a bay horse and looking spiffy in crisp stripes beneath a matching vest and wide-brimmed leather hat.

Melinda shot him a look. He tipped a hat to her.

"Not gonna apologize for jailing the two of you," he said. "If that's what you're expecting. I would've done it again, given the circumstances. Better to be safe than sorry."

"Fair enough," Lance said while they saddled up the horses. Melinda purchased a new saddlebag for Pepper, making sure

Abel's pouch, a canteen of water and wrapped dried jerky from the saloon were securely inside. They set off at a spirited pace down an east-facing trail, sidestepping dustings of snow.

At least someone's well-rested, Melinda thought and sucked in the crisp air, waiting for it to clear her headache.

"Sure hope your mystic can help us," she commented.

"She's guided us out of a pickle or two. Miss Candelaria has a keen eye for talent," Mathings said.

"So, Sheriff," Melinda said once the coffee finally hit her. "You and Miss Candelaria known each other long?"

He shifted, answering a tad too quickly. "A few years. Truth be told, never fancied myself a sheriff until I met her, but she saw something in me and sure enough, I seemed to have a knack for it."

"It's true what they say, she fought Edge monsters that put her in that chair?"

Mathings smiled. "There's a lot of stories about her, each as likely as the next." There was no denying the glimpse of admiration, and something more, in his voice.

She looked back to raise an eyebrow to Lance. "Won the bet. You owe me," she mouthed.

He shook his head, pretending to be flummoxed.

"This mystic lives on her own?" Lance asked instead while they took the last turn down the valley. A single house rose at its edge, with yellow painted wood and chimes made of hammered metal. "Could imagine someone trying to take advantage of such a gift."

"Candelaria set her up with a helper or two." Mathings tapped a satin bag tied with a ribbon on his saddle. "This'll get you a few minutes of her time."

A girl with hair the color of gold waved at them from the open window. "Welcome!" She wore a neatly pressed embroidered dress, a barrette in her hair.

Melinda assumed she was the helper, but a moment later, as Sheriff Mathings dismounted and gave a deep tip of his hat toward the window, she realized this was the mystic.

"May I introduce two visitors for Miss Aine Cary, Mr. Lance Putnam and Ms. Melinda West," Mathings called to the door.

A portly man came out to unlock the fence and accepted the satin bag from Mathings.

"Howdy. Gene's the name." The man stuck out his hand, cheery as a jaybird. Hair clasped in a long ponytail, checkered bowtie, and a trim beard framed his round face. He was big enough to be a brute in a fight, but, judging by the nervous way he ducked his head and held himself hunched, he probably couldn't even swing a punch properly. Melinda did a double take when she spotted his eyes, a peculiar shade of green like a lake on a summer day. Whereas Lance's eyes were bluish and gray, changing like a storm, Gene's eyes looked like something painted, like something *lit*.

"Howdy." She shook his hand warily. She never trusted folks who were too friendly at first, but Gene's smile was warm and sincere.

"How is Miss Aine doing today?" Mathings asked. "Hopefully receptive."

"No guarantees. But good day for it," Gene said. He spoke more formally than Melinda was used to, which made her think of some of the newer towns with folks that kept to themselves, following strict rules of one book or another. "The sunshine helps, and a bite in the air. And the gift, of course."

"Awfully young, isn't she?" Melinda said as they trailed behind him to the front door, sidestepping prowling cats and a chicken, and leaving Mathings behind to wait.

Gene smiled. "Mystic powers don't have an age or type it seems, miss."

Inside, between more chimes and the scent of muffins, Gene opened the ribboned bag, gently taking out Mathings' gifts: two coins, a bottle of brandy, a glass of perfume, and a small bound journal.

The golden-haired girl, Aine, wandered over, her dreamy gaze seeming to look right past them.

"Lovely," Aine said. She picked up and set down each item several times before sitting. "If I don't touch things in exactly the right way the universe begins to unravel."

Melinda couldn't help but raise an eyebrow and glance at Lance. This was the mystic that was going to help them track down Eloise? He gave a tiny shrug and they both slid into overstuffed chairs around a wood table. Aine's eyes were pale as clear crystal. *Unnerving,* Melinda thought.

Aine began to speak random words as though she were talking about the weather: "Eyes in the snow. Lines like arrows. Sugar and salt. Oh, so much salt!"

"Maybe tell her what you need," Gene suggested, heading to the kitchen. "Miss Aine, these fine folks are looking for your assistance."

"We need to follow a trail. Our friend's soul has been taken." Melinda knew it would sound strange but pressed on, guessing that a mystic would be more than likely to understand. "We followed a soul sucker this far but need your help."

"You got any dreambugs? Or any other ways to see the unseeable?" Lance chimed in as Gene set down a tray with a steaming china set smelling of black tea. "No price is too high."

Aine pressed bony hands together and murmured, "Pepper. And what strange, strange moons."

Gene shrugged and smiled, as if telling them to be patient, and sipped his tea. Aine started paging through a book.

After a few long moments, Lance stood. "We don't have time for this. We'd have better luck on our own, I'd reckon."

Melinda gaped at him. Usually, she was the one needing to work on her patience. "Let's give it a minute," she said.

Gene nodded and excused himself back to the kitchen while Aine murmured to herself.

"Why're you acting like a hen on a hot griddle?" Melinda said to Lance.

He blinked, looking distant before giving a small smile. "Haven't felt right today. My thoughts are all wrong, like I'm underwater. Hangover, maybe. Or a nasty bug."

"Exhaustion talking, I'd wager. I'm plump tuckered too," Melinda said, and he nodded. "And worried to death about Abel."

They both perked as Gene returned with a plate of hot strawberry muffins.

"My favorite," Melinda said before taking a bite. The muffin crumbled in her mouth, warm and sweet, the strawberry bits hot on her tongue. Picking berries with her momma had been one thing she looked forward to every summer when she was a kid. The strawberries were easy for her to reach even when she was little, and she'd fill up two baskets in barely a blink, to her mother's delight. That was when it was just the two of them, heading out early to the fields, the smell of spring in the air and a whole day of baking ahead. "My ma used to make these way back when."

"Miss Aine had a feeling. Asked me and my missus to bake them fresh this morning. Luckily, we had some preserves in the cellar." Gene said with a smile.

"How does all this work, anyhow?" Lance asked, sounding more like himself after a hearty bite.

"The way I understand it, there's lots of lines of information out there," Gene said. "You know the telegram? It's kinda like that, but with lots of invisible lines all over the world. Seems Miss Aine is able to hear all of those. Sometimes it takes a while to hear the one she wants."

"Ain't that something," Lance said. "Surprised everyone's not banging down her door."

"Miss Candelaria does a good job of protecting her. While we wait, tell me about yourselves," Gene said in an eager way that reminded Melinda of a pup. He turned to Lance. "Mr. Putnam, you have firstcomers' blood in you, yes?"

Melinda stiffened but Lance merely nodded. "Pa from the Northern People of the Horizon. Ma was a newcomer from one of the Grand Isles. She left quick after I was born. Pa's family didn't take too kindly to her. She tried her best, but it was too much, I guess. Pa and I set out to find her, but you know how that kind of story ends."

"Miss your home?" Gene said, helping himself to one of the muffins. Melinda tried not to stare at his eyes, which now looked like emeralds that belonged more on a rich woman's necklace than in a person's skull.

"It's not really home, considering I haven't been there since a swaddling," Lance said. "'Sides, home is what you make of it."

"How about you?" Melinda cut in. "Where'd you get eyes like that—is your family from the Grand Isles?"

"No miss, never even seen the ocean. I'm from a town not worth mentioning a few days East. Religious. Haven't been back since I got struck by lightning when I was a kid. After that, my eyes changed color and I got a sense of things—finding what's missing, guessing what people are gonna do. Nothing like Miss Aine's ability of course, but enough that folks didn't take well to it. People where I grew up are old-fashioned. Superstitious. So, I had to get myself out."

Lance whistled. "Who would've thought lightning could give a gift like that? So many things we can't explain in this world."

"Ain't that the truth." Gene looked sad for a minute but then brightened. "I met my missus here, made myself a home, and it's all been peaches since."

"He doesn't have much longer." Aine's voice rang out with more conviction than a preacher's, as if she were a different person. Her colorless eyes framed by golden eyelashes looked directly at Melinda. "Your Abel, that is."

Lance's face drained and Melinda felt the floor move away from her. They hadn't mentioned Abel's name.

"Tell us where to go," Lance said.

"She'll be in Goldie before tomorrow's sundown," Aine said in that same voice. "You must stop her before she reaches the Edge."

"The Edge?" Gene set down his muffin and quickly patted his face with a napkin. "You'll never come back if you go."

"She's not gonna get that far." Melinda stood, drawing up her mental map. Goldie was one of half a dozen border towns a few miles from the inaccessible ridge of peaks that made up the Edge, nestled into the Northern Ridge Mountains. Closer to the Edge than she'd like.

"You must go with them," Aine said, and they all paused. Aine fixed her marbled gaze on Gene with a clarity that sent a shiver down Melinda's spine. "Help them track."

"Pardon? I, ah ..." Gene sputtered. "I can't."

"We're quite capable on our own, Miss Aine," Melinda said. "You already pointed us the right way and we can take it from here."

"Floating fish and fire sticks," Aine shook her head and waved her hands, agitated. "He must. You must. You must."

"OK," Gene said, visibly shaken. "If that's your wish, Miss Aine."

"Might not be a bad idea," Lance said quietly to Melinda. "If he's got a bit of a sense for finding stuff, he could help us get to Eloise faster."

Melinda groaned inwardly. The last thing they needed was dead weight, someone to keep track of and protect.

"You have to stop him," Aine said, eyes unfocused.

"You mean her? Eloise?" Lance said.

Melinda shuddered and felt cold despite the proximity to the fireplace. "She must mean Harston. Who is he and what does he want?"

"Metal ... cylinders," Aine frowned.

"The canister," Melinda whispered.

Aine nodded. "Once he has enough ..."

"Then what?" Lance's fists gripped the table. "Then what happens?"

But Aine's eyes had gone unfocused again. Gene sighed and stood, guiding Aine to the rocking chair.

"She's spent for the day. You're not getting any more," Gene said. He penned a note and packed a small leather bag with food and a canteen before adjusting his bowler hat neatly atop his ponytailed hair.

"She'll be OK alone?" Lance asked.

"My missus will keep an eye on her."

"Your wife don't mind you leaving with us?" Melinda asked.

"We know when Miss Aine tells us something it's important," Gene said. "Missus will be back from the blacksmith soon enough. I'm hoping the sheriff can keep watch on Miss Aine until then."

"Thank you." Lance tipped his hat to Aine's blank stare and went out the door behind Gene. Before Melinda could follow, Aine's voice split the air.

"It's worse than you know." The woman's face was flush beneath her tangle of hair even though her lips were tinged the slightest blue, as if she had just taken a dunk in river water. "His soul is seeping fast. Fast."

"I know—the spider took Abel's soul—" Melinda started, but then noticed how Aine's gaze was fixed through the open door with a look like she saw someone riddled through with bullets.

A bolt seared through Melinda as she realized who Aine was talking about.

Lance.

"You're wrong. He wasn't bit—" Melinda cut off as she remembered how a wisp of smoke had remained after she shot the creature off Lance—and how the smoke had gone into Eloise's canister ... "*No.*"

"Has a little bitty piece of his soul." Aine continued staring at the door. "*He's* going to take the rest. And your soul too."

CHAPTER NINE

Melinda burst out into the sharp sunlight, her thoughts whirling. Part of Lance's soul stolen. That would explain why he had been so down. So off. Lance shot her a curious look as she joined the group by the horses. "All right?" he mouthed.

Melinda nodded. As soon as they had a second alone, she'd tell him, first chance she got.

"You go ahead and take my bay here," Mathings said to Gene, handing over his horse's reigns. "My deputy's on the way."

"You'll get the note to my wife?" Gene nervously passed his leather bag between his hands.

"Surely will." Mathings looked at his pocket watch. "If you hustle—and I mean really hustle—you might be able to catch the ten o'clock train. Fastest way to Goldie."

"Thanks kindly," Gene said with a wheeze. He leaned down, hands on his knees.

"You need some sniffing salts there, partner?" Lance asked as Mathings helped him up.

"Little nervous is all." Gene sucked in air like he had run a mile. "Haven't been out of town in ages."

Melinda couldn't help but groan, and Lance shot her a look. Having Gene tag along was going to be a bigger hassle than she'd guessed.

"You take care." Mathings gave Gene a friendly slap on the back. "Must be real serious if Miss Aine wants you to go."

Gene just nodded, stricken silent from panic, Melinda suspected. They didn't talk much as they cantered east along the valley.

She pulled Pepper in the back, keeping a keen eye on Lance. He seemed to ride fine enough, steadier than Gene at least. An hour or so of riding finally put the train into view.

"There it is." Gene sounded excited despite himself. "The H&NR."

"The High Hawk and Northern Ridge Railway," Lance guessed as they neared the transport coach entrance.

"Alphabet soup is all I hear," Melinda said while she coaxed Pepper up the wooden walkway into the coach. She tethered the horse into one of the stalls, next to roped-up boxes of crates. Pepper flicked her ears and snorted.

"I'd just as much prefer to be riding than on the train too," Melinda said with a pat. "But it's only for a few hours. I'll be a few coaches down."

"You look about as excited as a cat in a room full of rocking chairs," Lance said when she joined him in line. "All that we've seen, and a train got you nervous?"

"Why can't we just take the horses up?"

"Too steep. It'd take us days instead of a few hours. We'll get to the next stop at sunset, then take them a few miles to Goldie." He shifted from foot to foot, antsier than she had ever seen him. Partly from worrying about Abel, yes. But ever since Aine's warning, Melinda could see the signs of his soul seeping. It made sense now, why he seemed lost in thought, distant, even a little prickly at times.

"I gotta tell you some ..." Melinda cut short when Gene joined them.

"Beautiful invention," Gene said, beaming like he had built it. "Rode it twice before. Nothing quite like it. Eight cars. Two years in the making."

"So," Lance said while they inched up the line. "You track a lot of critters?"

Gene shook his head. "Never. Mainly just point folks in the right direction. Help them find a missing heirloom, or occasional cow."

"What does it feel like?" Melinda asked to get her mind off the train as the line shuffled forward.

"Oh, I dunno. Like a sense of something settling in just right. I don't actually see anything. More of a feeling. And I can't really control it."

Lance gave a low whistle as they climbed up the stairs and into the train, taking in its cedar wood frames and oiled leather seats. "Mighty nice contraption."

"I don't know about this," Melinda said and jumped as a steam whistle blared. Soot billowed into the air. The train lurched and she almost stumbled.

"Best to sit 'til we hit altitude," Gene said and handed them wrapped biscuits from his bag before biting into one himself. "You'll know when we see the first glimpses of Needleside. They say twenty some men died building this railroad."

Melinda and Lance passed two rows of ladies deep in conversation and a snoozing family until they reached the next pair of seats. "You got thoughts on our new companion?" Lance said as they hung up their dusters and settled in.

"Hoping he don't get in the way." She didn't dare look out the window, where a steep drop flashed between the olive-green brushes of fir trees.

Lance grinned. "We've been on more treacherous trails through this at least a dozen times."

"It's different when you're in a steel contraption," she said through gritted teeth. "Can't control much if she decides to veer off track."

"She won't." He tipped his hat back and closed his eyes. Worry spiked through her again as she studied the scratches and bruises from yesterday's wrangling stark against his tanned skin.

"I gotta tell you something," Melinda said.

"Can't it wait a bit? I'm tired."

"Not really, no."

A little snore escaped him, and she tapped his knee. *"Lance."*

He snored again. She studied his face for a second, wondering if it was the soul sucking. But he could always fall asleep faster than a fly on meat, so she decided to let him be, for now.

Her own eyes grew heavy as the train's clanking reverberated and the city of High Hawk and the other Western towns rolled away from them.

She jolted awake. She couldn't move, even though she was all too aware of the train chugging along. Lance still snored across from her and her fingers tinged warningly.

"Mellie," a voice said. *His* voice.

Harston.

She tried to shake her head, to yell, to move, anything. But her body was frozen, and she felt like she was rapidly sinking down a hole.

"Your little bag of charms won't help you now," Harston said, amused.

Abel's pouch—her heart sank remembering it was in Pepper's saddlebag, a few carriages away. She didn't know the radius of the damned thing but had assumed it'd work just fine.

She assumed wrong.

Melinda projected words in her mind: *"That's Melinda to you. We're going to find you."*

"Your beloved doesn't have long." Harston sounded smug. *"His soul is leaking out and I'll get the rest."*

"I'm going to shoot you and all your soul suckin' creatures." She tried moving her hands, even her eyes, but she was still frozen.

She could almost see, with her vision that wasn't quite vision, the form of Harston taking root, red as though drenched in a brilliant sunrise, standing between her and Lance.

"Tell me, Mellie, who do you spot in the shadows?"

She didn't answer, but the question sent a shiver of dread down her spine. Harston's sallow face and mop of black hair came into focus as he leaned in and made a sound like an inhale.

"Mmm, your spirit smells so delightful. Tasty," he said. A trickling sensation moved along her cheek and down her neck, like beads of water. She would've given anything to smack it away right then. *"Just as damaged as theirs. Just as tender."*

Damaged? She may miss her momma and not care for people much, but that didn't make her damaged. The trickling sensation moved down her arm and then under her shirt. Like fingertips, she realized in disgust.

"Appreciate you keeping your damn hands to yourself," she said, and the sensation paused.

"Tell you what. You want to help him," Harston continued. *"I'll give your lover's soul back. For a price."*

"I'm listening."

"All you have to do is call off your search. Leave Abel's soul with me."

"Ain't happening." The sinking feeling intensified, her stomach dropping away. She tried to hold on, to focus on forming words to her questions. *"What do you want Abel's soul for, anyway?"*

Harston smiled, but his eyes glared. *"Poor Mellie. Going to go to the grave for a man you think is so good, so pure. You know, I knew him long before you did. Your dear Abel isn't quite the saint you make him out to be. Dream, and see for yourself."*

His face grew, and transposed onto his smile was something else: another face, large and white, with two purplish pinpoints for eyes, like she was looking at a giant maggot or albino bull.

She tried to scream but the train and everything in it dropped away. A scene like a tiny stage zoomed up to her. Sand as far as the eye could see. Railroad tracks curled and blasted by an explosion. Blood ran like water between sand dunes. Screams rose, the wretched screams of those in pain. And in the center of it stood a figure with his hat cocked low, his soot-stained palms glowing white. Abel.

Melinda woke up with a gasp. All her limbs tingled but she could move, *finally*. She jumped up, taking stock. Time had passed; Lance's head had slumped to the side, still dozing.

No signs of Harston anywhere.

Outside, pale aspen trunks rose around them as the spruce became fewer amidst high piles of snow. She took a long chug from her canteen. The air felt thinner through the cracked window —she was sure she'd never been this high in the mountains before. Boulders and piles of stones seemed ready to give. Beyond, the sky stretched to endless gray, like they were at the ends of the Earth. The vision, dream, whatever she saw, couldn't be real. Just one of Harston's tricks.

Harston was powerful, no doubt about that. She looked over to Malgun propped up next to her duster for reassurance. She didn't like killing humans—or human-like creatures—but some things were non-negotiable.

Lance opened his eyes with a sigh and he rubbed his face. "You sleep?" His stormy eyes reflected the gray-blue sky outside as snow started to fall.

"I gotta tell you something." Melinda grabbed his hand, her head swarming. Where to even begin, Harston, Lance's soul, the vision of Abel? Before she could get out a word, Gene burst from the closest carriage.

"She's here." Gene grabbed the headrest of Melinda's seat, his face red under his bowler hat.

"Eloise?" Lance sat up straighter.

Melinda stood. Of course Eloise was here. Whenever she was close, Harston's power seemed stronger. She should've guessed from her nightmare. She unholstered her pistol and grabbed Malgun for good measure. "Where?"

"Back of the train," Gene said, sucking in shallow breaths.

"Breathe, Gene. You certain?" Lance spoke low, so as not to alarm the dozing passengers around them.

"Sure." Gene's eyes shone greener than fresh spring grass, reflecting some unknown light. "I got a strange feeling so I headed a few carriages down. Feeling got real strong toward the back."

"Harston knows we're here," Melinda said, and Lance shot a quick, puzzled glance at her. "So that means she might know too."

"Overkill?" Lance nodded to Malgun. "Don't want to light the whole train on fire."

"I'll figure it out. He said something before about having one spider left," she said. "Can't be caught off guard again. Gene, you wait here."

Gene nodded, his face a mix of relief and terror. Melinda and Lance hurried through half a dozen coaches, the seats emptying as they got closer to the back. The noise of passengers receded until only the clanking of the train was left. Melinda paused at the next coach's door to see rows and rows of boxes and luggage through the window. In the far corner, a broad hat lined with colored satin was just visible. Melinda moved a little closer to the window to see Eloise propped against a pile of suitcases at the end of the carriage, about twenty feet out. "She's ... sleeping." Her eyes fell on the two canisters that hung from Eloise's waist. Abel's soul. And now part of Lance's.

They're gonna be OK, Melinda thought and passed Lance Malgun. "I'll take Eloise. You keep an eye out for Harston and the spider," she said.

"Careful with bullets, we can't risk damaging Abel's canister," Lance said. "Remember what Beatrice said."

Melinda nodded, a flood of Aunt B's warnings coming back, most urgently to make sure the vessel containing Abel's soul stayed intact. If the soul fragment wasn't close enough to Abel's body when freed from its container, it could be lost forever.

Behind her, Lance breathed in sharply as they moved out of the coach and hovered between the two train cars, the cold wind whipping over their faces. Melinda made sure not to look too long at either side of her, where the steep drop to the right showed foaming whitewater and ice some 500 feet down, and the mountain to the left flashed sharp rocks. Below them, the train groaned and screeched as they rounded the mountain.

"You're surrounded, Eloise!" Melinda shouted as she swung open the door to the luggage coach. "Nowhere to run to this time."

Eloise jumped up, her hands splayed, blinking the sleep instantly out of her eyes. She held herself still as a cat on the hunt. "Guess you got me."

The piled luggage in the narrow space left them a few feet to maneuver. Melinda kept her pistol trained at Eloise's chest and leaned to the right. Lance went behind her to the left so they'd both have a clear shot. Something about Eloise giving up was too easy. Maybe another bluff.

"Awful calm for someone who's going to jail for a long time," Lance called from behind Melinda.

Eloise smiled, her eyes calculating despite her cocky shrug. "What can I say? Even the best have to face the music sometime."

"Stop, outlaw!" A voice shouted behind them.

Before Melinda could turn, a noise exploded, making them instinctively duck.

A gun shot.

They weren't alone.

CHAPTER TEN

Melinda and Lance whirled around, still ducking, to see two figures pushing onto the carriage behind them, a petite woman with a swinging, blue-streaked braid and sinewy man with a leather vest and gloves, both with weapons drawn.

"You could've killed us!" Lance shouted angrily. "Dammit, the canister!"

"Found her!" The woman said.

"*We* found her," Melinda corrected. "Stay back."

"I'm bringing her in." The man pointed his silver-embossed revolver past Melinda's head at Eloise, who raised her hands in surrender at the other end of the carriage. A respectably sized hunting knife swung from a holder at his hip. Lean beneath a beaded vest over rolled-up cotton sleeves, the man glared at Eloise with a hatred only the vengeful could evoke. Black hair curled behind his ears under a wide hat that he steadied on his head with his free hand.

"Get in line," Melinda said.

"You don't have any idea what you're dealing with," the woman said, her commanding tone making Melinda prickle with irritation. She wore no hat and had a fur-lined suede jacket. A coiled whip hung at her belt next to a large, holstered knife. Her braid, with streaks the color of the sky at midday, was unnerving; it reminded Melinda of northwestern groups said to have vivid, unusual pigmentations that were rumored to be caused by something in the water.

"We've been tracking her for a long time," the woman continued. "So step aside."

The man took aim, his jaw a determined jut behind a black mustache and chin scruff.

"Angelo Bravo and Topaz Starr." Eloise grinned. "Well, look at this reception—y'all know how to make a gal feel special."

"Looking forward to hauling your sorry carcass in." Angelo's free fist clenched. "You cost me everything, outlaw."

"Your own fault, bounty hunter."

"Wait a minute," Lance said. "We'll be getting the canister and then you can take her, all right? Just hold your fire so it doesn't get damaged."

"Mr. Bravo is a little angry at me," Eloise continued with a cat-ate-the-canary smile. Trying to bait him, that was clear as day. "Not my fault he was in the wrong place at the wrong time."

Angelo snarled and another shot rang out between Melinda and Lance. Eloise crumpled behind a tower of luggage.

"We finally got her," Topaz said in relief and glanced at Angelo. "Told you that tip from the jailbird would pay off."

"Dammit." Lance shoved Angelo backwards. "You didn't have to kill the woman."

"Damn you," Angelo pushed him back. "I'd rather haul her dead carcass than risk her slipping away again. I've waited too long."

As the others continued arguing, Melinda strode toward Eloise's fallen hat and braced herself for the sight. She had seen dead bodies before, but it never seemed to get any easier. It wasn't so much that blood bothered her, but the transition from a living, breathing, thinking human to an empty husk always made her pause. Anytime she saw a passing, two memories came back to her, bright as day. The first dead body she had ever seen: her momma's, face caved in, nearly unrecognizable after the sickness took her. The other time was the first human-like Edge creature Melinda had ever killed, an ape-goblin amalgamation that had been trying to tear out her throat. It hadn't been human, but it was close enough. And now, she'd have to contend with a human corpse. But Eloise hadn't given them much choice.

As she hurried to the end of the coach, she stopped mid-step. No body. Only a hat.

Before Melinda could back up, cold steel pressed against the side of her neck. Eloise moved from behind the tower of luggage so Melinda was between her and the others. She chuckled while keeping the 12-inch revolver steady. Melinda swallowed, the gun sliding with the motion, and glared something fierce at Eloise's alert, focused face.

Behind Melinda, Lance sucked in a breath.

"Told you she was slippery," Angelo snarled.

"No one move now," Eloise said and took Melinda's gun in her free hand.

"Making it worse for yourself, Miss Jackson," Lance called. "We can sort all this out if you come in peacefully."

"Without Harston's spiders, you're outnumbered," Melinda added, glancing around for anything she could use. The train jostled and she hoped Eloise's hand was steady. "You got nowhere to go."

"Awfully brave for someone with a gun to them." Eloise's smile was cool beneath her puff of hair.

"It's not the first time. Can't imagine it's the last." Their car floor tilted a fraction, the towers of crates and luggage held in place by ropes on either side swayed. The train was starting to take a sharp turn along the mountain. Behind her, she could sense Lance tense, too quiet. They had worked together long enough for her to know he was ready for the turn.

And so was she.

When the train lurched, Melinda grabbed Eloise's arm, shoving it up and out of the way as Lance rushed forward to tackle her. A shot went off and Melinda held her breath for an instant as she always did, half expecting the pain of a bullet. Another shot fired, exploding a crate next to her as she stumbled and fell.

Melinda turned in time to see Eloise spin and sink a kick into Lance's stomach, sending him backwards with a grunt and into Angelo and Topaz. Eloise quickly untied the thick rope next to them.

"No!" Melinda cried but the crates and luggage crashed down as the train turned again, completely sealing off half the coach.

Leaving her alone with Eloise.

Eloise crouched next to a pile of suitcases. Behind them, muffled shouts barely made it through from the other side of the mountain of fallen cargo.

"Guess I got a little luck left." Eloise's dark eyes focused, undoubtedly with the same adrenaline that was coursing through Melinda's blood.

"You're faster than a grasshopper in a chicken yard, but that won't help you now," Melinda's eyes fell on the canisters swinging from Eloise's hip. "I'm taking those, one way or another. You seem like a smart cookie. Thing is, I can't figure out *why*. Why are you working for Harston, whatever he is? He brainwash you?"

Eloise's lip curled and anger flashed in her eyes. There it was. A soft spot in her armor, something that might work as a distraction.

"Easy for you to judge. You ever belong to someone else? I'd rather go to hell than be set in chains again." Eloise unconsciously rubbed at the winged tattoo on her wrist, and something clicked into place.

"South Rim Bowl," Melinda realized. She'd heard of mega cities being built down in the 300,000-some mile valley in the Southeast. Not a problem in and of itself, until you heard the stories of people being branded and put in chains to work in the Bowl.

Rumor had it, it didn't matter if you were man, woman, old, young, newcomer or firstcomer. Between the Edge creatures to the North, railroad camps in the East, and forced labor in the Southeast, Melinda would take the monsters over the greed of humans any day.

"That's right." Eloise glared harder than granite. "Harston helped me get my freedom, and I ain't never going back."

Behind them, the pile of crates shifted and the others' voices got louder.

"Stealing souls to repay a demon man seems a bit much," Melinda said. If she could buy a few more seconds for the others to get in, they'd have Eloise cornered, surer than a rat in a barrel.

"I ain't got the luxury of being an idealist. Besides"— Eloise's smirk widened—"the way I hear it, your boy Abel deserved it."

"What would you know about it?" Melinda ground her teeth. Eloise was baiting her, that much she knew. Still, that know-all smile was getting under her skin.

"Harston wanted me to ask you one more time. You call off your pursuit, let me go on my way, and I'll give you back the pretty boy's soul. Last chance."

Melinda hesitated but shook her head. Much as she wanted to restore Lance's soul, she couldn't give up on Abel. "I thought I was pretty clear with your boss. No deal."

Eloise smiled. "Good."

Eloise swung a punch and Melinda turned to take it on the shoulder. Melinda grabbed the closest thing to her—an embroidered straw hat box—and flung it toward Eloise. Melinda used the split second of distraction to duck and twist, getting in one, two quick jabs along Eloise's chin. Eloise responded with a quick kick to the back of Melinda's knee. Eloise was a good fighter, that was for sure. And, Melinda realized as Eloise's grin came back, she *enjoyed* it.

The train tilted, heading toward a carved-out tunnel beneath a block of mountain. They'd have a moment of darkness, which Melinda could use to her advantage. Eloise's glance looked calculating, probably thinking the same. The cave enveloped the train and Melinda sprang forward, reaching for the canister. Her hand grabbed empty air. The light came back a second later to show Eloise kicking open a side door of the coach, the clatter of the train's wheels screaming up at them from below.

Eloise really was unhinged – she was about to jump from the moving train, most likely to her death.

"Don't!" Melinda shouted and rushed to yank her back, spotting the shift in Eloise's stance too late.

Eloise spun, using her momentum to hook Melinda's shoulder and shove her toward the open door.

Melinda twisted, grabbing the door frame as she started to fall out. Eloise's spurred boot greeted her in the gut, but Melinda grunted and held on, using one of her own legs to keep Eloise at bay.

Eloise clamped Melinda's neck and pushed. Melinda held onto the frame, tucking her chin. Both their hats flew off backwards into the coach and the sudden rush of cold air against her scalp helped her breath. The train's wheels screamed against the tracks; below, snowbanks loomed next to a sheer drop.

Melinda gripped onto the door frame with one hand, and with the other tried to reach for one of the canisters, Eloise's holster, anything to get a handle and hoist herself back up.

"Ever hear of that saying, if you can't beat 'em, join 'em?" Eloise shouted over the clamoring of the train. "Well, my saying is, if they don't join ya, get rid of 'em." She let go of Melinda's neck and jabbed a sharp elbow into Melinda's white-fisted grip on the door.

Melinda's stomach dropped away, faster than she could scream, as she fell.

Sorry, Lance, was all she could think as she plummeted.

And sorry Abel, Beatrice.

She braced for impact, hoping the pain would be over quick.

A yawn of cold swallowed her. The ground turned, for a second the sky and snow flashing like a flip book as she rolled. Snow filled her boots and sleeves and neck.

Not dead.

Melinda scrambled up to find herself in a snowbank. Not more than a foot away, the ground fell away to a sharp drop-off of snow-burdened firs and endless white. She spat out a mouthful of icy snow and tried to get her footing. A fire had spread in her chest where Eloise had kicked her. Probably a bruised rib, maybe cracked. The rest of her already ached with cold.

"Wait!" She staggered to her feet as the train disappeared around the bend.

She cursed. Her hand was already swelling from Eloise's quick work. While she waited for her breath to find her again, she took stock. No horse. No Lance. No coat. And no guns.

She was alone.

CHAPTER ELEVEN

The thunder of the locomotive had faded and the crispness of cold air, with its own absence of sound, grew oppressive, along with the blood rushing in Melinda's ears.

She climbed, slipping and stumbling, up to the train tracks. The train probably had a few hours left before their stop. The sun was low so she'd be out well past sundown when the temperature would drop even further. The bruised rib was already slowing her down. Thankfully, she had a few layers of cotton and her leather vest, but nonetheless, there was a very good chance she'd freeze to death. No choice but to try to hoof it.

She might make it. She might not.

Nothing left to do but start.

She made her way along the tracks, sidestepping patches of ice between the iron rails, her boots crunching. She turned up the neck on her shirt, wishing mightily for her duster and hat and trying to ignore the creeping pain in her hands, which she buried deep into her pockets. Her breath came short from the fight and the altitude, so she walked slow, sucking on chunks of ice when she needed water. Her teeth chattered so hard she thought they might break.

The smeared disk of faint sunlight sunk behind towers of gray clouds, and she tried to think of anything besides the knives of cold searing through her hands and feet, the aches that stitched across her chest and shoulders and neck as she hunched against the occasional wind. She blinked rapidly to keep her eyes from freezing.

Twilight was just hitting when the aches abruptly faded, and her limbs were flooded with warmth. An urge to sleep hit her as powerful as a hammer. A bad sign, she thought dimly. The bank of snow to the side of the tracks looked as inviting as a massive bed stuffed with feathers.

Just a minute, Melinda thought. *I'll rest for just a minute.*

A prickling sense came over her. And something else—the feeling of someone watching.

"Lance?" she murmured, but the tiny hairs along her neck suggested otherwise. She scanned for a branch or icicle, something she could use as a weapon, but then forgot what she needed it for.

"Like some help?" The velvety voice was like a shawl, wrapping along her shoulders and collarbone.

"Get outta my head," Melinda said to the still air. "You're harder to shake than a case of the fleas."

"I got a new deal for you." Harston's voice floated behind her, then in front. "You know your beloved is not well."

"Leave him alone."

"Some people can survive a little soul-sucking, but not everyone. Even though I only got a little piece, the rest drains out, yearning to be whole. I'd be surprised if he makes it to the next sunrise before he drops, empty as a husk," Harston said sympathetically. "Weak character, I suppose."

Melinda tried to make fists and failed. "You best hope I'm feeling merciful when I find you."

"Mellie, so quick to kill." Harston's voice felt like a thousand roaches running across her otherwise numb skin. "To murder. Even when you are yourself on the brink of passing into another world." He sighed. "Such a waste."

"I would hardly use the word 'murder' when it comes to monsters."

"Are you so sure they're monsters?" Harston's question hung in the air. "That I'm a monster?"

"Surest one I've ever seen." A red cloud manifested next to her, forming into Harston's curled mustache, his glowing eyes, and a shadow of a hat. "I've killed plenty before, and I'll kill more yet." She let the threat hang.

"Creatures, no matter where they're from, have the right to live." Harston's voice rang sharp, but he was still translucent, and she had a feeling a fist or bullet would fly right through him. "Some just need ... partnerships to survive. To thrive. Surely you must feel some remorse? With all your *murdering*."

Harston tipped his shadow hat toward her and touched his mustache. Melinda wondered if the red cloud was warm and snapped herself out of it.

"Your words sure are slick. Stealing souls ain't exactly the province of the benevolent." Her teeth had stopped chattering, she noticed. Another sign she was getting closer to the end. Not how she pictured it, arguing with a demon-man as she froze to death.

"Predators preying on predators. Your saint Abel is more a monster than me, as I've showed you. He caused the death of plenty of innocents." The outline of another figure formed behind Harston. Large, like a white bull standing on hind legs. "Truth is, I knew someday I'd find Abel again." He grinned wider. "Lucky for me, you made that easy."

Guilt shot through Melinda, hotter than an iron on a fire. For an instant she was back at Abel's house, sprawled on the floor, the soul-sucking spider about to strike her heart. But it hadn't. It had waited.

Waited for Abel. She had just been the bait.

If only she had left the damn eyestone alone.

"That's right, Mellie," he whispered. "You let me find him. That makes me partial to you, I guess you could say. Abel's pet. Now mine."

"Don't much care for your lies," she managed. The fire-colored cloud deepened, inviting. She couldn't help but wonder again if it would warm her up, long enough for her to survive.

Tingles slipped along her neck, as if a curious insect were running along her skin.

"Tell you what," Harston said. The cloud around him began to fade, or maybe it was Melinda's vision. "One more offer before I go. Your soul for your beloved's piece. Decide quickly now."

She hesitated. Just for a second.

"You'll freeze before anyone finds you," Harston said, almost kindly. "Why die a pointless death? This way you can at least save him."

She struggled to think straight, but she was so tired. "Why?"

"Your soul is sturdy." Harston's thin lips stretched out in a grin as his features started to blur. "And seems so delectable."

Melinda tried to stand steady but felt on the verge of falling. She couldn't just die and have her life mean nothing. It seemed like a small price to pay, even as everything in her screamed against it.

"Tell me what you do with the souls, first. What are you, a vampire? Sorcerer?"

Harston paused for an instant, his next words measured as he and the cloud became so faint Melinda could barely see him. "In my world, souls are not just substance but also building blocks. Abel's is too valuable to give up. But your beloved's, I don't mind swapping for yours. Hurry, now. I can't stay much longer."

Melinda didn't see she had much choice. She would freeze anyway, that much was clear. And even if not, she couldn't let Lance down. She thought of him and Beatrice and Abel and hoped they would be OK. "How?"

"Wait. It'll be lovely, like a warm, warm bath. See you in the shadows." She heard his smile more than saw it as he faded away along with the cloud. It was a minute later when she saw it. A dark blob skittered over the snow as heavy flakes fell.

The last spider. It shone black, bigger than her hand; its scrambling slender legs glossier than glass. Its cluster of red eyes rotated toward her.

She tried to stay calm as it approached. It couldn't hurt much or feel that bad. Lance hadn't even seemed to notice the bite himself.

"Go on then," she said. The spider crept up her leg, the eyes rolling up to look at her. If she didn't know better, she'd swear it was smiling. Snowflakes flecked over its body.

"Let me in," Harston's voice whispered.

The spider's mouth opened, clear fangs gleaming.

Melinda squeezed her eyes shut as the spider prepared to bite.

CHAPTER TWELVE

The spider's cold fangs started to pierce through her pants when a bullet tore through the air.

Melinda fell backwards into the snow, blinking at the potent gray sky. Her hand flew to her knee where the spider had been, now just a trail of black smoke drifting up.

It hadn't worked.

"Damn," she muttered. She'd stay here, no point in getting up anymore. Her vision dimmed and she wondered if Harston, the spider and the bullet had been an illusion. Not that it mattered.

End of the line for her.

Something moved ahead. Another illusion. She squinted through the gusts of snow.

A horse made it way toward her through the snow.

And on the horse, a figure in a hat—Harston—no, Lance.

She'd recognize Lance's broad-shouldered form at any distance, even bundled up and in a snowstorm. She did a double take as his face loomed over her. She'd never seen that look on his face before—so serious, grooved, with that particular configuration of folds along his forehead she'd rarely witnessed. It was the look when Abel had fallen, tenfold.

He was saying something. She fought to focus.

"… thought I lost you with that spider." The fault lines of tension along his forehead deepened as he helped her up. He threw a blanket over her shoulders. "Pretty good aim, if I do say so myself."

"Lucky shot ..." Melinda murmured, her voice barely working.

"Save your strength." He put his hat on her head and rubbed her arms, but she could barely feel it. His face close to hers burned like a lantern in the twilight. "Thought maybe you had gone off the side back there."

"Eloise?"

His mouth downturned and he shook his head. "Never mind that now. Let's get you warmed up. Stay with me."

He gave her a little shake and Melinda jerked awake, trying to focus on Lance's blue-gray eyes. She felt like she'd never be warm again. As he hugged her, doubt still flooded her mind—had she even talked with Harston out there or had it been a hallucination? She pulled back to look at Lance's face, so tired, so drained.

"I have to tell you." Melinda's teeth started chattering again and she fought to get the words out. "You're missing part of your soul. From when that spider landed on you."

Lance's gaze turned puzzled, then cleared. "That explains why I've been feeling like I have the worst barrel fever." He laughed lightly. "Let's get you back."

He helped her onto Mud and set them off at a fast clip. She sank into the heat of the horse and Lance behind her, but her thoughts were still foggy, half-formed. They reached Goldie sometime later, the moon high above them. Lance quickly settled Mud into a livery stable and then led them half a block to a nearby tavern.

"Any sign of her?" Melinda said but knew the answer already.

"As soon as you went over—" Lance's mouth set in a grim line. "We'd just gotten the luggage out of the way. She jumped out a minute later before we could reach her. But don't worry about that now, let's get you warmed up and make sure you're OK."

They entered a small but full tavern and the smell of cooked beef and spilt bourbon, laced with the slightest scent of darkbellas, hit Melinda hard. Gratefully, she noted the roaring fireplace in the corner.

"Miss West!" Gene exclaimed from a barstool and jumped up to hug Melinda, catching her by surprise.

The bigger man enveloped her, and she soaked up the warmth, even though she typically avoided hugs at all costs. He stepped back, holding her duster and bag, and Malgun, Melinda saw thankfully.

"We thought, well, after Eloise—Let's just say it's a miracle you survived." Gene draped another blanket over her and handed her a cup of weak beer.

"No thanks to these two." Lance marched over to a table full of empty plates and glasses where Angelo and Topaz sat in deep discussion. Topaz's azure-streaked braid and orange bandana were the only two bright spots in the dim light. Angelo's silver-handled pistol rested on the table between them like a pet. They stopped and looked up.

"Glad your miss is OK, but we're bringing in Eloise Jackson." Angelo spat his tobacco into a bucket at his feet. The tables nearest them fell a little quieter. "So don't get in the way."

Lance's fists balled. "It's a matter of life and death, so don't be getting in *our* way."

Angelo scowled at that, rubbing his chin scruff. "She's mine to kill or bring in."

"It's your fault we lost her to start, with your loose trigger finger." Lance took a fighting stance and Angelo tensed to stand. Topaz, despite being a good foot shorter than all of them, shifted her body weight, her hand floating toward her knife holster.

"Lance," Melinda hissed. It wasn't like him to be so hot-headed. "It can't hurt to exchange some information, as long as one of us gets her."

He considered and relaxed his stance. The tables around them resumed their normal chatter.

"Maybe we could work together," Gene said meekly. "On account of no one seeming to have any luck yet."

"We don't need help." Topaz piped up. "And we aren't interested in splitting the bounty money."

"We just want what she's carrying," Melinda managed to find words, though they came sluggish. Shivers still wracked her shoulders despite the roaring fireplace near them, though slower now. "Tell you what …" she glanced at Lance, and he nodded imperceptibly. "You help us get her, you can have the bounty money and the pleasure of hauling her in. As long as we get the canisters."

"Sounds like a fair shake." Topaz scrutinized Melinda and gestured to the open seats at the table. "Gal, take a seat before you fall over."

"Just a bruised rib." Melinda didn't realize how heavily she had been leaning into Gene until he helped her shrug out of her wet vest and into a chair. She winced, trying to ignore the stab of pain in her ribs. Gene passed her a hot mug, and she took an unsteady sip. Coffee, with a lot of sugar, sent a thread of heat into her core, along with the fireplace at her back. The barkeep set down plates, with his smile lingering on Angelo. Everyone enthusiastically dug into seasoned beef and dried fruit cakes, but Melinda's appetite seemed frozen out of her. She focused on sipping the coffee, urging the warmth to come back into her fingers and toes.

"What did Eloise do to you, if you don't mind my asking?" Gene said to Angelo. Angelo dropped his bite, his face tilting downwards, and Melinda saw something she recognized all too well: despair.

"That outlaw cost me someone I loved," Angelo said. He had a staccato way of talking that Melinda wasn't used to. "And her bounty will just start to make things right."

"Killed?" Gene's tone was hushed.

Angelo glared and didn't say anymore.

A beat of silence before Topaz cleared her throat. She sat close to Angelo, but Melinda didn't get the sense that they were a couple. Friends it looked more like. Melinda hadn't missed Angelo's glance toward the barkeep's flexing forearms as he plopped down a new round of foaming homebrew from the keg. Topaz, in the meantime, had squared her shoulders more toward

Lance, letting her braid shift in the lantern's glow as she pinned a piece of paper to the table with a pen knife. A crudely drawn map.

"The outlaw could be headed to any of the border towns if she survived the jump," Topaz said. "And I think it's safe to assume she made it, given her supernatural assistance."

"The Edge." Gene shivered. "That's where she's going. We have to get there before she does." The same urgency the psychic had conveyed that morning echoed in his voice.

"But *which* path? Which town?" Angelo growled.

Topaz tapped the paper. "Between here and there she'd have to cross haunted plains to get to the northern Edge towns. Trails due east have some of the nastiest bandits bound to give us a bit of trouble. And southeast's got the infected foothills."

"Gene, can you get a sense of her trail?" Melinda asked.

Gene paused, his green eyes looking distant before he shrugged helplessly. "Sometimes it takes a while to work."

"Then what use are you?" Lance burst. Melinda blinked at him in surprise. It wasn't like him to be so curt, but then again, they were grasping at straws.

"Maybe … I can soon." Gene's face sagged.

Angelo laughed mirthlessly. "We don't need no magical hoo-ha. We'll find her the way we always find her. Looking sharp, asking around. Let's saddle up."

"No," Lance cut in. "Melinda needs some time to recover."

"I'm *fine*," she protested. Even though she desperately wanted it to be true, her limbs were still too numb. She had warmed up a bit, but now it was a struggle to sit up and she tried not to waver.

Lance watched her and nodded after a second. "Thought so. We leave in the morning."

"Don't bother." Angelo stood. "We'll find her before then."

Topaz stayed seated. "Honey, we aren't gonna have much luck 'til we get some light and a better sense of direction. If the outlaw was on foot the rest of the way, she doesn't have a lead on us. And we'll have an easier time if Mr. Green Eyes there can point us the right way."

"First sensible thing I've heard. All of us"—Lance shot a look to the others, pausing on Angelo—"could use a night to get our heads on straight."

Angelo crossed his arms and finally sat back down. Relief flooded Gene's face. Another round of drinks came, and Melinda switched to the even weaker homebrew to get some liquid back in her. Topaz, Lance and Angelo drank brandy, while Gene stuck with coffee.

At Gene and Lance's urging, Melinda took a few bites of beef, barely listening to the conversation, before Lance ushered her up to one of the rooms. The bed was firmer than the one at High Hawk and piled high with sheepskins. Lance helped her out of her clothes, which had mostly dried, and settled one of the sheepskins around her.

"Don't coddle me. Just need to sleep it off."

Lance got the fireplace going before pacing the room. "Mellie, you nearly died out there." He rolled a cigarette with one hand, the other ran through his hair.

"I'm here now. Not our first close call."

He stopped pacing to grab her hand. She didn't recognize his clammy grip for a second. "Don't act like it was nothing."

Her head swirled with all she had seen. "Harston said something about Abel out there, killing during his time on the railroad. You know anything about that?"

"Sounds like a hallucination. Rest now, love."

She strained to see him, to say more, but each sentence was getting harder. "How about you, you feelin' all right?"

"Fine, just fine." His voice floated next to her while he sat, the sharp, familiar smell of fresh tobacco reaching her. She leaned back into the pillow, sleep taking over faster than a desert nightfall. She wanted to say more but couldn't, but there was one thing she knew while she sank into sleep.

It was the first time he had lied to her.

PART TWO:

THE BORDER

CHAPTER THIRTEEN

When Melinda woke, the air hung cold and bright. Her torso throbbed like a knife was stuck in it but at least her mind felt clearer. With the clarity, an image of Abel standing over the streams of blood came back to her, along with Harston's smug chuckle.

It was a dream. A hallucination. Had to be.

Nevertheless, she had to tell Lance. She washed up best she could at the basin, wincing at the darkening bruise along her side. She slowly dressed, tied her hair back, replaced her hat, and headed downstairs.

A handful of people were scattered bleary-eyed around the tavern, most of whom looked like they had never gone to bed. A few fellows at the table nearby, along with Lance, were all captivated by some story Topaz was telling, her hair loose and unbraided now with blue streaks flashing against black strands, her ruffled blouse beneath her open pinstriped jacket showing more cleavage than Melinda thought was respectable. Angelo next to her was eating a pile of bacon like it was his job.

Topaz isn't your enemy, she reminded herself, sliding onto a bar stool and squashing down any jealousy as she heard the group behind her laugh.

She kept talking to herself like her momma had taught her 'til she worked out her feelings. *You're just irritated cause she's holding court like a queen. She's got her strengths, and you got yours.*

"Here you go, miss." The barkeep set down a steaming cup of coffee and gave her a smile. He was stout with a meticulously clean cotton shirt and wool vest. Now that she was more lucid, Melinda guessed by the timbre of his voice and curve of his cheeks that he might've been a woman once.

"Better brew a whole kettle," Melinda said. Her appetite had returned, full force. She ordered eggs, bacon, beans. "You see any rodeo-looking gal pass through here on her way to a Border town?"

The barkeep shook his head, puzzled. "By herself? You must be new to these parts, if you don't mind me guessing. No one ever ventures around here alone. Strange creatures roam the lands more plentiful than cattle."

"Anything else a passerby might need to know about the town?"

The barkeep looked pained for a minute. "It's an odd place. Been here nearly ten years. Always thought I'd sell the place and go but ..." His gaze drifted out to the morning crowd as he poured her coffee. "You see a colorful collection of people when you set up shop near a train station. Everyone's mostly passing through, taking the train from High Hawk or going way north to Fifty Salmon Runs. We're just a stop in between. I like it though. Not many jobs you get to see little glimpses of so many lives."

"A transient town then." Melinda downed the drink like it was a lifeline.

"That's right." He refilled her cup. "Lot of wastelands for miles around. There aren't many places to stop and take a rest around here. I like being able to offer a little feeling of home for folks. Maybe 'cause I never really had one myself." He laughed ruefully and headed toward the kitchen. "Breakfast'll be right out."

Melinda nodded. That, she could understand.

"Doing better, love?" Lance appeared, touching her shoulder. He sat next to her at the bar and started to roll tobacco. "Didn't want to wake you, you looked dead to the world up there. How's the coffee?"

"Belly wash. But it's warm at least. Where's Gene?"

"Still upstairs. He swore a good night's sleep would get him a sense. We already talked to a few folks around here this morning. No one's seen her." Lance lowered his voice. "Wanted to talk to you about something. I think we oughta leave." His head tilted over to the others' table.

"Go on without them?" Melinda shook her head. "What about tracking?"

"Who knows how long it'll take Gene's sense to kick in. We'll find our way, always do. He'd probably be happy to save his bacon anyway."

"Angelo and Topaz?"

"They can find some other bounty."

Melinda shook her head. "This ain't about them. It's about Abel. And when the going gets tough we may need the help."

"Well damn," Lance's face drew, irritated. "It's not like you to want the company. You were more eager than I was to go it alone."

"That was before. It wouldn't be right to ditch them." More than keeping their word, it *felt* wrong, but Melinda didn't say that.

He groaned. "You're doing it again. Thinking of the faces in front of you rather than seeing the bigger picture."

"Oh, I see the big picture," Melinda retorted. "I know you care about Abel like he's your daddy, but it's blinding you. Making you reckless. We ain't going to abandon that lot, especially after giving our word. Unless you want to abandon me too."

Lance's mouth set in a grim line, and she thought he might actually do it. *So much for always having each other's backs. Well, you'll manage just fine*, she thought to herself even as her heart twisted in protest. *You always do.*

The barkeep set down two breakfast plates and excused himself. Once he was gone, Lance's face relaxed into a sad smile. "I just couldn't live with myself if something happened to Abel."

She took a breath too, letting some of the tension go. "I know. I can't either. We should take all the help we can get. For Abel." In the beat of silence, she was struck by the dark circles rimming his eyes and the almost death-like pallor of his skin.

"You seem less than peachy," she said.

He gave a wan smile. "Feeling like a boxed-up alley cat."

A fresh bolt of worry seized her gut. "Maybe you should hole up here while we go the rest of the way."

"It's nothing."

"Easy to tell when you're not being forthcoming. Which means you feel worse than you're telling me."

Lance's old smile broke through, but his gaze still looked faraway.

"Stop scowling at me," he said. "I can handle it. Honest."

"Seeing as how it's an unknowable situation, that just ain't true." She hesitated. "What does it feel like, to have some of your soul sucked away?"

"I'm having a hard time controlling myself," Lance confessed finally. "Yesterday I wanted to beat Angelo to a pulp. Almost couldn't stop. Half the time I feel like I'm dreaming, the other half like I'm going to do something I'll regret."

Alarm bells went off as his glance slid half a second in the direction of Topaz and then back to her.

"You got something to tell me?" Melinda crossed her arms. Not jumping the gun, just waiting, a crow testing wind currents. Whatever happened, they'd get through it. "Just spit it out, it'll be easier that way."

"I've never had a thought for anyone but you." He pressed his hand to his eyes for a long minute, a note of anguish in his tone that made her heart turn. "But lately—since the spider got me, I get these feelings, these *thoughts*. Haven't acted on anything, but it's getting harder. I don't know what tomorrow will bring."

"Nothing wrong with thinking what you're thinking." Melinda found his hand, cold like he had dunked it in river water. She squeezed, wishing she could bring him back to himself. "We'll get the canisters soon enough. I got your back. Always. Don't ever forget it."

Lance nodded, looking steadier. He went to the outhouse and Melinda shoveled in her breakfast. Nothing close to what Aunt B would've cooked up, but it would do.

Topaz joined her at the bar after a minute, leaning on the counter to shoot a plume of smoke upwards from one of Lance's hand-rolled cigarettes. Behind them, Angelo and the barkeep were in deep conversation.

"You gonna marry that charmer?" Topaz's gaze narrowed. Coal dust and beeswax mix lined her eyes. Sometimes it helped shield against a sun glare, but it also was something Melinda had seen people do to make themselves look nicer.

"Why, you fishin' for an invite to the wedding?"

Topaz smiled with half of her mouth. "Funny. Just a word from one lady to another. I can spot a heartbreaker a mile away. It's one of my many gifts."

Melinda put her fork down. "You have a lot of experience in that department, sounds like."

"Nah." Topaz put out the cigarette. "I'm not a homewrecker. But he's spinning like a top, anyone can spot that."

Melinda glared, hoping Topaz would get the hint and leave her be. "What kind of name is Topaz anyway?"

"At home, we're named from the color granted to us," Topaz said, absently touching her braid.

"That's nice," Melinda said grudgingly, and meant it. She glanced back at the empty table. "Angelo?"

"Saying a quick good-bye to the barkeep in the back, I imagine." Topaz smiled wickedly. "We're going to saddle up soon enough. Hoping your Green Eyes pulls through."

"Excuse me ladies." A youngish man, well-cropped auburn hair flopping to the side along with an artfully trimmed mustache, smiled at them. He held a red wood polished walking stick a little too comfortably. Singlestick fighter, she'd wager.

"Mr. Irvin Adrian Borsheim." He stuck out a hand and she shook it reluctantly.

"You got every letter of the alphabet in there?" she said.

He laughed loudly. Insincere. Like a man used to getting his way. Something about it sent her skin prickling.

"You don't sound like you're from around here, mister," Topaz said in nearly a simper. Melinda looked at her in surprise, but Topaz's voice stayed high and unnatural, lips pursed in a breathy smile.

"Clever girl," Irvin said. "I'm visiting from the South Rim. Talking to all the nice people in this town."

"Long way from home." Melinda took him in. No other weapon that she could see, though she'd guess he was sensible enough to have a pocket pistol stashed somewhere. The walking stick was engraved with something familiar, a tiny set of wings. Like the tattoo on Eloise's wrist.

Irvin nodded, taking off his hat and turning it between quick fingers as he spoke. It was constructed of leather and velvet, embroidered on the rim. "Got word of an outlaw on a train headed here. You happen to see her, you'll earn a pretty penny. Goes by the name Eloise Jackson."

Melinda watched Topaz out of the corner of her eye, but the woman merely crossed her arms, the same smile plastered on her face.

"What did this outlaw do?" Melinda ventured. No need to let him know what they did; she had an inkling he could cause trouble for them.

"She caused a pretty powerful explosion down at South Rim Bowl, like nothing we had ever seen before." He chuckled but something flickered across his face, like he had seen a gold nugget in the dirt. "Blew up some valuable construction site. She owes, well, let's say something substantial, and then some to pay off her debt. Her former bosses want to make sure she's not setting an example for the others."

"Wow-wee," Topaz said. "What sort of explosion?"

"You don't need to worry about all that. Just know that justice needs to be served." Irvin stretched his mouth, showing the whitest teeth Melinda had ever seen. "Hear anything, you head over to the nearest telegraph office and send a message to this town. I'll get it." He pushed over a torn-out page with scribbles across it.

"Yes sir," Topaz took it and folded it into her pocket. "Sure hope you get that outlaw!"

"You ever want to make some real money, you give me a call." Irvin leered at Topaz, then looked Melinda up and down. "You look stronger than a fiddle. You work a year or two for my employers, the South Rim Bowl Building Brothers, you could retire the rest of your life, live like a queen."

"Rings a bell. You have something of a reputation. Way I've heard it, you got a bit of a scam going on," Melinda said, enjoying the quick frown on Irvin's face before he smoothed it over. "You get honest workers to sign up, then they find themselves in some unforeseen debt and end up slaving away. Is that how it works?"

"Not quite," he said through the sourest smile she had ever seen. He turned to Topaz. "Consider it. We could always use girls like you, cheer up some of the workers."

"Will do, mister," Topaz gushed but her eyes were guarded, watching Irvin clamor out the door. Melinda looked at her and she shrugged, her voice going back to normal.

"You know a guy like that's trouble just by the looks of him. South Rim fellas, they ain't got morals," Topaz said and plucked one of the bacon strips from Melinda's plate. "People—*men*—see what they want. I make it easier for them by acting the way they expect. Gives me the upper hand, just in case. Don't tell me you've never put on a show for your man."

Melinda scowled and pulled her plate closer. "Everyone under the sun's looking for Eloise. That explosion's why Angelo's so keen to find her?"

Topaz's face sobered. "He and his man had been the best bounty hunters you've ever seen. They had taken a job to track Eloise. Needless to say, it didn't go well. I keep telling him Hans would've wanted him to move on." Her voice caught.

Melinda understood.

105

"Hans was your friend too." She couldn't help but think of her and Lance and how many times they'd come close to being half of a pair. "Sorry to hear that."

They turned as a flustered Gene clamored down into the tavern, straightening his bow tie with one hand, and smoothing his ponytail with the other. Lance trailed after him, alert as a wolf.

"I got it!" Gene's eyes glowed like sunlit moss. "Clear as day. Across those plains. Almost to a town…" He reached for Topaz's map and scanned. "Red Cliffs. She's gonna stop there."

"Due East, then," Topaz said, nodding to Angelo as he approached from the back door.

"Red Cliffs?" The barkeep resumed his place next to the glasses and frowned like he had sucked on a lemon. "Forsaken town with forsaken people. They say a fungus makes them all loopy."

Melinda and Lance exchanged a look. They had dealt with worse. "Let's jingle our spurs and get going," she said.

Outside, the winds blew worse than yesterday. Melinda was more than glad to have her hat back, plus extra layers of cow skin and horse blankets they had picked up. She felt too jittery; her burst of focus and impatience subsided to a more general uneasiness clawing at her insides, something she wasn't too used to. She downed more coffee from the canteen as Pepper fell into place behind Mud, each trot from the horse sending a snag of pain along her rib. Their breaths snaked out of them in long white plumes that the wind snatched away. Melinda alternatively touched Abel's charm pouch and the wooden talisman Lance had carved, both in her pocket and giving her some small peace of mind. At least Harston couldn't see them coming now. And neither could Eloise.

Topaz and Angelo rode ahead between fir trees through the tall snow, both with expert horsemanship, guiding their horses into a disciplined rhythm that Melinda reluctantly admired. Gene pulled up the rear, clucking to his chestnut mare and sliding slightly off his saddle.

"Doing better," Melinda said to him. "Shift your hips this way."

Gene paused before the lines around his eyes folded into a smile, face barely visible behind layers of woven scarves. "That helped mightily, Miss West. I always had a hard time with horses, but this one doesn't seem too bad. How are you faring?"

"Wishing for a hot spring about now."

She kept one eye on Lance while they talked and rode. He looked as though he hadn't slept in a week. Even when that was the case, normally he'd still have a spark in his eye. The spark wasn't to be seen; he looked more than grim—somber and distant. Almost mean.

Like someone she didn't know.

Ahead, the others had pulled to a stop at the edge of the tree line. An expanse of nothing but snow stretched out in front of them for miles, reaching the foothills in the distance. Topaz's blue streak seemed the only real color in the world.

Angelo studied the ground in front of them. Any tracks would be covered by fresh snow, but he seemed to be scrutinizing something that Melinda couldn't see. Lance cursed as he struggled to light his cigarette, and Gene scanned the horizon, his eyes without their green luminescence at the moment.

"Colder than a pawnbroker's smile out here." Topaz fumbled with a folded cloth. At Melinda's curious look she handed her the small handkerchief, in which nestled a glob of something that looked like a red piece of coal. "Heating powder," Topaz said. "Keep it, I got plenty."

Melinda rubbed off some the faint reddish powder with her fingers. A warm flush ran up her hand and kept the cold at bay. "Thanks."

"Someone passed," Angelo announced, looking up. "One horse. Maybe an hour or so."

"How can you tell?" Lance demanded.

"Difference in snow." He pointed but Melinda couldn't tell one drift from another.

"Hon could track bees in a blizzard," Topaz chuckled. "That's why he and—" she cleared her throat and corrected herself. "That's why *he's* the best bounty hunter. What about you, Green Eyes?"

"Can't say she's there yet but that's where she's headed." Gene pointed across the vast wintry hills. The group surveyed the just-barely visible plumes of fireplace smoke from the distant Border towns on the white horizon, harsh and brittle as bone under the cloudy sky.

Angelo spat. "People up there. Mean and lean. Seen too much."

"That's not all," Topaz said. "I heard things get strange closer to the Edge. Ghouls and what not." She glanced at Gene. "Keep your eyes peeled, you hear? Give a holler if you see anything."

"Well, y'all are in luck," Lance said. "You have here the two best monster wranglers you've ever seen, recently returned from retirement." The words were his, but his heart wasn't in it. He spoke deadpan, like he was reciting a line.

A cold that had nothing to do with the temperature settled like a mantle on Melinda's shoulders and she gnawed her lip. He was getting worse, and fast.

"We're not afraid of any bottom-feeding crowbaits." Angelo glowered. "Nothing much compares to the scoundrelly of people anyway."

"Have to agree with you there," Melinda said. "Let's get." She kicked Pepper into a trot but it was slow-going. The horses stumbled and slipped across the snowy expanse. They couldn't have been more than a few miles from the base of the ridge leading up to the Edge towns when Melinda got the same feeling she did on the train tracks, like someone was watching. But this was worse. Like many somethings watching.

"Hold up." Melinda was about to pull Pepper to a stop when the horse stopped first, shifting nervously.

"What is it, Mellie?" Lance paused alongside her.

Snow rippled up a few hundred yards away.

"Hell is that?" Angelo asked.

Lance flicked the butt of his cigarette into a snowbank and considered. "Avalanche?"

"Uh-uh," Topaz said. "That is definitely something unusual, if my eyes don't deceive me."

"Like what?" Gene whispered.

Melinda tugged Pepper in a circle, scanning.

"Miss West!" Gene shouted. Melinda turned to see three sets of orange eyes against the snow. The horses shifted uneasily and threw up their heads.

"Eekuts!" Lance said.

"Eeee what?" Angelo unholstered his gun. The Eekuts crouched larger than wolves, but instead of fur they looked jagged, like shards of ice smashed together to form bodies around orange-ringed pits for eyes. Two more appeared on the horizon to their left, not more than one hundred feet away.

"Ice canines," Melinda said, something stirring in her memory from one of Beatrice's books. "Scavengers." She strained to remember details. "Eekuts only live in the coldest parts. They trail other creatures to get food. Symbiotic."

"Symbi-whatnot, they better keep their goddamn distance," Angelo snarled and fired, but the gun misfired, and the bullet flew wide.

The horses' nostrils flared and their eyes widened. Gene panted, his fists white around the reigns.

"Try to keep your body relaxed so she won't bolt," Melinda said to him and pulled Pepper in a quick circle to scan the horizon. A few more Eekuts perched behind them. They were surrounded.

"Damn things multiplying like prairie dogs," Topaz said, unholstering her whip. Angelo cursed and reloaded.

"Malgun?" Lance said, holding onto his hat as Mud sidestepped.

Melinda tugged her reigns and pulled up her rifle. "This'll do."

She waited to feel the rhythm of Pepper's nervous steps under her, readied her sights on the nearest Eekut and—

The shot rang out.

She never missed.

But the bullet passed through the Eekut harmlessly. With a sound like glass grinding, ice reformed around its center where she had shot it.

"Goddamn!" Angelo said.

Before she could try again, the ground rumbled beneath their feet and a rope made of what looked like slick mucus popped out from beneath the snow, some twenty feet from her. *Not the ice wolves,* Melinda realized in a split second. *Snake?* But that was wrong too: the end was spade-shaped and covered in suctions, with the base of the cord buried in the ground.

The cord flung out a spray of snow as it wacked Lance in the chest, flinging him clear off of Mud.

Mud was trained well enough not to run but kicked up a cloud of white. Gene's horse wasn't so disciplined—the mare reared and sent Gene tumbling before it galloped in the direction of Goldie. The horse managed to dodge one Eekut, but two others pursued it, quickly closing in.

"You alive?" Melinda called to Lance. Her eyes swept the horizon for the remaining dozen Eekuts. They hadn't advanced or retreated, but merely watched. Surrounding their prey, she realized.

But what are they waiting for?

"Just a mouthful of snow," Lance yelled. The cord had wound both of his wrists and he pressed a boot into the tendril.

"I'm OK, too." Gene sat up with a gasp. He brushed off the snow, his bowler hat flung clear off.

"What in high hell is it?" Topaz yelped and tried to steady her horse, which ran a panicked lap around Lance.

More tendrils sprung up from the ground, spraying them with snow and ice. Angelo swung his pistol around, cursing as he fired at one and missed.

"Snow kraken," Lance huffed, kicking the tendril that held him. "Damn tough as a twenty-foot octopus. I can't get out of it."

From his other side, Topaz harnessed her whip. It hissed through the air and cracked against the tentacle binding Lance.

Instead of recoiling, the whip stuck onto the tentacle and Topaz gave it a yank. The tentacle wrapped tighter around Lance's wrists in response.

"Hold tight." Melinda dismounted, ignoring the hammer of pain along her ribs, and shoved the reins into Gene's hands.

"Don't," Lance shouted. "If you get closer, they'll get you too. Shoot from there. Dang, these tentacles have suckers. Prickers too."

Melinda glanced back to see Pepper and Mud had quickly retreated to a safe distance. Angelo was slamming the butt of his gun into a cord that had wound up his horse's leg. The horse screamed in panic as it sank into the snow. Another tendril wrapped around Angelo's neck and he gagged, eyes wild and angry. Gene stumbled over to help, and Melinda turned back to Lance to see more tentacles bound onto his arms and legs, rooting him to the spot and sinking him to his knees, helpless as a cow in quicksand. Topaz, yards away, struggled with her bolting horse and the whip, which had sunk into one of the tentacles like it was molasses.

The Eekuts watched the show, like hungry workers lined up for a potluck soup, their orange eyes glimmering.

"Hold still." Melinda took aim and shot a chunk of tentacle clean off of Lance. Before she could shoot again, the ground opened.

Right below Lance and Topaz.

CHAPTER FOURTEEN

A cry choked in Melinda's throat as Lance vanished, his body half twisting in her direction before he plummeted, and the snow closed up over him.

Gene's shout, more panicked than she had ever heard, froze her in her tracks. "Miss West, we need some help!"

She turned back to see Angelo's horse had fully disappeared beneath the snow, the hole that had swallowed it now closed. Angelo had managed to leap off before then but was turning purple as the snow kraken's tentacle around his neck tightened. Gene tried to wrench it off to no avail. Angelo choked, one hand at the tentacle and the other reaching for something at his belt. She followed his straining fingers to see the holstered hunting knife.

Melinda half-ran, half-slipped toward him in the snow, grabbed the giant knife and sliced off the tentacle around his neck. Round suctions on the sticky tentacle grasped the air, and hooks like rose thorns ran up its length. She kicked it away as a crack below Angelo widened and they both jumped to the side.

The crack turned into a hole wide enough for one person to fall through, then closed like something hungry. Before Melinda could make sense of it, Angelo, gasping for breath like a man that had been sucker punched, threw off the piece of tentacle still draped around his shoulder and hustled to where Lance and Topaz had vanished.

"Topaz!" Angelo screamed hoarsely. He grabbed his knife back and started stabbing it into the snow. "Goddammit, no!"

Melinda joined him, fell to the snow, and began digging with her bare hands. "Lance! Holler if you hear me!"

"Miss." Gene pointed to the horizon. "They're gone."

The Eekuts had vanished.

"We're not giving up on them." Melinda cataloged what little they knew. No reason to think the kraken wouldn't start dining on their friends, and soon. "What do you see, Gene?"

"They're down there." Gene gaped at the ground in front of them, his eyes flaring. "The Eekuts are down there with the kraken too, waiting. They look hungry."

Angelo kept digging with his knife, ignoring them.

"I got a theory." Melinda held her rifle and scanned the endless white. "The snow kraken controls these holes in the ground to pull down its prey. You see the kraken?"

"It's coming toward us." Gene shuddered.

"Holler when it's below." She trained her sights on the snow mound and held, taking a steadying breath.

"Now," Gene said, his voice louder. "Now!"

Melinda fired once, twice.

The ground heaved and they stumbled. Holes the size of doors sprung open around them. Through one, Melinda glimpsed a giant bluish eye in a mountain of mucus.

She passed her hat to Angelo.

"What in the hell are you doing?" Angelo demanded. "We got to draw up that thing, shoot it dead so we can rescue them."

"Big creature like that isn't coming up. If you see Eloise or a man in red, get Malgun from Pepper's saddle. Only one shot so don't waste it." She dangled her feet into the nearest hole.

"I'm going down too," Angelo said, and Melinda shook her head.

"Our best chance of getting them back is to stay split. I go down here. You see a chance to take a kill shot, you take it if Gene says."

"Wait!" Gene said. "What if the kraken finds you?"

"Make sure to round up the horses too for when I get back," was all she said.

"Take this." Angelo passed her his hunting knife. "Just in case. We'll be up here ready. If you're not back soon, I'm coming down."

Melinda shimmied into the crack, feet first, expecting she'd have to worm her way down. Instead, she started sliding as the surface closed over her head, Gene shouting something that she couldn't hear.

She was moving faster down some sort of chute, too narrow to move her arms.

A network of small tunnels, she realized as she braced for the inevitable end. Something the snow kraken had made, the whitish tubes barely visible in the blur around her. The tube widened and its incline leveled so she slowed, but something was wrong. The ice grew thicker around her. She slid to a stop, completely surrounded by ice. She couldn't move, couldn't see a damn thing.

She was in an ice cocoon.

She squirmed. Her rifle was crammed uselessly along her side and the knife in her hand flat against the ice wall.

"Anyone hear me?" she hollered. A little bit of light shone through the ice in front of her. Through the bumpy ice layer, she spotted what looked like a cavern. She forced herself to calm down, despite not being able to move her arms and legs.

Breathe, Melinda told herself and managed to flex her right hand, cold as it was from the ice. *You aren't dead.*

Not yet.

She scrunched herself as much as she could toward her left side. Gradually, she worked up her right hand in the bit of space, into an awkward chicken-wing shape pinned to her side.

But it was enough.

She started scraping at the cocoon with the knife. The substance wasn't really ice—more a combination of melting ice and sticky mucus.

"Ick," Melinda said aloud. Her freezing fingers gave her an idea. She worked the tie on the pouch Topaz had given her and sprinkled some of the reddish sand on the knife. She burrowed the blade into the cocoon, which immediately yielded, melting like butter. She worked on the hole until she could finally squirm through.

She fell a foot or so, landing with a grunt onto a ledge of ice. To her left, an ice wall curled upwards. To her right, a sheer drop of one hundred feet yawned into a massive cavern. Faint bluish light filtered from the ice ceiling. The ledge she stood on was wide enough for two people to stand abreast and lined the entire pit.

A few feet above the length of the ledge hung countless clear ice cocoons, dangling from cords in the icy ceiling like stalactites. All seemed empty, except for the two nearest her.

Lance and Topaz.

Melinda grabbed her rifle and crept along the ledge, trying not to slip. When she peeked down over the drop, she glimpsed a pack of Eekuts far below. They gnawed on the fresh remains and bones of a large animal—Angelo's horse, she realized. Other Eekuts sprawled out on piles of bones and nibbled each other's backs, occasionally spitting out tiny shards. She had seen enough creatures, usual or not, to recognize the activity after a second. Grooming.

"Don't mind me; just keep doing what you're doing," Melinda muttered to them through her chattering teeth. She side-stepped limp and grayish tubes—what looked like discarded tentacles from the ice kraken. As she neared the first cocoon, she spotted Topaz's azure-streaked hair through the icy mucus barrier.

It looked like Topaz was already thinning part of the cocoon with her heating powder; Melinda carefully carved around the softened layer. Finally, Topaz's hand popped out. Melinda grabbed it and heaved, until Topaz emerged, covered in the grayish ice goop. Her gaze darted wildly.

"Stay quiet," Melinda mouthed, and pointed toward the drop where the Eekuts still lounged, unaware, it seemed, of their movement. Topaz nodded and brushed ice from her shivering shoulders.

Melinda stifled a groan when she looked at the next cocoon, through which Lance's dark shirt was barely visible. The ice ledge had broken off, leaving a 12-foot gap beneath Lance's cocoon—directly over the cavernous pit.

"Damn," she muttered and glanced up. A few gray cords hung like vines from the ice-packed wall, but none within reach so that she could swing or climb over. She couldn't risk shooting at the cocoon to break it open; it'd alert the Eekuts and might injure Lance besides.

"Whip?" she whispered to Topaz.

Topaz spread her hands helplessly. The whip was gone. So was her knife.

"Got some boom powder." Topaz patted her pouch.

"Too loud." Melinda shook her head. Angelo's knife was the only choice. She wasn't as good with knives as guns, and if she missed it'd land on the Eekuts below. "You got any more of that heating rock?"

Topaz opened a folded cloth to sprinkle the last of the reddish coal-like powder on the knife.

Melinda readied to throw, guessing she had a fifty-fifty chance of making it.

"Let me." Topaz took the knife, weighing it expertly. "I got a knack."

"Hit center or high," Melinda replied. "Last thing we want is a hole that drops him down into the pit onto the Eekuts."

Topaz aimed and flung. The knife barely made it, piercing the side of the cocoon and causing it to sway an inch. The knife started to slice downwards, and Melinda thought for one horrifying moment that Lance really would fall out in a second or two. Before that happened, the knife disappeared into the cocoon. A hole widened in the side and Lance stuck his head out.

"Look sharp," Melinda hissed and pointed downwards. He nodded and started rocking the cocoon toward them. Above him, the cord holding it groaned, ready to snap. Topaz's breath went in sharply and Melinda braced for the worst.

Lance jumped during the next swing and the cocoon held. He landed on the ledge in front of them, slipping. Melinda clutched his arm, almost going over with him until Topaz pulled her back. Melinda helped him straighten, grabbing his shoulders to examine him. His arms were spotted in blood where the tentacle's hooks had dug in but, aside from that, he didn't look worse for wear.

"Thought you might've landed in a shallow grave," Melinda said.

Lance rubbed his face and looked at her with a ghost of a grin. "Not yet."

"Lady Luck must have a crush on you," Topaz commented.

"Now we just gotta get out of here. Maybe we can find one of those—" Melinda stopped as a screech shook the walls of the cave and ice started falling around them. Below, the Eekuts yipped in excitement.

"Hold on!" Melinda cried, but their section of the ledge plummeted with a crack. She didn't have time to shout as the ledge slid down along the side of the ice wall like a sled ride—right into the pit.

She stumbled to her feet amidst pieces of ice and horse bone as Lance helped a groaning Topaz up. At the same time, the Eekuts darted to the side. On the far end of the cavern, a hole appeared. Ice and membrane broke away to reveal a wheel-sized, pale blue eye.

The snow kraken was back.

"What's happening!" Topaz shouted.

"Feeding time," Melinda said grimly.

The snow kraken flopped into the pit. It loomed bigger than Melinda had expected, easily the size of several stacked wagons, with mucus glopping down its body despite the cold. Below its singular eye shone a black beak surrounded by flicking tentacles. Larger tentacles at its base propelled it forward.

They were cornered.

But not defenseless. Melinda lifted her rifle.

"Eye?" Lance said and she nodded. It was almost universally a weak spot for critters, natural or not.

Melinda fired. Instead of a gunshot, the gun clicked. And clicked again.

"Damn ice," she moaned and checked her pistol. It was likewise gummed up with ice and mucus.

"Any other bright ideas?" Topaz yelped as the three of them backed up against the ice wall.

The snow kraken rotated so its thicker tentacles coiled, ready. The beak at its center chomped with the sound of two machetes clanking together.

"We can distract it at least." Melinda gestured to the knife Lance still held.

"That's the ticket." He shifted his hold on the blade, aimed and threw.

The knife hit just off-center in the kraken's eye, sending out a gush of white goo. The kraken recoiled faster than a hand on a hot iron, squealing in pain. Melinda almost felt bad for it, until she spotted human bones scattered in the pit. As the kraken retreated, she spotted a clear passage to the gap it had come through.

"There's our way out!" Melinda climbed up broken ice to reach the empty tunnel. The Eekuts howled behind her, a sound worse than glass shattering.

They weren't waiting anymore.

Melinda whirled around to see the closest animal snarl and lunge at Lance, its claws gleaming like daggers made of icicles. He dodged it as they ran through the tunnel.

"They're too fast!" Lance shouted.

"I got 'em!" Topaz dumped the content of her pouch into a second bag and hurled the mixture behind them without looking. It exploded, filling the tunnel with a sickly sweet purple smoke, reminding Melinda of one of Abel's concoctions.

Coughing, they ran the rest of the length up the tunnel while snow and mucus rained around them. Melinda could see a gleam of sunlight at the end past the falling debris. Topaz made it, then Lance—but before Melinda could reach, the snow tunnel collapsed entirely, pouring in front of her vision and blocking out the light.

A hand punched through from above and grabbed hers, yanking her up.

Lance and Angelo heaved her out. Melinda wiped the snow from her face, readying to run or fight.

"Take it easy," Lance said. "The creatures retreated."

Mud and Pepper had wandered over, the other horses long gone. Angelo helped Topaz brush off the snow and gave her a long hug, while Gene laughed in relief.

"Let's get, before another critter decides to say howdy." Melinda quickly squeezed Lance's hand and tried not to think about what else might be lurking in the snow.

They followed their shadows to the rising peaks of Red Cliffs.

CHAPTER FIFTEEN

Between trekking on foot and sharing rides on Mud and Pepper, they didn't get to Red Cliffs until nearly twilight. The slushy, narrow path was empty of other riders. Air blew and the grit pricked their eyes and stuck in their teeth.

Not as bad as being stranded out on the train tracks yesterday, Melinda thought, though they were all covered in snow and shivering besides.

Angelo paused, staring at the ground. "Solo horse came through a few hours ago it looks like. Light tracks, so one passenger. Could be the outlaw."

The group pressed forward, following Angelo past adobe houses and tents. He yanked his horse to a stop a minute later.

"What's wrong?" Topaz pulled alongside him.

"Trail's cold. But ..." Angelo's gaze shot around. "Doesn't make sense," he grunted. "A horse can't just disappear."

"We're not dealing with something natural," Lance said. "Eloise has help. Someone who doesn't want us to find her."

Angelo sat back in his saddle in frustration.

"Gene, you got anything?" Lance asked.

"No, siree." Gene wiped his nose. His head titled; he looked more than dazed.

"You all right?" Melinda asked.

"Maybe if I ate a bit, warmed up ..." Gene trailed off.

"How long til your power comes back?" Angelo barked.

"Not sure if I got any left in me today," Gene all but whispered. "Maybe in the morning."

"We don't have time for that," Angelo said.

"It's the ..." Gene gestured toward the mountain ridges behind them and smiled weakly. "The Edge, I think. Giving me a bout of something. Y'all feel it?"

Melinda scrutinized him. "Little bit. Not like you. Think your sight makes you more sensitive to it?"

Gene nodded slowly.

"Well, not a bad idea to stop and dry off anyway." Melinda's heart fell but she kept her voice even; Gene clearly felt bad enough as it was. "Let's find the standing saloon and get our bearings."

"That's the first decent thing I've heard all day," Topaz declared, and even Angelo didn't argue. They were all shivering, and the horses were lagging. "Something about facing imminent doom makes me hungry enough to eat a cow."

As they walked, Melinda didn't see the normal signs of a working town. Something was off. No mills, no blacksmith, nothing. Just homes and a few saloons. Not even a butcher. No signs of kids anywhere. Laughter floated through the air, normally a good sign in a town, but this laughter sounded unhinged, two screws short of a full pack. They passed white bugs big as their hands scuttling along the dirt and a toad, light blue in color, staring at them.

"Edge creatures," Gene shuddered.

"How can you tell?" Lance flicked his rolled cigarette butt at the toad. "Your special sight?"

Gene shook his head. "Anyone can tell. They have a weird luminescence. If you squint, you can see it."

Melinda narrowed her eyes and could just make out a faint halo around the toad. "How about that." In all their time monster hunting, she had never really stopped to consider the critters. It made sense: Aunt B always said they had odd properties. They turned a corner, and the Northern Ridge Mountain range came into view. Above the closest peaks, the sky swirled purple with salmon-colored plumes, like a storm on the edge of sunset.

"Lemme wager—the Edge?" Melinda said. She had never seen it in person before and the sight turned her stomach into a rock. No one exactly knew how far the Edge expanded into the mountain range. It was near impassable; trying to find an entrance into the Edge left most people dead.

She couldn't tear her eyes away.

Now that they were seeing it in person—the symbol of everything Abel had trained them to fight against—the catalog of all the Edge monsters they had encountered clicked through her mind. Most of the monsters were mindless, akin to creatures that had been displaced and needed to be eliminated or relocated somewhere where humans weren't.

But other times … other times the creatures that emerged from the Edge seemed to have malice stitched in every fiber of their beings. Those made up the rarer and nastier creatures they had had to fight: swarms of reptiles that massacred towns; infectious flies that turned even the kindest among them into butchers and granted life immortal; a lake demon who set her sights on burning children alive.

Melinda bit her lip hard, trying to push back the wave of living nightmares. She already fought them off enough in her dreams, she didn't want to deal with them now, too.

"Well, if that don't take the rag off the bush." Lance gave a low whistle.

"Uglier than the last time I saw it," Angelo said, a new bleakness in his tone.

"How close did you get?" Gene spoke as though he didn't know if he was awe-struck or fear-struck.

Angelo rubbed his trimmed beard. "Near enough. Saw some things. Like a mirror. You see yourself, but in a bad way. Doing stuff you can't unsee. Wouldn't wish it on anyone really, except that outlaw, damn her to hell."

"Damn her to hell," Topaz echoed in agreement.

The sky gave Melinda a faint sense of vertigo, making her feel like she was about to fall off Pepper. All the horses seemed more nervous, sidestepping and straining against their reigns.

"Strange town," she muttered. And stranger still; she did a double take as they passed a knot of people walking past the newspaper office. At first, she thought it was the weird light from the Edge casting everything in a not-quite sunset hue, but then she realized the citizens of Red Cliff had hair pinker than a newborn kitten fresh out of the womb. Even beards were tinged salmon, the same color in the swirls of sky over the Edge.

"These Red Cliffions look cut from a different cloth," Topaz said. "Odd-looking folks."

"Guessing proximity to the Edge makes them look the way they do," Lance said. "I'd reckon we'll look like that too if we stay long enough."

Topaz smoothed her braid and shuddered. "Everyone's regarding us awfully suspicious."

"Downright hostile, I'd say," Angelo spat as they continued along the main road.

"People came in for the promise of gold, but it led them astray." Gene brightened and spoke a little louder, reminding Melinda of Aunt B giving a lesson. "Nothing useful in these rocks and nothing grows too well. Somewhere here was the start of the Monster Massacre of Double Moon a hundred years ago, when the Edge appeared."

Melinda nodded, history lessons that Abel and Beatrice had repeated swirling in her mind. When trade opened across the plains and western oceans, newcomers from the Grand Isles arrived, some fighting to take over land from the firstcomers. But once the Edge appeared and its hordes of monsters took out a good chunk of residents, newcomers and firstcomers banded together to fight back. Since then, something changed about the Edge. The majority of creatures stopped straying into human territory, though there were plenty of exceptions, as evidenced by Melinda and Lance's surplus of work.

"Don't know why anyone would live up here so close to the Edge," Melinda said. "Everything about the place feels wrong. Why would the Cliffions stay?"

The question hung, forgotten, when they turned into the square. A smell like dung and rotten flowers, but sharper, seeped from the ground, growing stronger near the standing stalls and bonfire. Dozens of people, most looking to be Cliffions with the pinkish hue in their hair and eyebrows, gathered in small knots in the dusty square, eating or talking.

"Let's see what we can find out," Lance said.

They got the horses settled at the trough and then Angelo and Topaz beelined to a stand with liquor, Gene to a seller holding meat skewers. Melinda and Lance stood to the side, passing a canteen of water and taking in the people around them. Melinda tried to scrutinize Lance without seeming too obvious. He didn't seem much worse now, just tired like the rest of them. Surely, he could hang in there until they retrieved the canister.

"Think Gene might be outta juice," Lance said, and they both looked over. The man had eaten his skewer already and slumped over on a crudely carved bench.

"Can't blame him. Maybe our new friends will prove useful," Melinda said, rubbing her side. Now that the adrenaline had dissipated, her ribs ached something awful.

"Don't be too sure," Lance said, and Melinda followed his glance. Topaz was chatting with a seller, and Angelo nodded his hat to a trio of dirt-covered folks. Both Topaz and Angelo shook their heads toward each other, a universal sign of *no luck*.

Before Melinda could suggest they try another part of town, two men passed, their eyes narrowed at Lance.

"Mixed," one hissed.

Lance's fists balled and Melinda shot them a look of disgust. After all they had been through, this was the last thing they needed. "Just another backwards town," she said loudly. Though they usually kept a low profile, she couldn't help it. "Can't wait to get outta here."

The men smirked at her and moved to join a crowd surrounding a hawkish woman laughing too loudly. She wore her pink hair piled in intricate knots on her head, and a cream-colored ruffled prairie dress, stained at the hem. Most people were angled toward the woman, so Melinda figured she must've been a person of importance. The crowd all laughed a little too long and a little too hard at what was said, like an amateur play.

Melinda pointed her chin toward the woman and spoke quietly to Lance. "If anyone in town knows something it'd be that one. Work your magic?"

Lance took another sip of water and handed her the canteen. "Wager she's a proprietress?"

Melinda shook her head. "She's not keeping an eye on the sellers or stands. Politician, maybe."

"We'll see." Lance sauntered over to the group and Melinda plopped on a bench beside Gene to wait.

"Eat something?" he asked.

"Too tired, Gene." She closed her eyes for a second, trying to will away the sharp ache in her ribs that emanated out to her entire body. Eloise could be anywhere, they might never find the souls.

She glanced over at Lance again.

He seemed all right. Maybe the missing bit of soul was something that he could recover from, even if they couldn't get his canister back.

She tried not to think of Abel.

"S-sorry, miss. Wish I could help right now." Gene gave her a small wavering smile.

"Call me Melinda, all right? No need to be so formal all the time."

Gene nodded, looking about as sick as a man who'd been drinking for days. "You ever lose someone and then feel like you see them sometimes, like they're right there with you?"

Melinda nodded slowly. Sometimes the way a sunbeam hit a leaf, or the stillness of a deer in a field of flowers, made her feel like her momma was just out of sight, about to call out to her.

"That's like the sight," he said. "Normally I only feel it when I'm looking for something. But right now, I feel it all the time, like there's lots of someones right here with me, scrambling my feelings. I can't explain it—"

"I know, Gene. It's all right. We'll sort it out."

Something caught Melinda's eye: an immaculate hat lined with velvet, twisting in its owner's hands in the crowd. She glimpsed two stern-looking men flanking the owner.

"Hey, I know that fella." She tipped her hat down quickly. "Mr. Irvin something-or-other, was asking about Eloise back at Goldie. Must've gone roundabout and avoided the kraken detour."

"He looks like a well-polished gentleman." Gene squinted. "What's he want with Eloise?"

Melinda sighed. "Seems like she's a popular lady. We need to be the first to find her. Make sure we can get those canisters and save our friend."

Topaz appeared in front of them with three shots. "Still no sight, Green Eyes? Maybe this'll help." She passed them each something that smelled stronger than firewater and took a shot herself, grim.

Melinda shook her head. "Not when I'm working."

"You gotta be highbrow all the time? Enjoy standing there, judging people all day?" Topaz rolled her eyes and passed the extra shot to Gene, who accepted gratefully. "Maybe this will get your magical sight firing again."

"Strong stuff!" Gene said, two circles of red appearing in his otherwise paper-white cheeks.

Topaz patted him on the back.

Melinda didn't blame them; an urge to drink gnawed at her, maybe from the jitteriness of being close to the Edge. She touched the reassuring fabric of Abel's charm bag—now tightly secured on her belt—and focused on steady breathing. A few feet away, Lance downed a shot and nodded at something one of the townsfolk said. Melinda stood and made her way to him.

"Want to introduce you to Mayor Lorette Pipens," Lance said, slinging an arm over Melinda. His words had a little coil to them, blunted at the edges.

"We don't get many visitors around here," Pipens said, and Melinda tried not to wince at her shriekish voice that managed to both sound like a rusted nail scraping against a chalkboard and a breathy girl trying to entice a suitor. "Well, except for a few troublemakers we have to shoo out now and then."

"We've been wagering why folks would choose to live this close to the Edge. Care to settle the bet for us?" Melinda said, trying not to seem too much like she was fishing.

The other Cliffions in the group had turned to Pipens, eager for something—information, validation, Melinda couldn't tell which.

"It's not so bad. That dizziness you might be feeling from the Edge, you get used to it if you're here long enough," Pipens said. "Believe it or not, there were others living here once." She grinned crooked as a lightning bolt. "But we won."

Melinda fought a shudder, not wanting to give the woman the satisfaction of getting under her skin. Pipens laughed again, bordering on hysterical. A pair of well-heeled men nearby chuckled along with her, making Melinda feel like they were all in on a secret joke.

"I was just inquiring about any oddities they may've seen here," Lance said. He seemed agitated by the way he shifted his feet, but she couldn't tell from what.

"Too many to count!" Pipens laughed and the other Cliffions chuckled as if on cue. Something deep in her bones told Melinda it was time to skedaddle. She tipped her hat a good-bye and led Lance away.

"That was about as useful as two buggies in a one-horse town," Melinda sighed and followed Lance as he bought another shot from one of the stands. "Hey, forget we're working?" she said.

"I work how I want." Lance's mouth narrowed into a thin line and for a second, she felt like she didn't know him at all.

"Hey." She grabbed his hand. "Think of Abel. We gotta focus."

"I haven't stopped thinking about him," he snapped and strode to the others. "I'm peachy."

He sounded like a stranger. Worry and anger crashed in her like a summer storm. How long until his soul was gone completely, and would that leave him a shell of who he was? What if they couldn't fix it?

She blinked back an image of him, gray and lifeless next to Abel, both lying in shallow graves. Back at the bench, Gene's head was nearly between his knees. Angelo and Topaz stood in front of him.

"What's going on?" Melinda's gaze fell to Gene who tried, and failed, to stand.

"The Edge is taking something outta me," he said. "I just need ... a few more minutes."

"He's more sensitive than a spring daisy," Topaz observed.

"We've wasted enough time," Angelo said. "Bandit is close. None of these pigeon brains know anything. We're scouting and cutting dead weight." He barely looked at Gene as he addressed him. "We can't wait around for you to recover from whatever's plaguing you. You're a grown boy, sure you can find your way home on your own."

Angelo marched off and Topaz looked between Melinda and Gene.

"We're not ditching anyone," Melinda said. "We've come this far together." Gene, pale and ashen on the bench, didn't look in any shape to walk, let alone track Eloise.

"Nothing personal." Topaz sent her and Lance an apologetic shrug and followed Angelo down the street.

"Lance." Melinda lowered her voice. It wasn't a question, but to her surprise, he hesitated. "Lance. The man's hardly traveled on his own. We can't leave him. And it's not exactly safe alone here."

Lance's mouth hardened. "The bounty hunter's right. We don't have time. Let's go." He glanced at her, giving her a look colder than she had ever seen. *Think of Abel.*

She recoiled like he had pricked her with a throwing knife. It wasn't like him to toss her words back in her face with a tone like sour milk.

"You go right ahead then," Melinda shot back.

She crossed her arms and watched Lance stomp off after Angelo and Topaz, his back hunched under his duster, hat pulled low, his easy saunter gone. A feeling like being punched spread through her gut. He was really walking away from her. After all they'd been through, after all the monsters and close calls and nights under the stars. It was really that easy for him to turn without even a second glance behind, as if she were no more than a passing stranger.

His soul is fading, she reminded herself, but it didn't make her feel much better. She had to find Eloise and the canisters, now.

She was about to plead with Gene to try to sense Eloise again but looked sharply at the crowd instead. Something in the way the Cliffions paused, like a pack of wolves sniffing the air, sent prickles down Melinda's arm. A sound drifted up.

Hooves and shouts. A lot of them.

"Riders!" Someone screamed. But it wasn't a scream of terror, rather of excitement.

The Cliffions around her unholstered weapons, something Melinda rarely saw before – in most towns, only the law keepers carried guns. But now she saw every last soul pull out something or another, guns and hammers and clubs and blades.

"Let's give a howdy welcome to our old friends," Pipens shouted to the group. Someone had handed her a long machete, finely polished. She held it expertly, more so than Melinda would've thought befitted a mayor.

"Double drinks for anyone who gets a head!" the barkeep yelled.

Melinda looked around for cover, for an easy way she and Gene could slip out. It wasn't their fight. But a dozen white horses thundered around the bonfire, their riders determined. Angry.

They were surrounded.

CHAPTER SIXTEEN

Melinda yanked Gene to the side as the brawl started. Blades clashed and bullets went off. She took in as much as possible before they ducked down behind one of the abandoned seller carts.

The riders wore a mismatch of outfits. A heavy-set man covered in black-and-white furs, and a tall woman in a clasped dress beneath a leather bodice, lifted their blades, both with looks of fierce concentration. Two more riders galloped up behind them, one with a sheet of black hair and a pregnant bump holding a saber, the other a curly-haired woman with spectacles and an axe. A tattoo of an intersecting double moon on both of their necks caught Melinda's eye. The same symbol flashed beneath the scruff of hair at the back of another rider's neck.

"Who are they?" Gene gasped.

A drawing of the intersecting moons stained the white horses' foreheads. The symbol sparked a memory, a roaming group that marked themselves—

"Edge Riders," Melinda said. "Self-appointed guardians of our world. Mix of people that come together when they have the 'calling' to roam the Border towns and make sure monsters don't stray too far."

Gene snapped his fingers. "Their ancestors helped bade back creatures during the Double Moon Massacre."

"That's right. But why on earth are they attacking this town? They're supposed to be protectors of the land." Though the Cliffions she had met left something to be desired, they weren't monsters. Although, glimpsing more than one Cliffion grinning in pleasure as they fought, she had to wonder. A horse thundered past, the sudden motion nearly making them stumble backwards.

"It's not our fight," Melinda said. "Let's make like a shy rattler and go."

They headed into the darkening forest behind them, where sickly trees faded up and over a hill.

She cast one last glance behind them, but the brawl had kicked up thick billowing clouds of dust that stank like something rotten. She hadn't seen Lance in the fight, but a pang of worry ran through her nonetheless.

He can handle himself, damaged soul or not, she told herself.

They ducked under branches, Melinda pushing them forward until Gene stopped abruptly.

"Miss—uh, Melinda," Gene said. He was looking paler by the minute. "For a second there, I got a sense of Eloise. Not too far off. East, in something that looks like a barn."

Melinda stiffened. "Where?"

He pointed and they hurried to the edge of the forest, the shouts and grunts from the fight growing more and more muted behind them. She scanned the roads to either side and motioned him out.

All was silent, save for Gene trying to catch his breath. No sign of Lance and the others.

"There." He pointed to a barn off the path. A cold breeze emanated from the direction of the building in the gloom, making her shudder.

"Eloise is inside," he whispered.

Melinda unholstered her pistol. Eloise had gotten the best of her twice. Not this time.

"Should we wait for the others?" Gene said. "She's a dangerous outlaw, after all, and I can't be much help to you, I'm afraid."

"I can take care of her myself. I don't need help."

"I don't doubt that at all. But maybe it would be prudent if I go find them." He fidgeted with his bowler.

"If they want to be strong-headed fools, let them," she said. She shoved away her worries about Lance. She had to stay focused on Eloise and get his soul back. "I told you, I got this. You hold tight here."

She didn't wait for Gene to answer but quickly crept up along the side of the path until she spotted Eloise.

The outlaw stood framed in the open barn door, loading up a chuck wagon. Her hat was a little worse for wear, her fringed jacket streaked with mud in spots. Two new pistols sat at either hip between smaller leather sacks hanging from her belt.

Melinda froze as she saw more clearly into the barn. Two horses stood to the side, harnessed and ready to go. But that wasn't what caught her eye. The back of the wagon where Eloise worked held a caged sheep, as well as a crate. And in the crate peeked the tops of twelve canisters entwined with wire.

Souls.

So many more than just Abel's and Lance's.

"Hush now," Eloise drawled at the bleating sheep as she checked the rope securing its cage in the wagon. "Not everyone gets the honor of becoming such an important sacrifice."

Melinda was close enough now to scope out the inside of the barn. A gray light came in from the left—one window, all but boarded up. The entrance was the only way in or out.

"Ready to ride, lovies." Eloise checked the horses' hitch, giving the leather a tug.

Melinda couldn't wait any longer. If Eloise started off on the wagon, she'd lose her chance. "Eloise!" she shouted, inhaling the stench of rotting wood and old rainwater as she stepped into the barn with her pistol pointed. "Raise 'em."

"You again? You remind me of a roach, I swear." Eloise's smirk vanished, replaced with surly resolve as she lifted her hands.

"Still got that ugly hat I see. Skin yourself, real slow." Melinda scanned the inside of the barn with her periphery as she kept her center of focus on Eloise. Hay strewn across the dirt. Oil lamps set up for extra light. Water trough half full of black water. Broken wheels piled against bales of hay. Rotting wood rising in a loft above them.

With one hand, Eloise slowly unbuckled her gun belt and eased it to the ground.

"You sunk lower than I thought. Stealing so many souls." Melinda took a step closer toward the crate of canisters, glimpsing what she could from the side of her vision. The canisters looked identical; she had no way of telling which were Abel's and Lance's.

"It's a simple equation, really," Eloise said. "Boss pays me, and I do what he asks." Her gaze darted to the side and her lips flicked.

She was repressing a smile at something, Melinda realized. *Harston.* She spared a split second to scan for the red cloud.

She realized too late it was a bluff.

Eloise dove forward, barreling into Melinda and slamming her arm to the side. Pain spiderwebbed into Melinda's gut and into her ribs. The handle slipped from her grip, sending the gun to the ground. She winced as a wayward shot fired, making pieces of wood rain down and the horses buck.

The ache she had from the train fall had come back tenfold and she struggled to stand. Before she could straighten, Eloise grabbed her duster collar, holding it so tightly Melinda started to gasp for breath.

Eloise glanced at Abel's charm sack hanging from Melinda's belt. "So that's how you keep Harston at bay. Well, your little charms won't help you now."

Melinda's duster collar ripped with a groan as Eloise shoved her backwards. Melinda stumbled, a pile of stray hay cushioning her fall. She looked up in time to see Eloise lifting a piece of wood. Melinda threw up her hands to block, bracing for the impact.

Eloise stopped. Her mouth, which had started to curl in triumph, twisted into a snarl.

In a second Melinda saw why. A few feet away, the steel muzzle of Angelo's gun moved closer.

"Gotcha now, bounty hunter," Angelo said.

CHAPTER SEVENTEEN

"I found them, Melinda," Gene called, hurrying in. Topaz stomped into the barn with a coil of rope. Lance followed, blue eyes strained beneath a streak of dirt across his forehead.

Lance hurried toward Melinda to help her up. She waved him away, staggering to her feet on her own. Anger swelled up in her, drowning out the relief of seeing him. She willed herself to ignore him for now, at least until the urge to slug him had subsided somewhat. She examined the ripped neckline of her duster. Still hanging on, still wearable, but dang that was her favorite.

"You again," Eloise said to Angelo. "I swear, you're all worse than a case of fleas. Couldn't help making your lover a bed of dirt. He shot first, after all."

"You're buzzard food, lickspittle." Angelo's eyes narrowed to pits of rage, but he held his gun steady.

"Don't let her get under your skin, hon," Topaz murmured as she looped rope over Eloise's wrists.

Lance stepped back and turned toward Melinda.

"Can't believe you all but left me," Melinda said quietly, debating if she wanted to punch Lance or ignore him, as his words came back to her. His *tone*. Soul sucking or not, it still made her pause. *Not fair*, she told herself. *He's not feeling himself.* Still, she couldn't seem to make herself look at him as the coil of anger in her waited, ready to spring. He sensed it but stepped closer anyway. He shot her a look, apologetic and mixed with pain.

"Hard to think straight." Lance shook his head like a cow swarmed by gnats. The knot in her chest twisted at the grayness of his face and her anger finally relented. "Please don't mind what I say, Mellie. My whole head is swimming. Like a nightmare. I'm sorry." He grabbed her hand and squeezed.

"It'll be in the past soon enough," Melinda said, trying to sound more confident than she felt. He looked tired, more so than she had ever seen him, and she wanted nothing more than to find the nearest room so they could rest. "Just another story we tell someday. But first ..."

They turned back to see Angelo motion his gun toward Eloise's forehead. Topaz finished tying the rope around her wrists.

"Won't be so cheery once you're facing your trial," Angelo was saying.

Something flashed in Eloise's face—hesitation maybe—before her mouth tightened. "I didn't have a choice and I don't regret it," she said. "Your man got what was coming to him when he tried to send me back."

Angelo lifted the butt of his gun as if to strike her.

"We're bringing her in alive," Lance said, a note of warning in his voice, and Angelo lowered the gun back to pointing at her forehead.

"You handsome fellas sure know how to make a lady feel loved," Eloise said. "But lemme tell you how it's going to go. We're near the Edge now, so game's changed. Now that I know you're here, Harston's gonna find out too."

"Funny how someone can act like a high roller even as they're being tied up," Melinda commented. She tapped Abel's charm bag, getting the satisfaction of seeing Eloise's eyes narrow.

"That little charm bag isn't gonna help you for long," Elois scoffed. "Harston's gonna track you down and flay you all alive. Just a matter of time."

"Please." Topaz rolled her eyes. "Give it a rest, hon. At least have some dignity to know when to fold your hand."

Melinda tuned out their bickering and turned to scrutinize the canisters loaded on the back of the wagon. Twelve of them, lined up nice and neat.

All those souls …

Melinda's stomach turned thinking about them. How many others were like Abel now, in a near-death trance or maybe worse. Were there kids in there?

Lance joined her, scanning them solemnly.

"Now you have a quandary," Eloise said louder to the two of them. The sheep shifted in its cage as Topaz examined the inside of the wagon. "You're not going be able to tell which soul is which."

"Any of them calling to you?" Melinda murmured to him.

Lance's hands hovered over one, before moving to another. "This fella," he said. "Feels like home."

"You sure?" Melinda caught his second of hesitation, and her heart fell.

"No sweat," Lance said finally. "Let's try it."

"Might want to hold off darling." Eloise grinned. "If you're wrong, the soul is gone forever."

"Gene?" Melinda called. Eloise was bluffing again. Had to be. But Gene's next words made her stomach drop.

"She is correct; no way to tell whose is whose, as far I can see. Maybe a mystic can help." Gene chewed on his lip, examining a canister. "Why do you want these poor souls?"

"Answer, outlaw." Angelo raised his free hand toward Eloise, fist clenched. "Or you're going to feel a world of pain before I drag your sorry carcass to jail."

"The souls are like bricks. Building material for a doorway," Eloise said reluctantly. "There's no way to stop him, you know. You're just buying time." Her eyes flicked toward Lance. "He only takes souls that deserve it anyhow."

"That's what he tells you so you can do his bidding and still sleep at night," Lance said tightly.

"She's just trying to bug you, that's her game," Melinda said.

"Miss Aine can surely help us sort out the souls." Gene carefully put the canister back in the crate. "Suggest we wait until we get these back to her to open them."

Melinda glanced at Lance. "Aunt B can probably figure it out too. Gene's right; best to wait, make sure we do it right."

"We'll take all of them with us," Lance said curtly to the others. Melinda nodded in agreement. They would track down the owner of every missing soul as fast as possible. She shook off an old burlap sack they could use to hold the canisters when a boom echoed outside. The walls shook and everyone ducked.

"What in the high hell was that!" Topaz shouted.

Melinda recognized the sound immediately and locked eyes with Lance, catching his look of dawning.

Shotgun.

"Who?" he said.

The horses whinnied, and the sheep bleated in panic. As she swung her gun toward the barn doors, Melinda didn't make the mistake of taking her eyes off Eloise this time and neither, she noticed, did Angelo. Gene, who was closest to the door, peered out cautiously. Lance drew his pistol next to him.

"Edge Riders?" Melinda guessed.

"I don't think so. A man, standing by the bushes."

Melinda sidled up to glimpse an immaculate hat and a red, polished walking stick in the last few rays of twilight. And a shotgun.

"Irvin," she groaned. "He's more persistent than a horsefly at a picnic."

Lance peered out next to her. "Good or bad?"

"Hard to say. Don't shoot!" Melinda hollered out the door. "We got the outlaw."

"Glad to hear it! Send her out, please," Irvin called back.

"Hell we will," Angelo snarled. "I've been hunting her for too long. I'll be damned if someone else takes her in."

"That South Rim boy seriously thinks he's splitting the bounty after we did all the work?" Topaz said and laughed. "Uh-uh."

"I don't much care who gets the bounty." Lance shot Angelo a steely glance. He glared with that new look he had, one that sent a bad feeling snaking in Melinda's gut. "Let her go for all we care. Long as we get the canisters."

Topaz looked startled, then her eyes narrowed. "Really? You'd let justice go unserved?"

"Might as well kill me now," Eloise all but shouted. "You don't watch out, he'll take the lot of you in for forced labor."

"We're not criminals like you," Topaz replied.

"People like him find ways," Eloise said. Her eyes shot upward, looking, Melinda realized, for Harston to help her.

"Maybe we can talk with him, work out a way—" Gene offered.

"Uh-uh. She's mine," Angelo said. "I'm sending her to jail for a long time. Either that or I'll put the bullet in myself."

"We aren't executing anyone," Melinda snapped. She needed a second to think, but everyone was still bickering.

"Miss Melinda! I'm gonna need you to send out Miss Jackson, if you please," Irvin called, as amicably as if he were telling them the weather.

"Mellie?" Lance stood next to her, speaking low. "Let's take the souls and go. Let these guys figure out who gets what for the bounty."

A warning gunshot fired into the barn, this time splintering the wood next to them.

"Gene!" Angelo barked. "Make yourself useful and go out there and tell them to go to hell."

Out of the corner of Melinda's eye, while Angelo shooed Gene outside, Eloise moved her bound hands toward her side. Too slickly, pulling something out of her jacket pocket.

Melinda swung, preparing to fire when she saw what it was. Not a gun. A thirteenth canister.

"Gotta have an ace up my sleeve," Eloise said and held the top of the canister lid nearly twisted off. "You help me, or I release your friend's soul."

"Wait!" Melinda lowered her gun, but Angelo kept his pointed at Eloise.

Topaz had materialized a knife behind Eloise and pressed it against the back of her neck.

"Hand it over," Topaz said.

"Nope. You shoot or slice me and this soul is gone," Eloise said, her gaze sliding to Melinda. "Get me outta here now, or you lose it forever."

"Put the knife down," Lance snapped.

"She's lying," Topaz said. "Obviously."

Melinda exchanged a quick look with Lance. She wouldn't put it past Eloise to have a backup plan like this. And even though they had no way of knowing whether it was Abel's soul, they couldn't take the risk.

"It's simple," Eloise purred to Melinda. "Get me on my wagon here, and I'll make sure this soul doesn't vanish into the ether. Heck, I'm feeling generous, I'll even give you this one. Let it be said that Eloise Jackson always keeps her word."

"What choice do we have?" Melinda murmured to Lance. He nodded slowly, pained. They'd have to get the other canisters later. He shifted his weight, taking a small step toward the other side of Angelo. Melinda moved opposite, closer to Topaz.

"Let her go," Lance said.

"I've been looking for her for years. I made a promise," Angelo said slowly. Dangerously. *Like someone about to do something stupid,* Melinda thought. "I'm not about to give her up now. Not after what she did."

"She's bluffing, hon," Topaz said to Melinda. "it's an empty canister for all we know."

"No choice," Melinda said. "You know that. What if it was you in there? Or Angelo?" Maybe Lance had been right; they should've ditched the rest back at Goldie. Would've kept things from getting complicated.

"Don't want it to go like this, but I'll take you down if I need to," Topaz replied.

"Your vengeance isn't worth it," Lance told Angelo, who merely spat in response.

Eloise's eyes locked on Melinda. "You better get me outta here intact, understand?" In her hands, the canister lid was just barely on top. The tiniest wisp floated around it and Lance tensed. Melinda's stomach clenched and she deepened her stance, calculating how quickly she could disarm Topaz.

"Hold on," Lance said, loud enough to draw their attention. "Just hold on—"

"Enough!" Angelo roared.

Topaz gasped and Melinda turned to see why.

Angelo's gun was still raised, level.

And pointed straight at Melinda.

Chapter Eighteen

"What the hell are you doing?" Lance held tenser than a rattler about to bite as Angelo pointed the gun at Melinda.

Normally a gun pointed toward her didn't faze her too much—it wasn't the first time—but she saw how steady Angelo's hand was, his finger taut to pull the trigger. He'd do it, she saw, if he thought he had to.

"You really gonna shoot me?" Melinda gave a good scowl, one evoking Aunt B's disapproval when Melinda forgot a critical fact about an Edge creature. *Knowledge is an indispensable tool to help you from getting killed out there*, Aunt B would say after the full force of her glare made Melinda feel like crawling under a rock. Melinda got her facts straight after that.

Now, Melinda was glad to see her glare made Angelo falter a second before his face hardened again.

"Outlaw's lying through her teeth anyway!" Topaz growled, pressing the knife.

"Seems like my hand is played." Eloise hands moved a fraction of an inch, a puff of smoke no bigger than a dandelion seed escaping it.

"Stop!" Melinda shouted.

In the corner of her eye, Lance tensed. Melinda ducked as he jumped toward Angelo. Topaz shouted while the two men struggled.

Both with pistols in their hands.

A stray bullet could go off at any second.

"Leave him alone!" Topaz yelled at Lance. Lance buried his free fist into Angelo's gut, and both guns clattered to the ground, miraculously without firing.

"Keep on the outlaw, Topaz!" Angelo wheezed, jumping up to hook Lance around the neck and they spun. "I'll handle rodeo boy here. Yee-haw, huh cowpoke?"

While Topaz was distracted, Melinda darted forward to grab Topaz's knife hand, swinging it upwards and knocking the weapon away. She tracked each instant as though everyone were moving through molasses. Topaz tensing with a look of surprise, followed by grim resolve. Eloise ducking out of the way and hurtling toward the wagon, canister tight in her hands. Lance and Angelo still tussling.

"You hold them off another breath, then I'll roll you your canister!" Eloise yelled.

"I don't want to hurt you," Topaz growled at Melinda and swung her free hand in a claw that Melinda caught and forced away.

"Oh, please," Melinda said. Topaz let the tone get the better of her, flushing and flailing more wildly, losing momentum. Without a weapon, Topaz's small stature wasn't a match against Melinda's size and skill.

She couldn't say the same for Lance; he could hold his own in a fight normally, but Angelo's sinewy arms moved fast and strong like a snake, nearly getting Lance in a full head grip. Another few seconds and he'd be down.

She couldn't think about that now. She batted Topaz back but kept one eye on Eloise, who untied the horses and clamored up the wagon.

"The canister you promised!" Melinda shouted and shoved Topaz away. "Now!"

The metal cylinder, lid fully secure, rolled on the wood. Melinda snatched it up. She didn't fully trust Eloise that it was Abel or Lance's soul, but it was something at least.

KC GRIFANT

Topaz scooped up her knife and Lance had a few seconds before Angelo got his full weight around him. But Melinda had to ignore them and get the other canisters before Eloise skedaddled.

Eloise drove the wagon forward to the front of the barn, protected from any gunfire. Melinda ran to jump onto the back of the wagon when a shot went off in the barn.

Lance or Angelo must have gotten the upper hand.

No, she corrected herself as her ears rang from the blast. That wasn't one of Angelo or Lance's pistols. It was the shotgun.

The wagon screeched to a stop.

"Melinda," Gene called from the side of the barn with a strained note in his tone that made her turn. He hurried back into the barn, a glazed look in his eye like a deer deciding what to do. "I tried talking to them, but they couldn't wait anymore, they said."

They?

Irvin strode in, jaunty as could be. A dozen shotgun fellas poured into the barn behind him. They were all tall as Melinda and wider than barrels, with broad-brimmed bowler hats and gold chain watches hanging from their vests.

"Pardon me, but y'all look in need of some help," Irvin said. A wave of relief hit Melinda as she hugged the lone canister to her and watched in a near daze. Irvin's men surrounded the wagon. Eloise yelled and the canisters rattled as the wagon stopped. All intact.

All safe.

Angelo brushed himself off as Lance beelined toward Melinda.

"First and last time going up against a bounty hunter," Lance announced, wincing as she checked the start of a shiner Angelo had given him.

"We did it." Melinda squeezed his shoulder and handed him the canister.

"Tall lady, we meet again." Irvin approached.

"Gotta admit, you have better timing than a circus barker," Melinda said.

"Nice work cornering the criminal," Irvine murmured appreciatively. He looked Lance and Melinda over like he was sizing up workhorses before two men yanked Eloise in front of them.

"Not again," Eloise said hoarsely, with a note of something Melinda hadn't heard before in her normally cocky demeanor. Pure panic. Warning bells went off in Melinda, chasing away her relief. But that was silly; the canisters were safe now.

"There she is." Irvin planted his feet wide and moved his walking stick from one hand to the other. "The slippery fish who somehow destroyed one of our premiere operations."

"The bounty is mine," Angelo said as Topaz holstered her knife and joined him. "I'm gonna see her pay for what she did. So, you can just back on out."

"You know." Irvin took off his hat, running the thumb over its felt rim. "We don't have the same issues you all have here. Criminals have an opportunity to pay off their debts in the South Rim Bowl, fairly. We have a streamlined and effective rehabilitation process."

"Is *that* what you call it? Rehabilitation?" Eloise gave the slightest tremble, but her glare was fierce, fiercer than Melinda had ever seen. "I saw the people, the *families*, in your chains. Thinking they could quickly pay off their debt or make some money for the future. Some of them had been there for a decade. Some of them there 'til they died—" She blinked rapidly, her mouth twisting.

"Mister, you heard the man." Topaz interrupted. "She's our bounty. We tracked her. You can buzz off."

"We're reasonable," Irvin continued, addressing Eloise. "We still can't figure out how you and your supernatural friend blew up the building; the power was enormous." His eyes widened a bit, insincerely. "We could harness that resource. Use it to better society. You have my word we'll make your sentence less if you cooperate. All I'm asking is that you broker an introduction to your unusual friend, maybe see if he could do us a favor, and I'll do you one. That's it. Whaddya say, Miss?"

Eloise spat on the ground and strained against the two men holding her. "I know what your word means."

"Let's try again." Irvin swung the stick with a neat smack into Eloise's stomach and she doubled over. It was more of a warning blow, but Gene, who hovered nearby, gasped, and Melinda winced all the same. Nothing fair about that fight.

"She's going to jail." Angelo stepped in between Eloise and Irvin before Irwin took another swing. A hardness jutted Angelo's bearded jaw, and he wiped beads of sweat from under his hat rim.

Irvin studied him, as if for the first time. "You don't believe in the rehabilitation of those who have made mistakes, friend?"

"She's a murderer ..." Angelo's eyes narrowed, and his fingers twitched. If Melinda didn't know better, she thought he'd try to strangle Eloise on the spot.

"She put his boyfriend in the shallow dirt," Topaz chimed in, indignant.

Eloise didn't say anything, just kept her glare on Irvin as her breathing evened out.

Irvin snapped his fingers. "I know you," he said to Angelo. "You're the B&W Duo."

Angelo nearly grimaced at the name; Topaz had no such filter and frowned, her lip twisting sourly.

"The B&W Duo, that's right," Irvin continued. "Highest bounty yield in the last four years. Consisting of you, Angelo Bravo, of course, and, oh, it's on the tip of my tongue ... *Hans Weber*, that was it. Mr. Bravo and Mr. Weber." He glanced at Topaz. "But this isn't Mr. Weber, is it?"

"You got no right saying his name," Angelo said, voice taut as a bowstring.

"No disrespect, truly. It's coming back to me, what I read," Irvin said. "The B&W Duo, sweeping from coast to coast for any outlaws. The press loved you, or at least, you made sure the newspaper men knew what you were up to, documenting your wins, helping you get more fame. Smart." He nodded appreciatively. "Boosts your reputation and, I imagine, your fees.

The two of you unstoppable together. Until ... *oh*, I read about what happened next."

Angelo's face seemed to hollow out, the shadows eating it up.

Irvin looked to the barrel-chested man to his left, whose face had settled into a bulldog-like focus. "Help me out here, Henry?"

"They met a bounty that gave them more than they bargained for," the man said. "Bank robbery."

Their gazes shot over to Eloise, who stared stonily at a spot against the barn wall, looking for all the world like she was trying to materialize something. A ghost. *Harston*, Melinda thought.

"That's it! Thank you, Henry," Irvin said, voice as smooth as just-churned butter. "Shame. Tragedy, in fact. I remember the news now. Mr. Hans Weber murdered."

Irvin's glance slid toward Topaz. "And now you're training a replacement."

Something stirred in Melinda at the sight of Angelo's face growing longer, his shoulders heavier. There was no replacing someone that was lost—she knew that from her momma's death—whether it was family or friends. The loss left a gaping hole that one learned to work around, even though it was never quite the same. She tried not to think of Abel, miles and miles away, who knew in what condition.

"Awful lot of talking," Angelo said, an edge to his warning, like a dog about to bite. "Doesn't solve our impasse."

"Tell you what," Irvin said, the more-than-reasonable salesman. "I understand you need some atonement. We'll give you 20 percent of the bounty award, even though technically you didn't assist in the capture."

Angelo shook his head, his cheeks flushed beneath his meticulous goatee. He gave a dead, dry grin, one of the few times Melinda had seen him smile. "Not exactly in the negotiating mood."

Melinda noticed the men slowly flanking them and caught Lance's eye. He spotted the same thing and gave an imperceptible nod, realizing what she did.

Irvin wasn't looking for a deal, he was buying time.

Melinda let her gaze fall onto an old rope by their feet under the strewn hay. Eight feet maybe. The other end lay near Lance's boots. She looked back up at him and he gave another nod to let her know he was thinking the same thing: they could lift the rope together and rush the row of goons and Irvin. It'd give them a moment of distraction to draw their weapons and gain the upper hand if things went sour.

"Criminals, then, if you refuse to comply with reason." Irvin smiled like someone presented with a buffet. "Luckily, we have openings in our rehabilitation program."

The danger in the barn became palpable, and Melinda spotted the way Topaz and Angelo shifted their stances, recognizing the warning signs too late. Irvin's men lifted their shotguns.

Melinda exchanged looks with Lance as they had their silent conversation:

Ready?

Ready!

His shoulders tightened as they both prepared to duck and lift the rope together.

But something was wrong—instead of squatting down Lance's eyes fluttered.

He heaved forward.

"Lance!" She darted forward to catch the canister as it fell out of his limp hands. Gene, who was closest, helped him steady himself.

Lance groaned, touching his chest in a daze.

"Shot?" Melinda scanned for a bullet wound. Nothing.

"Don't think so. Feels hard to ... breathe ..."

Gene looked alarmed. "It's his soul, miss!"

Before she could respond, Irvin's South Rim men rushed them and the room erupted into chaos.

Melinda twisted back as a man large as an ox planted himself in front of her. She kicked up a cloud of dust and straw and got in a good shoulder shove at his moment of distraction. Two more goons, built like bulls, seized her arms. They wrenched her pistols and Malgun away.

And the canister.

Maybe with Lance they'd have had a chance, but he staggered, looking worse than his hangover after the Full Moon Festival. He leaned against a bale of hay, eyes glazed and unresponsive. Gene and Topaz protested as men seized them.

Angelo lunged, all but ignoring the shotguns before four goons tackled him.

They were overpowered.

"You gotta help him!" Melinda's gaze locked on Lance's slumping figure.

Irvin ignored her and instructed the others. "Gather all this up and move out."

"Told you," Eloise spoke up, sullen. "We're all going to the South Rim Bowl now."

"Howdy!" A voice trilled through the barn entrance. Mayor Pipens trounced in, her skirt swishing, and Irvin tipped his hat in greeting.

"Thank goodness," Gene said. "There's been a misunderstanding—"

"Tell these crooks to let us go!" Topaz hollered.

But Pipens smirked in a way that reminded Melinda of a bully she knew as a kid, who liked to tell everyone how Melinda's momma had died and her pappa had left her.

"Well, what do we have here," Pipens purred. "A whole host of misfits, it looks like."

"What are you talking about?" Topaz said.

"A few folks here were abetting a known criminal and interfering with her capture, wouldn't you agree, Mayor?" Irvin said smoothly.

"Public menaces, all of them," Pipens agreed and simpered as Angelo and Topaz shouted in protest.

Irvin offered Pipens an official-looking paper and lead pencil from his pocket. She signed with a flourish, passed it back to him and accepted a thin envelope of what Melinda could only assume contained bank notes. Pipens strode out without a second look.

"As decreed by the mayor of this town, for disrupting peace and abetting a criminal, we'll need you all to come with us." Irvin smiled greedily. "Resist and your sentences will be longer, I'm afraid. Nothing personal. Just business. And justice."

"And a hefty profit for you," Melinda muttered.

"It's not true that we're criminals," Gene said meekly. "It's just not—"

"You'd better let us go!" Topaz shrieked. She shook out a small knife from her sleeve, flicked it up and stabbed one of her restrainers in the back of the hand. Angelo shouted and strained against the men holding him tighter than a bound pig.

Irvin stepped forward and spun his walking stick into Topaz's arm with a sickening crack. She screamed and dropped the knife. Angelo aired his lungs with a good stream of cusses until one of his restrainers smacked him on the side of his head.

"Nothing I can't shake off, hon," Topaz called to Angelo, but her voice trembled as if she was hiding a good bit of pain.

"Damn grass-bellied bottom feeders," Angelo spat, looking like Irvin had just taken the top spot on his most wanted list. A gash along his forehead bled.

"As I was saying," Irvin said. "Criminals."

It was like a bad dream. Melinda struggled against the arms holding her, to no avail.

Eloise, who hadn't moved during the brawl, locked eyes on Melinda. "Let him in!" she said urgently.

Melinda didn't understand at first until she felt the weight of the small bag bump against her hip.

Abel's charm bag.

Melinda twisted slightly, her fingers just brushing the edge of the rough fabric. She could almost hear Harston's velvety voice and his deep chuckle echoing in her mind. His voice tickling over her name: *Mellie*.

She let go of the bag. She couldn't risk it.

"Let him in!" Eloise said again, this time her voice ragged with panic as the South Rim gang shoved her forward, along with Angelo, Topaz and Gene. Someone started taking the wagon away with all those canisters to who knew where. Two men leaned over Lance's limp form and Melinda hollered at them to stop, but they weren't listening. No one was listening.

She reached again for Abel's charm bag.

It was a risk to let Harston find them, but it seemed like whenever Eloise needed assistance, Harston sent some kind of creature to help, if he couldn't do it himself. That would at least distract the South Rim gang and give Melinda a fighting chance to get Abel and Lance's souls back.

With a pang, she rubbed the rough sewn fabric between her fingers, crushing the desiccated herbs and watching the tiny shards of crystals tinker to the ground.

"Harston!" Eloise howled.

Rustles started above them. Some of the folks nearest Melinda paused, glancing up into the dark shadows of the barn's ceiling.

"What the hell?" The one holding her left shoulder said, his meaty brow furrowing.

"Oooh, you're in for it now!" Eloise threw back her head and laughed as the skin along Melinda's neck and arms tingled.

Something was there in the barn with them.

CHAPTER NINETEEN

The rustling sound grew louder, sending shivers down Melinda's back. She shuddered and hoped she had made the right call.

"What on Earth?" Topaz gasped. She, along with everyone else, was staring up.

"Harston," Gene squeaked.

Melinda nodded grimly. The horses bound to the wagon shifted and whinnied, trying to bolt. She held her breath as the canisters almost tumbled out of the crate. Irvin's men struggled to calm the horses and finally got them retied to their posts.

Eloise, meanwhile, started to chuckle.

"Calm down, everyone. Smoke and mirrors, smoke and mirrors," Irvin said over the murmurs. He looked positively rapturous as he scanned above. "Guessing this is the force that caused the devastation back at South Rim Bowl." He rose his voice toward the ceiling. "We'd love to come to an understanding with you, whatever you are."

"You're barking up the wrong tree," Eloise said with a smile sharper than a butcher's knife.

"Whatever deal you made with Miss Eloise here, we can double it," Irvin called. "We'll make you a sweet offering."

The barn grew darker in response. Something—a shadow—shifted along the ceiling.

It dropped.

Right onto one of the men holding Eloise.

It was a slug, no—a centipede or some combination of the two, albino, easily the size of a calf. Melinda's mind put together the pieces as quickly as she could amidst the rising shouts. Four pairs of orange eyes the size of poker chips. Hundreds of rippling legs beneath it. The creature draped over the back of the man's head like a snowy cape. The man's long peppered beard wagged as he struggled to yank the leech off.

Melinda had only ever seen something like that once before, in one of Aunt B's books.

A cereleech.

What looked like tiny hooks in its countless legs dug in along the man's temples and cheeks as he pounded his fists uselessly into the cereleech's gooey body. The creature blinked all its eyes as it extended two pinkish tentacles into the man's ears, behind bushy sideburns.

The bearded man's eyes filmed over in the same glaring white as the leech's body.

"Holy hell!" One of the men holding Melinda's arm cursed and let go. He backed up, and all the way out of the barn. She used the opportunity to elbow the other man holding her and wrench back the canister.

"What is *it?*" Topaz moaned.

"Cereleech. Whatever you do, don't let it get on you!" Melinda shouted.

The brainwashed goon turned and fired his gun at Eloise's other assailant, a looming beast of a man, who took four bullets before falling back with a gargled grunt.

The cereleech sprung off and the bearded man staggered. The white film left his eyes as he blinked in confusion.

Melinda ducked down and tried to register the cereleech's movements so she could shoot the damned thing. The cereleech was faster than any creature she had seen before, seeming to defy the laws of nature as they knew it.

Eloise dusted herself off and stepped back as the leech propelled forward to the next of Irvin's men, a redheaded fellow who was spitting some of the most colorful curses Melinda had ever heard. His eyes turned white as the cereleech settled onto his head, and he fired at the previously possessed, bearded goon.

Half a dozen of the South Rim guns, along with Angelo's, fired toward the cereleech as it jumped again to the next person, but bullets passed right through its fleshy underside. Eloise took the opportunity to shoot the two men closest to her.

Gunshots shredded the shirt of the next possessed man, but he simply stepped back from the force, ignoring the freshly gaping bullet holes, before shooting the redheaded man in the chest. Like a sick game of tag, Melinda realized, the cereleech was jumping to whoever had a loaded weapon to take out the previously possessed.

In the chaos, Topaz ducked down beside her, while Gene and Lance froze a few feet away.

"Guns aren't stopping it," Topaz hissed. "What do we do?"

"The possessed don't feel any pain and are strong besides when that little bug is on 'em," Eloise said, almost sounding proud. "Isn't it neat?"

"Unbelievable!" Irvin looked upwards. "Harston, is it? You need souls, right? Bodies? I can get you anything. More than Miss Eloise here. Let's talk—"

The cereleech shot toward Irvin. With a deft grip, Irvin hoisted his walking stick and twirled it in time to deliver a hardy smack to the creature. The cereleech turned into a white blob, splitting and flowing over the stick, easy as water. It jumped past Irvin's startled face, knocking off his nice hat as it settled onto his head like a billowing hood. Irvin's eyes blinked white, and his face went slack as the cereleech dug its legs into his cheeks and stuck its tentacles into his ears.

Two South Rim men rushed forward. One raised a knife, pointing it to the cereleech.

"Wouldn't do that," Eloise chuckled. "You try blasting it or removing that little guy, it injects a poison from the ears into the brain. They also reproduce faster than horse flies."

One goon glanced at her. "How do we stop—"

Irvin swung out his stick, quickly disarming the pair of men and slamming the weapon into their faces. He moved jerky but fast, nearly as fast as the cereleech. Over their muffled grunts and screams, he whacked them both again in the heads until they slumped over. Irvin stepped over their bodies in front of Eloise. Eloise scooped up her pistol and pointed it at Irvin.

"Please ... I'll make ... you ... deal," Irvin managed, slurring. A vein along his temple tightened with the strain of talking through the cereleech's control.

He dropped his stick with a clatter and fell to his knees in front of Eloise. He peeled back his vest with hands trembling from trying to resist, and then his shirt, exposing the scruff at his chest. His filmed eyes blinked at the same time as the cereleech's orange gaze.

Eloise smiled.

The cereleech shot back up into the rafters a split second before Eloise fired. Once, twice, three times at Irvin's heart. Red blossomed down his stomach and belt.

"You'd better give me Malgun back, if you want to live through this," Melinda said to one of the four remaining South Rim men, the one holding her guns. His mouth was agape, framed by a mustache that looked like two gray caterpillars stretching down to his chin.

The goon hurriedly passed the weapons to her.

"Irvin's dead!" The goon shouted as the others stared helplessly at Irvin's body. Like a flock of birds turning in the wind, the rest of the South Rim fellows ran out of the barn.

Melinda hooked the soul canister on her belt and hustled next to Lance, who breathed heavily against the straw bale.

But his eyes were unfocused, his mouth moving like he was trying to talk. "I got your back," she told them. "Just hang in there."

She shifted Malgun's hefty weight in her hands.

Finally, it was time to use it.

"The rest of you, stay on the leech. Gene, you see Harston?" She pointed Malgun up, sweeping her sights along the top of the barn.

Gene shook his head, terrified. "Nothing."

Eloise took a few steps and donned a smile that nearly split her face. "See that? All's right with the world!" She placed one boot on Irvin's still chest. "Unlike others I know, Harston always keeps his word," she said to Irvin's body and spat next to it.

"You can't trust Harston," Melinda said. "Whatever he says or promises. You can't believe him."

"What do you know of anything, gunslinger?" Eloise squashed her heel deeper into Irvin, sending a small geyser of blood up before it spilled over his side. "For all your little monster facts, you don't know squat of real power. Beings like him, they gotta keep their word. It's the supernatural in them. Now, who wants to be my helper?"

Above them, the cereleech chittered and ran along the wood in the dark, its legs like dry leaves brushing together.

"Where is it?" Topaz said. She had retrieved her knife and readied to slash with her good arm. The arm that Irvin had hit hung limply at her side.

"Shoot it!" Angelo bellowed. "Melinda, shoot it with your gizmo!"

Melinda ignored him; she only had one shot with Malgun and was saving it for Harston.

The shadow hovered above them, and she tightened her grip. She hesitated only a second.

It was a second too long.

The cereleech dove down with an unnatural speed and plopped onto Topaz's knife. She flailed with her knife but the cereleech scurried onto the back of her head as she screamed.

"Get the hell off her!" Angelo scooped up the knife and was behind Topaz in an instant. He lifted the blade.

"Stop!" Melinda shouted. "It's like a tick. You try to remove it, you'll make things worse. Put the knife down."

Topaz whirled and threw a punch, her eyes snow-white. Angelo ducked and caught her wrist, holding it back. Melinda rushed forward to hold her other arm as she wrenched, trying to fight.

"How do we get it off?" he growled.

Melinda shook her head helplessly.

In a flash, Angelo rose his pistol toward Eloise again, but she had already pointed hers at Angelo. Melinda mentally tallied up their remaining bullets. One each.

A draw.

Melinda sucked in a breath at what Angelo did next.

He holstered his gun.

"Let her go." His voice lost its hardness, became ragged as torn skin. He locked gazes with Eloise. "You owe me this. I'll ..." He spat out the words like they were coal. "Give up hunting you."

"Not a bad deal," Eloise said, considering. "But I need a helper for Harston."

"Take me instead," Angelo said. "You let her be, and leave the rest of them alone too. Deal?"

She tapped her chin. "Hmm. All right, all right. Let it be said that Eloise Jackson has mercy." She grinned. "Hey little critter, you mind doing the old switcheroo?"

The leech shifted, slowly pulling its legs off Topaz's head. A single blue strand of her hair caught and fell to the floor. Topaz nearly collapsed, and Melinda grabbed her.

"I'm OK," Topaz gasped. "I think."

Angelo looked at Melinda. "Make sure she—"

The cereleech jumped onto the back of Angelo's head, knocking off his hat as it settled. Melinda bit her lip to keep from yelling. Gene let out a dry sob.

Angelo, his eyes bright white, jerked suddenly to elbow Topaz in the temple. She dropped like a sack. Gene knelt quickly down next to her.

"Can't have you all following us, messing up my plans," Eloise said.

"Dammit, Eloise!" Melinda hissed. "You told Angelo you'd let us be." She glanced at Lance again to see if he might be any help. He was still awake at least and fumbling with his gun like a drunk man taking on a dare. He tried to reload but dropped the bullets on the ground.

"I am." Eloise blinked innocently. "Now you're free to go. It's not a bad deal for your friend, you know." She gestured to the cereleech pulsing on Angelo's head. "Can't feel pain with that thing on. Doesn't that sound grand? Only downside is he has to listen to me now." She straightened her hat and started toward the wagon.

Angelo groaned and lurched forward, grabbing the canister from Melinda's belt. She twisted away and threw a punch to the man's nose but what Eloise had said was true: he didn't seem to feel any pain. Angelo's head merely flicked back and forth as he wrenched the canister away. She shoved him and gave him a quick kick to the back of the knee, making him stagger. Before she could retrieve the canister, Angelo pointed his pistol first at her, and then at Lance.

"You wouldn't want to cause anyone's untimely demise now, would you?" Eloise called. "One bullet left, and I'd prefer he save it in case we run into any more trouble."

Just as Melinda considered firing on Eloise, Angelo staggered in front of her, acting as Eloise's flesh-and-blood armor, his pistol pointed toward Lance all the while.

"Can't stop … myself …" Angelo's mouth moved, words slurring. He twitched and moaned, walking backwards toward the wagon like a marionette in the hands of a novice puppet master, gun still raised.

"So you don't keep your word," Melinda called to Eloise. "Figures."

"Way I see it, we're square since Harston saved us from the South Rim fellas," Eloise shot back. "Too bad there aren't more grown cereleeches closer for Harston to summon. I could've had a whole army of you. This cutie pie will have to do."

"Shoot ... dammit." Angelo's eyebrows furrowed over his blank gaze and his neck muscles strained. He managed the words haltingly. "Shoot ... me."

Melinda raised her gun in frustration. With Angelo as a shield, she couldn't get a clear shot at Eloise, and she wasn't about to take his life.

"Oh, and gunslinger?" Eloise called as she climbed up on the wagon. "You might not want to look behind you."

Melinda glanced over her shoulder.

In the remains of Irvin, white film with small balls had bubbled up along his face and bleeding chest. A few more of the balls were growing in the other bodies littered around them.

Not balls, Melinda realized in horror.

Cereleech eggs, readying to hatch.

CHAPTER TWENTY

Gene picked up Irvin's stick. He was holding it all wrong, but looked ready to swing it into the nearest group of eggs. Melinda would've been proud of him, if their odds weren't so lousy. She spotted dozens of eggs already in the other bodies, swelling rapidly and about to burst. Good thing she had Malgun.

She hoisted it when she heard mutters behind them.

"People coming our way, miss," Gene said. "They got weapons."

Great.

"More South Rim?"

"Cliffions."

Melinda tore her eyes away from the eggs to take in the figures that poured through the door and streamed around the wagon, where Angelo was untying the horses. A man with a snarl as mean as a kicked coyote held a brick. A scrawny woman swung a machete. A teen chubbier than Gene with hacked-off hair casually twirled an iron pipe.

"They're in here!" Mayor Pipens sang behind the crowd.

"Well shoot, ya'll make it easier than slicing hot butter," Eloise purred from the wagon. "C'mon lover boy, we got places to be. Let them have their party."

Melinda rushed forward, but the incoming Cliffions stood in her way. Ten, twenty of them, creating a human blockade between her and the wagon.

"Stop that wagon!" Melinda hollered.

Pipens stepped over Irvin's body with a fleeting glance. "Pity. Oh well. Get the eggs," she instructed the others. "Quick."

"You lost your marbles?" Melinda said. "You know what they'll do to you?"

"Baby cereleeches don't have the mind controlling power. But they do confer the very useful trait of not feeling pain." Pipens scooped up an egg and examined it like it was a fine pastry.

Melinda lunged forward as the wagon started off, but the townspeople still stood firmly in her way. "Why are you helping Eloise?" she cried.

"We make deals." Pipens smirked. "We funnel some of the Edge creatures for certain buyers. People who want to sabotage their competition. Maybe a bordering town."

Her words chilled Melinda to the bone. All this time they were fighting, she never suspected humans themselves were helping the Edge creatures.

"Some are also useful for us," Pipens continued. She gently cracked open the egg and a small leech the size of a rat scooted out. "During your little fight, a Mr. Harston appeared to me and made an introduction, offering these eggs so we can kill the Edge Riders, finally. And all we have to do in exchange …" The mayor lifted the baby cereleech to her ear where it explored before extending a small pink tentacle. "Is make sure you don't disturb that naughty outlaw again."

Melinda drew her gun and fired at Pipens.

But she was too late—the baby cereleech had already taken hold.

The bullet hole in Pipens' shoulder streamed blood. Pipens ignored it, her eyes white as maggots. She nodded to the Cliffions, and they rose their weapons. Machete. Pipe. Brick.

"Now what do we do?" Gene gasped, and Melinda shook her head grimly. It was a losing bet. They were outnumbered, and most of the Cliffions had already cracked open eggs and bonded with the baby cereleeches.

"Got any bright ideas?" Melinda fired off another shot into the crowd. It made the closest Cliffion, a young man with wild hair, stagger back. His cheek flapped off, white bone exposed. He grinned and lunged forward. Gene lifted Irvin's stick and swung it wide, missing.

"Melinda!" Gene's eyes glowed. "They're coming. Any second."

"More Cliffions?" She debated using Malgun, but it would be wasted on the crowd. And the wagon had already driven off, out of sight beyond the barn door. Her heart sagged. She couldn't do it anymore. She knew a rigged game when she saw it.

Gene's next words gave her a spark of hope.

"Edge Riders."

Another clamor at the door and she saw a flash of a white mane. Yells erupted outside as the Cliffions turned toward the source of the noise.

Thank goodness.

But the Edge Riders didn't seem to see, or didn't care about, Melinda and the others as they hurled glass containers stuffed with flaming cloth into the barn. The sound of smashing glass and shouts heightened to a frenzied pitch.

Melinda ducked as another glass jar exploded a few feet away. Flames licked up from the broken glass, climbing hungrily along the hay.

Half a dozen Riders crowded at the entrance, holding what looked like thin swords and leather pouches. They tossed more flaming glass bottles and threw their small leather satchels, which opened on impact to send a fine dusting of clear glittering powder in the air.

They want the Cliffions to burn, Melinda realized. And she and the others would burn right along with them if they didn't get out.

The mayor, a few steps from Melinda, screamed a garbled battle cry and charged. The Cliffions' faces were lit in flickering orange as they attacked the Edge Riders, hurling their weapons and pieces of rotten barn boards with unnatural strength. Lines of fire ran to the sides of the barn and quickly up the walls. Any remaining cereleech eggs on the ground liquified like massive bird stool.

"We gotta get out of here, now. Can you carry Topaz?" Melinda shouted over the din. Gene nodded and delicately hoisted her limp figure up. Melinda threw Lance's arm around her shoulder and looked for an exit.

Lance rubbed his face, blinking. "Mellie ... let me help."

"Just follow me, OK? We got to get out of here before we're fried to a crisp."

"Melinda!" Gene coughed through the smoke and pointed to the boarded-up window closest to them.

She used Irvin's stick to break away the rotten wood, Lance weakly yanking away the pieces. When the opening was large enough, she helped Lance climb through, then she and Gene gently slid Topaz after him.

"Go," she told Gene.

Gene shook his head, looking defeated. "I won't fit, miss. You go on."

"I'll make you fit!" Melinda knocked away more wood to expose the full frame of the window. "Go now!"

He shook his head again, but she shoved him hard. Gene huffed and put his arms through, then his head. His middle bulged around the frame, stuck as he had predicted. She gave his butt a push but he didn't budge. She coughed harder as smoke billowed around them and slumped down, trying to take in some air. Something suddenly gave—as if another force were pulling Gene through—and he slipped through the frame easier than a fish in water. She reached for the window and strong arms grabbed her, yanking her through.

Melinda fell on a patch of grass next to Lance. She tried to suck in the cold air, tinged with smoke, and nearly coughed up a lung. By the fire's light, Melinda could see Edge Riders hurling their bags at the half a dozen Cliffions who had made it outside. The bags opened on impact, sending the cloud of clear, sparkling particles around the Cliffions and their cereleeches. The baby critters squealed, shriveled, and fell off immediately.

An Edge Rider, not clearly male or female as far as Melinda could tell, stood over them. "Desiccating mix," they said conversationally. "Kills the unnaturals." Their hair was even longer than Gene's, neatly braided. Though their face was stern with sharp angles in their cheeks and chin, their black eyes flecked with gold took them in warmly. They were skinny and straight as a willow trunk, and taller than Melinda, a rarity. A double moon tattoo peeked out from beneath their ear.

Gene stopped coughing first and managed to choke out, "Thank you, um …"

"Tsen." They nodded in acknowledgment and ran back toward the front of the barn. Mayor Pipens and a handful of other Cliffions scrambled into the woods, two Edge Riders in close pursuit.

Melinda felt a hand on her shoulder as she finally stopped coughing.

Lance, next to her, his eyes wandering, still unfocused. "You all right?"

She clasped his hand. It was cold, too cold, despite their proximity to the fire. The barn gave a groan and collapsed in a heap of flames. "*Me*? I should be asking y—"

Lance pitched forward, out cold like a switch had been thrown. She could see it in the way his eyes fluttered shut and all the strength seemed to drain from his body, as if he had fallen into a sleep.

"Lance!" she screamed hoarsely and knelt next to him in the grass. The smell of burning hay and wood wafted through the air.

She scanned him, relieved to see his chest heave up and down. At least he was breathing. But slowly, too slowly. A tightness seized her lungs, the same tightness that had gripped her all those years ago while she watched her momma die.

"Harston said his soul would keep seeping out," she said as Gene knelt next to them. Her voice fought to get out of her chest, each word scratching against her raw throat. She coughed again. "You see any way to help him?"

Gene's eyes flared green for a moment. "It looks like he's in a trance."

"How do I fix it?"

Gene shook his head, helpless. "I reckon the soul seeps out to try to find its missing piece. I'm sorry, Melinda."

Melinda brushed her lips to Lance's scruffy cheek, which was cold and still. "Bet you ten pieces you'll be OK," Melinda whispered to him. "I'm not giving up on you. I'll get the canisters back before you know it."

"The wagon's gone," Gene offered timidly. "They're probably at the Edge by now."

"Then I'm going to the Edge. I'm getting those souls back."

She crouched over Lance as the Edge Riders holding torches thundered around them. The dust settled, and six horses stood stiller than statues, with garlands of charms swinging from their necks. Their riders spoke in a rapid language she couldn't make out. Gene watched them intently.

"You understand what they're saying?" Melinda asked.

"A little. Not really. I recognize bits and pieces from other dialects. Sounds like they sort of made a language, I gather, to help bridge their communications," Gene said. "Guess that's what happens when you have a lot of different people coming together."

He ventured closer and exchanged a few halting words with the spectacled, curly-haired rider they had run into earlier.

"This is Bina," Gene gestured to her. "And Kaki." The black-haired, pregnant woman nodded in curt greeting. Kaki gestured to Tsen across the field and moved her index fingers in a circle. She pointed to the fallen forms of Topaz and Lance, then their horses.

"Tsen is their translator," Gene said. "And I think they want us to come with them."

"I'm going to the Edge," Melinda said.

Four of the riders had dismounted. Two hoisted Topaz up. Bina and a man draped in spotted furs reached for Lance.

"Leave him alone!" Melinda shoved Bina's hand away.

Bina brushed back a short curl from her brow and frowned. She glanced up at Kaki, who was clearly in charge. Kaki looked irritated and made a quick hand signal. Bina started to lift him, slower.

"Miss!" Gene said before Melinda swatted again. "They want to help."

"Can they save his soul?"

Gene shook his head. "I don't know. But reckon it'd be worth a try, wouldn't it? And Miss Topaz is hurt. I think we ought to go with them, really I do."

Melinda's head spun, her lungs and ribs ached. She closed her eyes against the exhaustion, against how very wrong everything had gone. "OK. But if they can't help, I'm leaving for the Edge first thing." She tried not to sound as bleak as she felt.

She'd follow Eloise to the ends of the Earth if she had to. And it was looking like she'd have to prepare to do just that.

After retrieving the horses, they followed the Edge Riders toward the rising moon, Melinda on Pepper, and Gene uneasily on Mud. Melinda kept her eyes glued to the group in front, where Bina and another Rider carried Lance and Topaz. It took every inch of her willpower to trust them and let them lead to who knew where. *It might be the only way to help him*, she told herself for the hundredth time.

After twenty or so minutes of riding, flapping tents of buffalo hide came into view. The Northern Ridge peaks that contained the Edge loomed right above them, the closest Melinda had ever been. Vertigo rocked her every few minutes.

"You all right, Melinda?" Gene asked, slowing down next to her. Mud flicked his ears, probably disgruntled at having a new rider, but Melinda clucked at him to behave.

"Soon as we stop, we'll see if they know how we can get to the Edge," she said, her voice still hoarse from the smoke.

Gene nodded and they both fell silent as they reached the camp. The smell of what she guessed was squash soup and something else she couldn't place—sharp, like cinnamon—floated through the air. Despite her exhaustion, she couldn't help but marvel at the set-up, well-lit by rows of torches. The tents, dyed canary yellow and crimson, lined the base of the range. In the gleaming foothills and rocks around them, patterns of stones spiraled into fractal colors, like agate but brighter: moss green on sparkling gray, lava orange on black. The Edge imbued border stones with odd properties, Abel had always said.

The Edge Riders had woven pieces of the stones into tapestries and clothing hanging out to dry, giving the materials a luminescent look. It was clever, Melinda thought. A powerful wave of missing Abel and Aunt B came over her. They would have oohed and aahed like they did whenever finding something they hadn't seen before, excitedly jotting it down in their books for future generations to read about someday.

Abel would've loved the weapons too. Glossy obsidian spears topped with intricate crystal hooks hung from the Riders' saddles. One Rider had a netting coated in tiny spikes.

"Welcome to our home," Tsen called as the group stopped next to a narrow stream running through the camp. "You can see we're a mix of all ages, backgrounds, languages. Whoever has the calling to come and fight the unnatural forces from the Edge are always welcome."

Melinda and Gene dismounted, letting the horses eagerly lap up the streaming water.

"I hear they have to take a lifelong oath," Gene whispered to her. She watched them hustle Topaz and Lance's limp forms into one of the tents. Somewhere nearby, kids burst into peals of laughter.

"Keep an eye on Lance?" Melinda asked, and he nodded. As soon as Gene had left, she leaned over. The combination of the nearness to the Edge, the fight in the barn, and her worry over Lance and the canisters all came out in a flood of bile and vomit onto the nearest bush. When she was done, one of the Riders, the man in speckled furs, appeared, handing her a cup. She took it, sniffing and finally tasting. Tea, sweet. The drink calmed the knots in her gut as she downed it. He pointed her toward a campfire some fifty feet away, in the direction of milling figures and the scent of soups and hot milk. Her stomach growled but she didn't have time. She headed toward the nearest tent instead.

Inside, she was relieved to see that Topaz was sitting up on a cot, shaking her head over a basin and cursing. Her arm was already wrapped in a sling. Small eggs that clung to her hair fell into the basin as Bina shook more of the glittering clear dust— what Tsen had called desiccating mix—over Topaz's hair.

"I'd rather swim in cow guts than see those eggs ever again." Topaz shuddered and noticed Melinda. "Hey hon, could you please tell me where the hell Angelo is? Making friendly with the handsomest man here, I'm guessing, and leaving me here to deal with these head maggots on my own?"

One look at Melinda's face and Topaz grew somber.

"Where is he?" Topaz asked.

"I'm going to find him," was all Melinda said.

"I'm going with you." Topaz started to stand. Bina shook her head and pinched more of the mix from a ceramic pot. She gave Topaz a shy smile and gestured frantically for her to stay.

"Thanks, hon, but the clock's singing my tune," Topaz said.

"Please," Bina said, the word formed carefully, followed by a few more words that Melinda couldn't make out. She adjusted her glasses to peer at Topaz and frowned in displeasure.

"I'm guessing you need some more treatment to make sure the eggs are gone," Melinda said dryly.

"I'll take the mixture with me. Drown myself in it, if I need to." Topaz grimaced, and Melinda couldn't help but notice the dark circles under her eyes, and how her plump lips were drained of their usual flush.

"No offense, you look like hell," Melinda said. "Most people can't shake off a brain parasite overnight. Arm hurt?"

"It's all right. Fractured maybe." Topaz's face darkened. "At least Irvin got what he deserved."

"Stay here with Gene and Lance. I'll get the souls back and Angelo. If I don't make it, then you try."

Bina patted the cot. "Please."

Topaz settled back with a groan, closing her eyes.

"I'm glad you're all right. Rest up." Melinda leaned over and, to her surprise as much as Topaz's, gave the woman a quick hug.

"Bring him back to me," Topaz whispered.

Melinda hurried into the adjacent tent. In the expansive interior, Gene sat next to Lance's cot. A few feet away, Kaki, Tsen and another Rider were in deep discussion. "Well?" Melinda sank down beside Gene and grabbed Lance's hand. Clammy. She stared at his still face, unmoving like he was in the deepest sleep. *Don't you dare hang up your fiddle yet*, she silently told him.

"Not good, I'm afraid," Gene said. "They said if we had his soul canister here, they could help him." He looked miserable. "They said he doesn't have much time."

Melinda squeezed her eyes shut. She wanted nothing more than to climb into the cot beside Lance and sleep until he woke up. But that wasn't happening.

She opened her eyes to see Gene breathing hard, nearly wheezing. She touched his shoulder. "Hey, you did good back at the barn there," she said. "I owe you one. When I get back from the Edge, drinks on me."

Gene rubbed his face. "You'll never come back from the Edge. Demons dominate that land. Horrible things happened there during the Massacre, soaking into it, turning it evil. Making people lose their minds."

"I don't have a choice. I have to try. For Lance and Angelo." *And Abel.*

Melinda turned when Tsen approached, a board of small ceramic jars in their hands. It reminded her of Aunt B, mixing up salves for their various injuries, and a pang rocked her hard enough to bring the sting of tears.

"Melinda the Gunslinger and Gene the Empath, yes?" Tsen said.

"Something like that, mister—er, miss—um," Gene said.

"Healer Tsen is fine," they said and Gene nodded. "You're hurt," they continued, studying Melinda. Their voice was soft, soothing as though Melinda was a kid. "Ribs?"

She gingerly touched the sore spot on her side. "It'll heal."

"Throat?"

She swallowed, testing. "Still scratchy from the smoke, but that tea outside helped."

"Take a few drops of this the next few days. I made it myself." Tsen handed them each a small jar.

Gene examined it, then smelled it. "Fascinating. Herbs?"

"And minerals, and a few other things." Tsen motioned to the tent entrance. "Please, eat. Rest."

"I can't." Melinda stood. "I have to leave. Now." Eloise was already too far, and who knew how long the stolen souls had. "You got anything that can help with going to the Edge? Any weapons I could borrow?"

"You can't go to the Edge," Tsen said, like it was a simple fact.

"Why on Earth not?" Melinda demanded. "I thought you were all about monster hunting."

"We are, when they escape from the Edge. But you going into the Edge may provoke them. You never know what might happen. We've seen people go in. Sometimes they think they're helping, but they come back and make things worse. New unnatural things follow." Tsen's face grew full of sadness, which disappeared a second later into a more neutral expression. "Please try to understand. We have lives to protect here. And we have to think of future generations." Tsen glanced over at Kaki, who was absently rubbing her pregnant belly.

"I'm not releasing any new monsters. I'm going to stop a bigger one," Melinda said, and at Tsen's unmoving face, added, "you haven't met a monster like Harston before. I have to stop him."

On the other side of the tent, Kaki broke off from a conversation with a Rider to say something sharp and emphatic to

Tsen. Melinda didn't need a translator to understand. *She can't go to the Edge.*

Tsen tucked a strand of loose hair behind their ear. Their intense gaze seemed to drill into her, not annoyed like Kaki's look, but more curious. Their gentle scrutiny put Melinda at ease and made her feel like they were really listening. They could've been friends, it felt like, if they had met under better circumstances.

"I understand your friends are in trouble," Tsen said. "Odds are they are probably gone and that's the unpolished truth. I'm sorry, truly. There are already rips in the Edge. Your presence could make it worse."

"I'm going to the Edge, one way or another," she said. "And that's that."

Tsen raised their eyebrows, undoubtedly noting the threat in her voice. As did Kaki, who stared at Melinda with a mix of contempt, anger and disbelief that she was being so stubborn.

I don't care what Tsen or Kaki think, Melinda thought.

Gene grasped her hand, warm and dry.

"I know you're hurting, miss, I am too," he said softly. "And I understand that you're going to the Edge. Maybe these fine folks can give you a tip or two, to make it a little easier."

Tsen sighed, a mix of emotions on their face. They crossed their arms. "You have no way of getting into the Edge on your own. Only a mystic or unnatural can find the paths. Everyone else who tries to enter the mountain range dies."

Melinda crossed her arms right back. "Gene can help me."

"Oh." Gene paled.

"Just point me in the right direction," Melinda told Gene and he relaxed a bit. "I need you to come back here and stay with Lance while I go."

Kaki waved at them, spitting a stream of words.

"She says we officially do not condone your endeavor, as it is dangerous," Tsen said, somewhat ashen and speaking more formally than they had before. "We'll house anyone harmed by the unnaturals, so your friends can stay here to heal. But we cannot offer you assistance on your death march. You're on your own."

A bitter laugh escaped Melinda. "Always am. Thanks anyway." She didn't let herself look at Lance while she strode out in case she lost her composure entirely.

Under the moonlight and purple glow emanating from the Edge, Melinda sat on a boulder, waiting until her breaths slowed and the urge to scream or throw something faded, slightly. She'd save that rage for when she found Eloise and Harston. And she'd get through this on her own. She always did. The conviction, even to herself, rang hollow.

Someone appeared next to her, a lanky form against the dark horizon. "Take this." Tsen handed Melinda a bowl of stew before gently stringing a green leather satchel around her belt. She recognized it. Something the other Edge Riders had worn.

"It's made of hide stitched from one of the unnaturals," Tsen explained, sitting next to her on the rock as she ate. "Counters the ill effects of being too close. And the desiccating mix inside will help your friend."

"I appreciate that." She meant it. A gesture like that made her feel, at least for a minute, a little less alone. "But why the change of heart?"

"I feel like you're on the right track. And I've learned how important it is to follow those feelings." Tsen shrugged and leaned back to look at the nearly full moon. "I guess you could say I have a perspective most people don't. Helps me be a good chemist. And …" Their eyes flicked back toward the tent where Kaki was. A smile played at their lips. "Makes me not the best at following rules I don't agree with."

She caught a whiff of their scent of cinnamon and grass, horse musk and ointment. Something about it reminded her of home. "Thanks, Tsen. More than you know."

"If—*when* you return, think about joining us. I saw you back at the barn. You had a sense for fighting those things. Might be able to put your skills to better use here."

"Not exactly my type of rodeo. But I appreciate the sentiment."

Tsen leaned down and brushed their lips to Melinda's cheek, soft like a petal. She looked over in surprise. She felt herself blush and was glad for the dim light.

"Good luck, Melinda Gunslinger. I hope you find what you're looking for."

A ball of dread still hardened her chest, but Tsen's kindness made her feel a bit better. She plunged her hand into her pocket for the comforting feel of carved wood. With the desiccating mix to free Angelo from the cereleech, maybe she'd have a better chance after all. She tried not to think about how even the experienced Riders wouldn't go into the Edge. How it was the last place on Earth she wanted to go.

Above, the violet and salmon glow of the Edge brightened, like a dare.

Melinda stood and, with a heavy heart, prepared to follow Eloise into the Edge.

PART THREE:

THE EDGE

CHAPTER TWENTY-ONE

A mauve and periwinkle haze settled over the Edge as though it was forever on the verge of a thunderstorm at sunset, whether day or night. Around the base of the Northern Ridge mountains, a few signs scrawled on wooden posts of Xs and "DO NOT ENTER" were written in various languages. Aside from a few glowing bugs that scuttled in the dead grass, Melinda spotted no signs of life.

Gene walked slowly alongside of her and Pepper, breathing hard and looking like he was on the verge of puking. He stopped in front of one of the many steep trails that led up the closest mountain and raised his torch.

"There." He pointed to what looked like a dead end a hundred feet up where the trail ended in an abrupt drop. "You can find a way into the Edge at that gap, even if it doesn't look it. There's some sort of invisible walkway up there. I think it'll take you into a cave."

Melinda tugged Pepper toward the path. "You sure?"

Gene's green eyes gleamed. "Sure as sure can be. Be careful. Sounds like things are up instead of down and left instead of right in the Edge. Get out quick as you can before it gets to you."

"I will. Hey, Gene? Some people wouldn't have gotten as far as you did. Thanks for hanging in when the going got tough."

"It's something to write home about, that's for sure. I'll keep a good eye on your mister while you're gone." Gene looked solemn as a preacher, and Melinda clapped him on the shoulder, fighting back a bite that came to her eyes. "Good luck."

A trickle of cold rain started down from the strange purplish hue that never faltered, as Melinda urged a reluctant Pepper up the steep ridge. The smell of whatever fungus plagued the border of the Edge and the towns grew stronger, making her nose wrinkle. Pepper stopped when the trail appeared to abruptly end.

Melinda dismounted and tapped the toe of her boot over the edge of the cliff above what looked to be a sheer drop. Her foot hit an invisible boundary, firm as rock.

"I'll be," she said to Pepper. "This should be interesting."

She touched the pouch Tsen had given her for reassurance and walked a foot or two out, trying not to look down. The rain continued to fall, making her skin itch. Her heart hammered like she was about to plummet, an automatic reaction to seeing the distance between her boots and the ground one hundred feet below.

"C'mon, gal." She gave Pepper a firm tug of the reigns but knew the shift of solid muscle all too well as the mare settled into her stance. Pepper wasn't going anywhere.

"I get it," she said. "No sane animal wants to go near these parts."

Pepper regarded her with liquid eyes, and she sighed. Something about a horse's watchful silence always seemed to bring about confessionals. "I don't know, dammit. What else am I supposed to do? I have to try. Go ahead and wait for me or find your way back to Gene."

Pepper clipped back down the trail, looking for some palatable grass.

Melinda slowly inched along the invisible path, the cave twenty or so feet ahead. She tried not to look down but it was impossible. The yawning distance made her want to drop to her knees and crawl backwards.

There's no other way, she told herself firmly, digging her hand into the side of the rock as she forced herself to take another step. She didn't let herself think what might happen if the invisible path suddenly disappeared.

Finally, she reached a cave with solid-looking rock underfoot and breathed a sigh of relief. She turned a bend and the cave ended abruptly.

She stepped out, squinting against the sudden brightness.

It was as if she emerged into an entirely different landscape. Thick trees of a forest knotted upwards toward a colorless sky light enough to feel like morning. Even the atmosphere felt different; the rain had stopped, and the air was warm and heavy. No mountain or any type of topography in sight—the cave behind her stood alone between the trees.

"So, this is the Edge, huh? This place is strange as all get out," she said to herself, knocking the water drops from her hat. Talking aloud helped ease the silence, sharper now without the chatter she was used to from the others. She didn't let herself think about how lonely it was, ten times worse than after she was tossed from the train.

"Where's the dang sun?" she muttered. Even though there was light, she couldn't pinpoint the source, destroying any sense of direction.

At least it was a welcome change from the rain. *Pleasant even, under different circumstances*, she thought as she passed enormous trunks and sidestepped branches. She listened carefully, ready for an attack, but after a few minutes of walking, still nothing. The glimpses of sky between lush leaves arched in a clear, hard gray. When she looked up too long, the landscape around her ebbed and wavered, as though she were in a warped glass orb.

Stranger and stranger.

She spotted wagon tracks in the dirt and hurried forward, every sense on alert. Something skittled around her, like bird wings. Movement blurred at the corner of her eye, once, twice, and again. Then she spotted it.

A face in the dark bush next to her, followed by three more, then a dozen. The faces glimmered white and black, all with their mouths opened in silent screams. She drew her gun but paused when they disappeared. They reappeared a second later, children and adult faces flicking in and out like candles, in various stages of soundless shouts or glares. Some of the faces looked melted or charred.

Ghosts, she realized, from the Massacre. Before the Edge had appeared, a wave of newcomers had poured into the region, some bringing a wave of destruction, the likes of which were unfathomable to those who heard about it later. Lining up and shooting children point-blank. Hundreds of innocent souls, slaughtered. No wonder the Edge was located on this fault line of sorrow—some suspected the blood-soaked grounds made it easier for the monsters to enter the human world. A written line floated to her, maybe something she had read way back when in one of Aunt B's books.

The land, wrought in violence, blood and tears.

Melinda could feel the weight of the ghosts the deeper she went into the Edge. The ghosts wouldn't relent as she pressed on, some stepping out of the bushes now, partially visible. A child with a head mostly blasted off. One man had his eye socket pecked out, globs of blood hardening along his sunbaked cheek. A young woman gestured at her chest, where a hatchet blade neatly split her. Another woman swollen with pregnancy had half of her belly missing, like a caved-in shell, revealing a writhing mass of a baby.

Between the staring figures crawled ghost critters—a snake body topped with a chomping fish head slipped between a pair of children. An owl with the legs of a giant arachnid spun a web around a family of six, all missing their heads.

How do you do deal with ghosts? Think, dammit. Her mind was sluggish, blank in the thickness of the Edge's atmosphere.

The ghosts' anger hung heavy in the air, making each footfall drag. All she wanted to do was run backwards, flee from the accusing figures. Worse than the monsters coiling between them were the ghosts' eyes, unyielding, sharper than any arrowhead, and filled with a rage that comes from the deepest grief of lives snatched.

"I'm sorry." The words fell from her mouth as more and more mangled ghosts appeared. She racked her brain to remember what she had learned about ghosts. Some things, too horrific for this world, left their mark, like a scar in space, demanding attention. In those places, ghosts stuck and grew, chewing at nearby minds. But here in the Edge, the ghosts' presence was amplified tenfold, their forms seemingly *solidified*. She wondered with a shudder if the ghosts could reach out and grab her if they were so inclined.

Who do you spot in the shadows?

Harston had asked her that back when he appeared to her. The question hung now, like a cruel joke about to be revealed.

A more solid figure hovered in the leaves, one that the silent ghosts turned to. Melinda skidded to a stop.

It was herself. Brown duster sweeping the ground and a smile on her face as bullets whizzed from her guns, tearing into the figures around her. The other Melinda laughed, strands of hair whipping under her wide hat as drops of blood flew.

That's not me, she thought, squeezing her eyes shut. A trick of the ghosts, a trick of the Edge. But fear like she hadn't felt in a long time clamped into every inch of her and bolted her to the ground like a spear of ice.

Snap out of it, she told herself. *It's not you.*

But what if it was? What if she was the shadow self, and that Melinda over there was the real Melinda, slaughtering the ghost children?

It's just the Edge, playing tricks. She plunged her hand into her pocket to feel the reassuring smoothness of the wooden figure Lance had carved. *He needs you.* Abel and Angelo too. She couldn't give up on any of them yet.

One method of dealing with ghosts—that *sometimes* worked— was to really see their pain, acknowledge it, and make past wrongs right if possible. But that required looking at them straight on and letting her fear bubble up to the surface.

181

Only problem was, occasionally that tactic backfired and set the ghosts into a frenzy.

She didn't have much choice.

She opened her eyes and forced herself to look at the closest figure, a girl about seven or eight, with stringy hair and missing her body from the torso down. She was dragging herself toward Melinda as her doppelgänger reloaded, preparing to shoot the girl again.

"I'm sorry for what happened here," Melinda said, trying to still the tremble in her voice. It was the honest truth. "I won't forget the horrors you've shown me. I swear."

It worked, a little. The girl stopped scooting. The copy of Melinda faded somewhat, now a still shadow between the trees. The remaining faces looked on from the bushes, scowling, but fainter now.

That was the break Melinda needed. She hurried on with a new blurst of energy, the leaf-covered dirt giving way to rocks. The air grew thinner and—damnest thing, she couldn't tell if the ground was inclining or declining. At least the ghosts were gone, but this topsy turvy world was hitting her harder than she expected. Talking to herself helped. She thought she'd pretend she was talking to Lance, or maybe Abel or Aunt B, but when she started speaking, she found addressing her momma came naturally.

"Stranger than anything I've ever felt before, Momma. That's a funny thing to say to you, I suppose, seeing as how death probably feels the strangest. Maybe it's like this. Like lightning in my teeth, like my eyes are burnt out. Like the ground is just about ready to give out below me." She trailed off, willing back a prickle of tears. "Hope you didn't end up here, whatever this hell is."

The wagon came into view at the next bend. And Angelo. She crouched low, taking in the scene.

Angelo was setting a canister down in a ring with others on matted grass. The cereleech hung onto him like a hat, its fringes of legs folded comfortably along his sideburns and ears. At the center of the ring sat a carved-out sheep carcass, blood and guts pooling around it.

Eloise lounged back on a grassy knoll, watching with amusement and drinking out of a burgundy bottle.

Melinda quietly reloaded her revolver and double checked Malgun.

"Woo-wee, I should have had a helper like you years ago," Eloise said as Angelo carefully set the remaining canisters next to her. "Getting paid for doing nothing. And the view's not bad either."

Melinda took stock. Six canisters around the ring and seven strung together with rope at Eloise's side, as if ready to be carried. Thirteen total. No telling which was Lance's and Abel's, now. But why half of them were set to the side, she couldn't fathom.

Angelo's muffled anger came through as he muttered something. Eloise just laughed and took another swig. "You as touchy as a teased snake. Relax. Not much longer now. Might keep you for a while. My bonus for a job well done."

Melinda raised her six shooter and, with a twinge of regret, pointed it at Eloise's chest. Now that she knew what Eloise had been trying to escape, some of her hate had eased up. But the outlaw had gotten away from them too many times now. Melinda couldn't risk another escape, even if it meant killing her.

"Don't have a choice," she whispered to herself as Lance's ashy face came back to mind. She shifted her eyesight to Eloise's leg. It would slow her down, maybe not kill her.

Melinda took aim when something tightened around her boot.

Her feet were rooted to the spot, vines curling up and around her. She was stuck.

"You make it too easy, Mellie." Harston's voice rang out. *"Your soul gives off such a pungent scent of, mm, what is it? Guilt."* His words purred like someone about to dive into a steak. *"I can sense it so easily now that you don't have Abel's charm."*

On the knoll, Eloise snapped to attention like a good soldier. Melinda fired just before a vine twisted around her gun.

But her aim was true: Eloise crumpled with a shriek.

Angelo darted over to Melinda in that jerky motion, like strings from above were pulling him. Under his white-film eyes she could see the strain in his jaw, the twist in his mouth as tried to resist the cereleech's control.

"I'll shoot you too if I have to," Melinda said to him, lifting Malgun. It was a bluff—she wouldn't roast him, but she could knock him out. She shifted her grip to use Malgun as a blunt weapon, but Angelo, despite his twitchiness, was faster.

He anticipated the swing of her weapon to duck and pummeled her with two sharp jabs. She blocked as best she could with her forearm and Malgun, but the vines tightening around her made it a losing hand. He delivered a hard swing to her ribs, right where she was bruised. A long vine wound around her wrists as she doubled over.

"Sorry," Angelo slurred. "… you." He grabbed Malgun and threw it to the ground.

"We're in a real pickle," Melinda gasped through the pain. "Tell me some good news."

He shook his head, holding the piece of vine that bound her hands like it was a pair of handcuffs. "Done …" he managed. "Har … open."

Once she was able to breathe through the pain, she stayed doubled over to pull her bound wrists as close as she could to her belt and strained for the leather satchel of desiccating mix Tsen had given her. Just out of reach.

"You gonna pay for that bullet, gunslinger." Eloise winced, cinching a belt above her leg. It was a clean shot. Not too much blood, Melinda noted. But it would slow her down. "But first, I'll finish the ritual. Keep an eye on her, pet. It's always good to have a backup soul or two, just in case."

Eloise hobbled around the circle to open the first canister. A white wisp shot out and hovered above the metal tin, as if caught in a mini tornado.

A soul.

"No!" Melinda screamed.

"Keep it down," Eloise grunted and pointed her chin toward the pile of canisters that sat outside the circle. "Your friends are saved for later. Gotta keep some backup collateral around in case the cavalry comes, take my meaning?"

Melinda struggled as hard as she could against the vines, but the damn things were stronger than cattle rope and stung her skin the more she wiggled. She watched, blinking back tears of rage as Eloise eased open the next canister in the circle.

"Whose souls are those? No one deserves this!" Melinda shouted, trying to get Eloise to pause or reconsider, but she kept on going. The white whisps—the souls—floated up and hovered over each canister.

When Eloise released the sixth one in the ring, lines appeared like captured lightning, flaring from one soul to another, creating a circle on the grass around the sheep carcass. "Here we go," Eloise spread her hands. "You ready for a show?"

Melinda nearly fell as the ground shook. A sound like thunder boomed and crimson smoke condensed in the center of the circle. Even Eloise jumped and Angelo gave a stifled groan.

"Ooooie, that feels good," Harston said as the red smoke congealed into his floating figure.

Under his hovering feet, a hole formed where the sheep carcass had been. Like a sinkhole, the crater grew.

"Howdy, boss," Eloise said.

Harston landed on the ground in front of the hole. He appeared fully solid now, in a white hat trimmed with purple and a smart black suit that made his pale skin all the sharper. His thin mustache turned up neatly in the corners. He glanced at Melinda and she blinked. For a second his eyes had looked almost normal, brown, unbearably tired.

Now, Harston's glare was the color of amethyst.

"What did you do to those souls?" Melinda demanded, working her fingers faster toward the satchel with the desiccating mix. Harston looked more like solid flesh and blood now.

Which meant maybe she could shoot him.

Around them, the sky darkened as the lightning circle from the six suspended souls intensified to a nearly blinding glow. Behind Harston, the hole grew rapidly, ground falling away like sand. The edge of the pit reached the wagon, which creaked before tumbling into the gap.

"People like to be useful during life. Why not after also?" Harston arched an eyebrow in a feign of innocence. "There's still time to join. You can be with your hero Abel for all time, and your lover boy too."

"Don't know why you bother trying with her," Eloise said. "She'd rather be a self-sacrificing fool."

"Take a look," Harston invited. He gave an I-dare-you grin that, for some reason, made Melinda's blood boil. He spread a hand toward the pit, which had grown to the size of a small pond and held steady now. The six souls trembled in their spots, laced together by the lightning. "A sneak peek of what's to come."

The vines binding Melinda's legs retreated, and Angelo dragged her by the vine handcuffs closer to the hole. Almost against her will, she peered down.

Her brain fought to understand what she was seeing. An enormous creature—no, millions of creatures—squirmed within the pit. Limbs mashed together and stuck out, looking sharp as splintered sticks. In long shadows of faces, eyes glimmered pinpoints of yellow like Fool's Gold. But the worst part was the noise; they hissed and clinked similar to all matters of insects and snakes merging into one skin-crawling cacophony.

And they *whispered.*

Melinda didn't want to hear them, even as their words pressed up into her ears. *Killer. Pathetic. Failure. Unlovable.* She shoved the thoughts back, walling them up as best she could.

"Hell is more crowded than I thought," Melinda managed. "What are they?"

"Edglings." Harston smiled fondly. "Fledgling demons, if you will. Ready to make this world their own. Stuck in my world right now, but soon they'll be able to come right out to play. Isn't that right, my little ones?"

Next to her, Angelo grew pale, and even Eloise looked shaken. Angelo's hold on the vine had slackened, Melinda realized. She readied and seized his distraction, hands finally closing around the pouch of desiccating mix. She untied and threw it, best she could, onto him.

The glittering clear particles sprinkled over the cereleech. The creature made a sound like glass popping and shuddered. Melinda held her breath, watching the cereleech curl and foam, pieces falling on Angelo's shoulders and sticking to his hair.

Angelo staggered and dropped the vine. His eyes cleared. And hardened.

"Throw me Malgun, now!" she shouted. Angelo ignored her, beelining for Eloise.

Eloise tried to limp away but Angelo pounced, knocking her hat off. She tossed a punch but the shot to her leg made her sluggish. He locked both of her wrists in one hand and used the other to begin to choke her. She dropped her chin and slammed a knee into his, but Angelo held firm.

"Angelo, stop!" Melinda yelled. They needed to focus on Harston, but Angelo was ignoring her.

She'd handle it herself.

She tossed off the rest of the vines and scooped up Malgun. Harston waved a hand and more vines rose from the ground, readying to slam into her. She had half a second. She took a fraction of that to aim and fire.

She never missed.

Malgun's green blast tore through Harston, neon and bright. Harston shot backwards, his hat disintegrated and his suit shredded to tatters.

Red smoke billowed off him like a forest fire.

"Adamophelin," Harston moaned and fell over.

CHAPTER TWENTY-TWO

"Yee haw!" Angelo shouted. "Damn that sucker to hell! Now, it's your turn outlaw."

He shoved Eloise to the ground. She landed with an *oomph*, glaring up at him and rubbing her throat. "You have no idea what you're dealing with."

"Stay right there or I'll shoot you dead, I swear," he snarled.

"Something's not right," Melinda said, kicking off the limp vines from her feet. The hissing of the Edglings in the pit grew louder. Gray fingers longer than tree branches clawed upwards. The red smoke stayed suspended over Harston, like a cloud of ruby particles. "We have to break that ring of canisters."

"Help me," Harston moaned and grabbed his chest. He staggered to his feet. Howls from the Edglings rose from inside the circle, like the yipping of mad coyotes.

"Break that dang circle while I finish him!" Melinda said.

"I'm not losing this one again," Angelo said, looping one of the vines around Eloise.

Melinda yanked out her pocket knife and ran forward. Malgun was done, so she'd kill Harston and the creatures the old-fashioned way.

"Help me," Harston muttered again. Above him, the maroon cloud hung heavy enough to cut.

"I'll help you like a tick on my arm," Melinda said, and brought her knife to his pale throat. Killing was never easy, and she steeled herself for what had to be done. He was a murderer. Worse, a soul snatcher. He couldn't be allowed to live, and she couldn't risk him escaping again.

"I'm sorry," Harston looked up. Some color had returned to his face, though it contorted with so much sorrow that she hesitated. Something about his anguish looked real. And utterly unlike the Harston she was used to.

"*This body will be useful to me*," a new voice boomed above them.

"Dammit," Melinda cursed and lowered the knife. That voice— *the cloud*—was the source of whatever was causing this mess, she realized. "Whatever this monster is, it isn't dead yet. Angelo, knock one of those canisters out of the ring, maybe that'll stop it!"

Angelo tied off the last piece of vine around Eloise and started for the nearest canister. The ruby smoke suspended over Harston suddenly shot toward Angelo.

"Watch out!" Melinda hollered.

Angelo threw himself to the side and the smoke swirled past. It streamed to Eloise instead, rushing down over her head like a waterfall of blood.

"What in the high hell?" Angelo said.

Eloise coughed and her eyes widened for a moment, uncomprehending, until the red smoke faded. Her face smoothed over. She locked eyes with Melinda and smiled. Not her coy smile. Instead, it was a façade of a smile, as if someone was stretching the face of a corpse.

Melinda shuddered. She would recognize that smug gleam anywhere. "She's possessed—"

Eloise broke the vines apart and jumped up as if she had never been shot. Before Angelo could react, Eloise shoved him with a new surge of strength.

Directly into the pit.

"Angelo!" Melinda lunged to grab his hand.

He shouted and kicked, hanging onto the edge of the pit. One Edgling extended an arm as long as a snake and dug its fingers into his neck. Angelo howled in pain as more Edglings squealed and plunged their hands into his torso.

"Hold on!" Melinda tried hoisting him up, but the gray hands were too strong. They yanked him down, sucking him into the center of the writhing creatures.

He disappeared into the Edglings.

Melinda turned to see Eloise—or what had been Eloise—grabbing the bundle of the remaining seven canisters with the captured souls.

"No!" Melinda darted forward, but Eloise sprinted toward the pit.

"It's been fun, sweet Mellie!" Eloise called as she dove and vanished neatly into the writhing Edgling bodies.

Melinda grimaced and readied to follow Eloise into the pit. But her feet stayed rooted to the spot and this time it wasn't vines keeping her stationary.

Do it. Jump, she told herself. *You have to.* Her body wasn't listening. Fear spread icicles through her, the same fear she felt when she saw the purplish spots of infection along her momma's skin and realized she was going to die. A chunk of ice had slammed into her chest then and returned now, freezing her sure as a river in the dead of winter.

Lance is down there. And Abel.

She had no choice. She fired her revolver into the center of the pit once. Didn't do much but maybe it would make the Edglings think twice before attacking her.

She tensed to jump when the lightning circle around the canisters flared—and winked out.

The now ordinary, empty metal tins clattered to the ground. The suspended souls and Edglings vanished. All that remained was a regular hole, made of regular rock.

"No." The word escaped her, rasping against the newfound silence. The Edge had grown stagnant, its perpetual twilight wobbling in the stillness.

She has missed her chance. And the stolen souls were gone.

CHAPTER TWENTY-THREE

"*You.*" The rage laced Melinda's voice tighter than a barbed wire as she marched over to Harston. "I'm gonna make you a bed of dirt and flowers, right here."

She kicked as hard as she could into his chest. It felt good, solid. He curled up on the matted grass. He looked at her and, for a moment, Melinda didn't recognize him. His face tensed differently; his eyes were wide and clear and tired.

"Do it already. I deserve it," he said.

"*Why* did you do it—" she choked and bit her lip to press back the tide of fury that made her want to smack him again.

"The demon. Adamophelin. I unleashed it. It possesses Eloise now." He bowed his head, his black strands of hair drenched in sweat. "I was a fool. I wish I could tell Abel and her I'm sorry."

"Abel?"

"Yes, he ..." Harston looked crestfallen. "We did it together, long ago. We had no other choice. It doesn't matter now. I'm sorry. I can see you were close to him."

She stared at him. "You're *sorry*? You gotta do more than that. Help me get the souls back."

"I can't." He shuddered. "I can't risk possession again. You have no idea what it's like. I wasn't ready. I wasn't strong enough."

"Look, I get you're like a babe just born," she snapped. "But you got to do whatever you can to fix this mess, now."

She crouched and peered into the pit.

Darkness pooled downwards. But to where, that was the question. Cold air wafted up. No shadow creatures, no Eloise. Just an ordinary hole in the ground.

"No point in going down there. It was a one-way, temporary doorway to Adamophelin's world. There might be a remnant opening for a few minutes, but it'd be shrinking by now, possibly gone," Harston said, watching her. "No one is worth it. Your friends are gone."

"I don't have a choice."

"Hmph," he grunted in a way that was bittersweet and pained. "That's what I had thought too. Don't you, though?"

Melinda considered for an instant. She could walk away, leave Lance and Abel's souls, which could be irrecoverable anyway. Start her life anew, make amends where she could. The thought barely formed before it disappeared. "Nope. Gonna die trying, I suppose. And you're gonna try with me. You can save them still. Make your amends."

Harston's gaze looked faraway as he gave a small nod. Melinda supposed that was what he might have looked like normally, thoughtful. It reminded her of Abel.

"And you don't actually have a choice here, you know." She yanked him up to his feet. "You're coming with me. Gunpoint if I have to."

He nodded, resigned. "Suppose ..." His voice was barely a whisper, though doubtful. "I owe it to them."

"You have any insider know-how that might help us defeat Adamophelin?" She looked down the edge of the pit again. The coldness seeped right into her bones, and made her skin prickle. They were losing time.

"The details are fuzzy. Possession is like a dream, part of which you remember too much, but other pieces are gone." Harston jabbed a finger at his temple. "But the horror ... the horror is crammed in here for all time."

"Skip the melodramatics and tell me something useful," she snapped and readied to climb down.

"Wait." Harston smoothed his ripped suit and stood to gather the empty canisters. "These are how we can carry the souls back."

Melinda adjusted her bag to make room, cramming in three of the canisters and hooking the other three on her belt.

"Now let's get. You first."

He climbed down gingerly. She watched his movements, slow but steady. She found the first few foot holes and slowly made her way down after him.

They climbed, maybe 150 feet, Melinda guessed, until they hit the bottom. Black obsidian rocks and clear quartz jutted out at every angle, like the inside of one of Aunt B's geodes. She grimaced as her jacket and hat caught on the sharp stones.

"Start talking. Anything and everything that can help me stop this thing," she said while they walked, single-file, down the narrow, steep tunnel. The air grew chillier than a dead snake, and Melinda turned her collar up, ripped as it was. *At least I have my hat this time.*

"Adamophelin is the first part of its name, as far as I can translate it," Harston said. "Essentially, it means 'a monster making and feasting on an abundance.' It dominated humans hundreds of years ago, or so it claims, before it was banished."

She rolled her eyes in the dim light. Embedded in the cave walls, transparent flecks in the stone emitted a faint glow, just enough to see by. "Skip the history and get to the part where you tell me how to save the souls."

"You can't, most likely. Adamophelin will be doing everything it can to build a permanent bridge from its world to ours."

"I don't understand," she said, her mind ticking through the endless monsters they had seen. Scorpions, ice kraken, fire cattle. "There's already plenty of creatures that come out of the Edge. Seems like a doorway's already here."

"It's a small one, all but closed up. Most of the monsters you see are like animals, not really capable of sophisticated thought. Their souls are lighter, able to pass. Adamophelin is different, obviously." Harston breathed heavily in front of her, but moved, wry and nimble enough. "Bigger, more conscious beings like Adamophelin usually can't make it through the Edge, but when Abel and I did our spell, well … we temporarily opened a bigger doorway. Let the demon through. Now that Adamophelin has had a taste, it wants to bring its Edglings over to help it collect more power and souls."

"The Edglings." A shiver ran through her. "What the heck do they do?"

"Shadow jumpers, those Edglings you saw, will feed off humans and bolster the demon's power. Adamophelin figured if the Edglings could hunt humans, it'd be able to grow bigger, faster." Harston sounded resigned, and she fought an urge to shake him. At least he was talking, maybe something he said would be useful.

"So it used those canisters to carry souls here. Why?" Melinda prompted and paused as something odd struck her. The air should be getting damper, more claustrophobic as they descended.

But the air was getting thinner. Almost like they were on a high mountain.

Harston didn't seem to notice as he continued. "Adamophelin used some of the souls to construct this temporary doorway so it could get back home, and will use the rest to build a large, permanent doorway, a bridge from its world to ours."

"There's got to be a way to stop it."

"Once the souls are fused and the door opens there's no closing it again. And your Abel, well, he's the centerpiece of it. I …" Harston trailed off before continuing, quieter. "I needed help with the spell. I didn't mean for it to go so badly. I didn't mean for all this. We were too young to know better."

"So you both released Adamophelin on purpose," Melinda said in disgust.

"You don't understand the power Adamophelin can give. Erasing all your pain, giving you whatever you want. It gives you a bigger high than darkbellas. That's how it possesses people. And then it takes over completely. I was a fool." His voice twisted bitterly. "And we were trapped. Working conditions meant to kill us. No way out. You don't know the suffering we saw; we were going to die building that damn railroad."

"Spin your wheels and drown your sorrows later. Self-pity isn't gonna get us through this."

Eventually the tunnel leveled out enough for them to walk side-by-side. In the whitish glow of the cave walls, she couldn't help but notice how bony Harston's arms were, how pale.

"Doing all right there?"

"Just a little worn. Possession will do that to you." He smiled, but his face was humorless.

The tunnel declined sharply, making her feel like she wasn't just going deeper into the earth, but deeper into something unknown. All her hair was on edge and her skin had broken out in gooseflesh, but the thought of Lance and Abel and all those innocent folks—even Eloise, with her look of surprise before the demon took over—made Melinda walk faster.

You might not be able to save them.

She had to try, at least.

Her breath caught as the chill seemed to worsen. No sign of ice or snow or frost. Not even their breaths showed in front of them. Just the jutting stones of the tunnel, glittering like mica.

"I see something," she said. A narrow light emerged ahead. They pushed through the tunnel until it widened into a small cavern. At their feet glowed a lake, but the shimmering pale surface sloped down into darkness at its edges in a way that didn't make sense. And in its rippling reflection shone two orbs.

Melinda stopped when her mind figured out what she was looking at.

It was a sky.

And a moon.

Two moons in fact.

"Are you seeing this? Where are we?" She blinked hard but the sight didn't change. It looked like the *reflection* of a sky, but only darkness loomed above them. She knelt to look at the scene more closely. Those were definitely two moons, surer than the knuckles on her hands. Purple and milky gray rocks larger than wagons floated by the moons in glob-like formations. The rocks seemed to float up toward the surface of the lake before bouncing back, as though they were colliding with an invisible barrier.

Had to be the bends, a hallucination. She reached out a hand toward the moons, expecting to feel lake water, but a pressure pushed her back, like a strong wind, or tautly stretched hide.

She glanced at Harston. He crossed his arms, regarding the view at his feet impassively.

"This is it," Harston said. "I guess it's pretty in a twisted way, if you're seeing it for the first time."

The realization punched her in the gut. "The Edge doesn't mean the edge of land …" she started, still not quite believing it even as she was saying it. Harston nodded slightly and she finished the thought:

"It's the Edge of worlds."

CHAPTER TWENTY-FOUR

The alien skyline stayed hazy in front of them, as though they were looking down at it through a warped glass.

"A topsy turvy world." Harston laughed bitterly. "Well, one of them. There are several membranes like this in these mountains. Sometimes they break or bend and monsters escape through. When Abel and I opened this membrane to summon Adamophelin's power, we had no idea the demon could exist as a semi-tangible form and influence creatures from the Edge, even after we had absorbed its power." He grimaced. "Hold onto your hat, this is where it gets fun."

"Just get us through," she said.

"The membrane is solid, so we need to thin it to pass. It's easier with a soul, but obviously we're not going that route. Luckily for you, I've done this before." Harston whispered a few sentences of long syllabled and staccato words she didn't recognize, waving his hands like he was petting a lamb. The way Harston concentrated made her think of Abel.

They were probably good friends, she thought, and her heart twisted at the vision of Abel in bed. She didn't let herself think of Lance.

The cosmos below sharpened like a magnifying lens coming into view. Harston raised a boot to step onto the membrane. It wobbled like water disturbed and his foot disappeared next to one of the moons.

"Aren't we going to fall?" Melinda said.

He gave a ghostly smile and vanished through the membrane entirely.

"Here we go," Melinda told herself, and stepped in after him, bracing herself for a tumble.

She stumbled as if she had stepped off a two-foot drop, but her feet quickly found ground solid. The alien world was now right-side up—the two moons gleaming overhead, like eye sockets scraped out. The cave was gone; they were now in a purplish-black, rock-studded desert. Behind her, the membrane they had passed through rested in the dirt like a dark pool of water.

Melinda nearly fell over at the stench of weeks-old fish, an outhouse, and something acidic, all baked together. She swallowed back the bile creeping up her throat and focused on the rocks around her; massive slabs floated overhead and peppered the ground as far as she could see. The glittering boulders swelled out in spots and thinned in others, like the work of a novice glassmaker on the verge of madness.

"This way," Harston said, and she followed him between the rocks. The packed dirt and rock gave a slight yield like a sponge and shimmered dark one second, bile-yellow the next.

"It seemed easy enough to break the membrane, with your magic. Can't Adamophelin do the same?" Melinda asked.

"It's possible for a human mystic to manipulate the membrane —demons, not so much. And it's temporary." Harston waved a hand at the shadow figures, spiny and twig-like, that had started to dart around them and flit between the boulders. The Edglings. One brushed up against her arm, its coldness piercing through the duster as though she had no layers at all. She shivered at the stab of ice and flinched as others bumped into her. The sensation was maddening, like a crowd gone out of control, like a current she couldn't fight against.

"What are these Edgling things, exactly?" She tried to shoo them and, just like flies, they came back a second later.

Harston stomped away one that scrambled forward. "The little ones are easy to keep back if you don't let fear take hold. They started as disjointed spirits, wronged in the blood-soaked lands that powered the Edge. Eventually, they make their way down here where Adamophelin fashions them into the beginnings of demons. Try not to look at them, it gives them more strength."

Whispers started up, and she could almost make out what they were saying.

"Death. Killer. Killer. Killer."

A flash of memories came back to her, of shooting the snow kraken, the momma scorpion and her eggs, the countless creatures she had hunted.

"You were killing. Murdering. Innocent creatures. Families. Murderer, murderer."

"Stop it," Melinda said aloud and slapped her ears. The Edglings skittered around them and before she knew it, one crawled up her fast as a gecko, cocking its head in her face. Its mouth contorted in silent fury, eyes tiny pinpoints of yellow light that drilled into her like a shark.

More Edglings leapt and washed over her like a bucket of ice water.

Their whispers rose to screams that drilled into her chest and ears and brain until she couldn't breathe. Their hands seemed to reach into her very blood, twanging her every nerve. In an instant, grief swelled up. It was like everyone she had ever loved was blown apart in front of her, or an invisible hand tore out her organs and ripped every inch of her in opposite directions. She screamed with them, but couldn't hear herself, couldn't hear—

Harston grabbed her elbow and yanked her up. He kicked dirt toward the Edglings and dragged her away from them. She shook her head, trying to focus on his words.

"... with me here?" Harston said. "Think of your friends. And for goodness' sake, listen to me when I tell you not to look at them."

She nodded shakily and the whispers subsided. The Edglings had dispersed.

"Look." He pointed to the ground.

A glistening trail, like tiny fireflies caught in the thinnest of liquids, lay past their feet. "A trail of the souls."

Melinda knelt to touch the soul residue. It dissolved around her hands and reformed. She reached for one of her canisters, but Harston shook his head.

"These are just the traces. You'll know the souls when you see them. In our world they look like smoke, but here they'll look like—" he swallowed. "Like lanterns containing little moons. Or a flare at sunset."

"Poetic. So, we'll just scoop them up?"

Harston tugged on his mustache. "Something like that. If we can get the souls back through the membrane, Adamophelin won't have any way to follow us. It'll be stuck here forever." He looked up and she followed his gaze. The trail of light wound up among the rocks, a good steep climb that made her wish Pepper was around.

Silence hung like a thundercloud over them while they continued. Even the Edglings seemed to have vanished. She felt for a wild moment that she and Harston were miniature, walking through a dark-stained amethyst split open and tossed onto the ashes of a campfire.

Don't let this place get to you, she told herself. She broached a question to break the silence, something that had been bugging her.

"You knew Abel back when. How did he get all mixed up with this?" She didn't ask the question she really wanted to know, not yet.

Harston looked solemn. "We were on the verge of death, dozens of us, held captive—by force or poverty—to build the railroads that made the lifeline out of Granite Run. Conditions were bad, just as bad as the South Rim Bowl, mind you. Abel would do anything to free himself, and the others. They kept us in literal chains, it was—" he broke off and rubbed his eyes. "I had bartered for a spell book from a merchant. I knew something of the magical arts, but I wasn't powerful enough. I needed a partner. That's why we made a deal to summon a demon who could give us freedom." He hung his head. "A dozen people died that day when its power was released. We were fools."

"You summoned Adamophelin to free you." It hit Melinda how Abel—kind, gentle Abel—must've carried that guilt for years. Now the slightly haunted look in his eye made sense.

Harston nodded as they picked their way over the path where violet-tinged stones littered the ground, broken from the undersides of the floating rocks.

"We each absorbed a part of Adamophelin. I wasn't strong enough and Adamophelin started to possess me, fuse with me, *grow* in me. Abel saw what was happening," Harston said. "He knocked me out good, sealed me and Adamophelin up in a casket and took us out down into a cave in the middle of nowhere, and sealed it shut to keep us contained. I stayed there for years, but even in our weakened state, Adamophelin kept me alive, a half ghost-half man. The demon slowly gathered the bit of power we had left to attract whatever we could—Edge creatures, humans— in the hopes that a visitor would eventually free us. Finally, it worked, and we escaped." Harston looked ashen, plagued, Melinda saw, with the same guilt she felt. "Even though Abel carried part of Adamophelin's power, he could handle it, whereas I never could. Adamophelin was obsessed with finding Abel again."

Melinda's head spun. "All this time we were fighting and exterminating monsters, he always suspected you—*Adamophelin*— might come back for him. And I brought the eyestone right to him." Guilt flooded her again.

Feeling bad is not going to help anyone now, she reminded herself and forced her fists to uncoil.

Harston's voice dropped lower as he continued, lost in his memories. "When Adamophelin—and I—were freed, we were half in this world, half in the shadow world. We needed a human helper. It was easy for Adamophelin to find a flesh-and-blood human—Eloise—desperate enough to help. And Abel's soul, well, Adamophelin knew Abel was strong enough to be the centerpiece of its plan, the catalyst for the doorway."

Before Melinda could respond, a cluster of the Edglings around a figure caught her eye on one of the floating rocks, some fifty feet above them.

"Is that ..." her voice faltered.

"Your friend."

Angelo's face was frozen in a twist of agony and half a glare, as only he could do. Edglings half the size of humans crowded around him on the floating rock. Their features blurred save for muscular gray hands, dozens of which disappeared into his chest again and again. No blood or obvious injuries as far as she could see, but his stillness made her think he was dead.

Until his eyes rolled, looking down at her.

"We have to help him." She unholstered her gun.

"That won't work on them. Shadow guts, shadow blood." Harston looked disturbed. "The Edglings are deep into his mind now, he won't be able to fight them off. You could try to shoot him from here, free his soul. If the bullet doesn't do it, maybe a well-aimed rock at his skull."

"I'm not going to let him die here," she snapped and paced beneath the floating rock. No way up, none that she could see. She hurled a stone toward one of the Edglings that was digging into Angelo's body as carelessly as a butcher jaded by his job. It ducked, then continued rummaging.

She swore in frustration. "Free his soul to where?"

Harston shifted in the strange gray cast of the moons' light. "Wherever they go when they ain't here. Back into the ether."

"Comforting," she said dryly and looked up at Angelo again. "There must be a way to save him. I'll drag him back through the membrane after we get the souls. And you're gonna help me."

Silence.

Melinda looked over to see Harston shaking his head, eyes closed. He sank to his knees.

"It's my fault. It's all my fault," he said.

The Edglings flitted closer, drawn to his anguish. Three attached on his back like a hump, making Harston groan.

"Not that again. Stop it now." Melinda's voice rose in alarm. "You're attracting them with your guilty moaning."

She used her pistol to shove the Edglings away but they dissipated and reformed.

"Get!" she said, taking a firm tone as if they were a pack of circling coyotes. She made sure not to look at them too closely and gave Harston a shake. "You're making up for your mistakes now Harston, if you can just stay with me."

He opened his eyes and took a breath, looking for all the world like he had lost something irreplaceable.

"Thanks," he said shakily. He stood and went to the nearest rock. He started hitting it with a shard of stone.

Great, he's losing it. She just needed him to hold it together a little longer.

"Harston," she called cautiously. "What on earth are you doing?"

Once she was next to him, she could see that he had almost knocked off a long, jutting piece of stone, one of the dozens sticking out like massive horizontal icicles. A spear-like piece of crystal and purple stone about the length of her arm dropped to the ground at last.

"Best to have a weapon. You should find something like this. Your guns won't do any good against the Edglings. Matter doesn't work the same way," he said, examining the stone spear. "May I?" He grasped a strand of her hair and yanked before she could protest.

"Try that again and only one of us is leaving this place intact."

"Sorry. Mine is too short." He wound the strand of hair around the sharper end of the stone and knotted it. "I have a theory. Pairing some natural material from our world can help make this weapon more effective. Together the natural and unnatural materials will create a resonance that doesn't follow the rules. Makes a more potent weapon to slow Adamophelin down."

She scowled, rubbing the sore spot on her head. If it might help, it was a small price to pay. "Couldn't you use a piece of your shirt?"

He almost rolled his eyes. "Basics in alchemy. Biological substances are always infused with more power. And they should have some similarity when mixing. Shape or size, for example. Guessing Abel didn't teach you much?"

"Not that line of study. He didn't talk much about what he did before." She cast another look at the mass of shadows over Angelo. "Can you make a weapon to help him?"

"If we weaken or stop Adamophelin, the Edglings should disperse," Harston said, though the doubt was clear in his voice. "Then we can figure out a way to retrieve your friend."

She shot one last look at Angelo floating on the rock. *I'll find a way to get you back*, she swore before they headed up a sharp mountain path to follow the trail of souls.

As they started around the last bend, Harston crouched and pointed. She ducked behind a boulder next to him to get a better vantage point around the bend. Their trail ended several hundred feet ahead in a sheer cliff.

At the end of the cliff, the trail of souls streamed around what looked like a spiderweb, three times as tall as Melinda and the reddish-mauve color of thousands of sunsets after a storm. Eloise's black hair stood out just below the web, eyes dazed and shoulders drooped. Long glittering purple chains wound round her wrists and bound her to a boulder close to them. Edglings writhed in excitement around her.

"There she is." Harston tensed. "Being kept as a back-up soul, mostly likely."

Melinda only needed to know one thing. "How do we stop Adamophelin?"

A flicker passed over Harston's face. "Timing. And luck."

They darted behind the crystal boulders, staying as low as possible, and stopped once they were almost within arm's reach from Eloise. Between the rocks, Melinda glimpsed a figure ahead, about one hundred yards. She reeled. It was what she could only assume was Adamophelin, its back to them.

You've seen worse things, she tried to reassure herself, but couldn't think of a single one.

Adamophelin rose, human-like, the color of a crusted maggot and the size of a stallion, on its back legs. Its limbs gyrated in some energy or reality of their own. It turned for a second, and she glimpsed pinpoints of purple glowing in eyes between folds of white. A mouth that was too long, too loose, flashed dark pink depths from fleshy lips. Everything about it looked wrong, turning her stomach.

"What the heck is it?" she breathed.

"Adamophelin takes many forms," Harston whispered. "I don't know what its truest form is, to be honest. It may not have one."

Adamophelin worked on adhering five glowing orbs in an almost complete circle onto its giant crimson web. Another orb, larger than the rest, wobbled in the center.

The souls.

On the other side of the web, a sliver light reflected like glass and flashed colors. Green leaves, fir trees. Robin-blue sky. The vision of her world wavered, faint as a mirage.

The doorway was about to open.

Chapter Twenty-Five

"Stay calm," Harston whispered even though sweat dripped down his forehead.

Adamophelin lifted the last cannister to the web, where a seventh glowing orb flew out and stuck onto the last open spot in the circle.

"What's it doing?" Melinda hissed.

"The souls are all in place. Any second now, Adamophelin's going to put some of its own power into the web to kickstart the process of widening the doorway. That's when we strike."

She tapped one of the empty canisters on her belt. "How do I work these things?"

"They're just containers infused with its intentions. It's not hard," Harston said, as though she were a student that had failed the most basic of tests. "We infuse objects with sentiment and power all the time. You have a favorite book or gun, something that just feels right? It's like that."

"Save the magic lesson. I just need to know how to get the souls in them."

"Open them near the souls after we disrupt Adamophelin's power."

"Easier said than done." Melinda took stock. She had two guns, two knives, some ammo. The three canisters on her belt, three more in her bag. One boomstick. Enough for a few seconds of a distraction maybe. But she had no idea how long it took to capture a soul, or how Harston was going to take down Adamophelin.

"I told you your weapons won't work here." Harston quietly scooped up a handful of dark purplish gravel. "But I can contain the demon this time." He sounded more determined than she had ever heard him.

"How exactly, are you going to do that?" Melinda glanced back out from behind the rock. Adamophelin was still facing his soul web some hundred yards away. Closer to them, Eloise stood motionless like she was in a trance, the purple chains sparkling on her wrists.

"We'll release Eloise first. Then I'll use her chains on Adamophelin. This time *I'll* be the one possessing it." Harston's face settled into something that reminded her of Angelo. A little vengeful maybe, and a warning bell went off in her. Vengeful people did stupid stuff.

"You lost your marbles? We don't need to possess it, we just to get the souls."

"You want to stop it, right? I can lasso it with those chains. Undo what I did." He spit into the handful of gravel.

"What makes you think it's going to work this time?" She gave him her sternest look.

"I learned from my mistakes. Trust me." Harston shoved the spear of stone into Melinda's hands.

"It's not a real good sign if you need to tell someone to trust you," she said and tested the weight of the crystal spear in her hands. Solid, heavy. Swirled with purple and something more luminescence than quartz. It might have been pretty, in other circumstances.

"Listen," he continued. "Hit Adamophelin whenever you can. Enough that I can get the upper hand."

Melinda shook her head and tried to hand back the spear. "Spear throwing isn't my strong suit. Why don't we create a diversion instead so I can get the souls and we can skedaddle? That way you don't have to face it head on." A simple equation.

This was Adamophelin's territory, so it had the upper hand. That, and it was easily twice the size of them. Better to evade and play it quiet.

"This *will* work," he retorted.

"I hope you know what you're doing," she muttered. "Don't see how some spit is gonna stop him."

"Some of the material from this world and ours, mixed together." Harston showed her his hand of glistening gravel and again she was reminded of Abel and the spark in his eyes when he came up with something new. "Together, they make a substance that doesn't follow the rules of either world, remember? It's easier to persuade the matter, to encourage it to do what you want."

"Like a wish?"

"Like willpower. It should let me break the chains and, hopefully, turn them against Adamophelin. Watch." He tossed the gravel toward Eloise and tensed.

The purple chains around her wrists looked hard as amethyst one second, and like circus smoke the next. The chains vibrated and dropped a second later. Melinda held her breath while Eloise blinked and rubbed her wrists. Adamophelin didn't seem to notice as Eloise limped toward them.

Melinda tensed, ready to sock Eloise for all she had done but stopped herself. It could wait until they had gotten out of this forsaken place. Eloise looked at them, her face streaked with dirt. In one quick motion, she unholstered one of her guns and pointed it at Harston.

"Bastard," Eloise growled. Her eyes were etched with a haunting that Melinda recognized. Harston had the same look, like he'd been hollowed out from the inside.

"I never meant to hurt you," Harston said, raising his hands. "I'm sorry. I wouldn't wish possession on anyone. I know the mental pain it causes. Like every thought, every belief you have gets swept in a tornado. You're left picking up the pieces."

Eloise breathed heavily and glared, looking like she was still a second away from shooting Harston.

"Keep cool—and quiet. We need him to stop Adamophelin," Melinda hissed. "You'll get us all killed. Settle your debts later."

Without a word, Eloise unholstered her second pistol and swung both of them to Adamophelin's back.

"Wait!" Harston said.

Melinda quickly assessed: Eloise straightened her shoulders, undoubtedly taking aim. No time to stop her, and there was probably only a second or two before Adamophelin noticed. She dove back behind a boulder, warped but large enough for cover. Harston did the same.

At least they still had the element of surprise.

"*Eloise.*" Adamophelin's words sounded worse than Melinda could've imagined, like a snake learning to speak through a human mouth. "My dear."

She heard Eloise laugh bitterly. "We had a deal. And you couldn't keep your damn word, demon or man."

"But I did. You had greater power than most can even dream of."

"As your *host,*" Eloise shrieked. "You took my freedom."

"That's the funny thing about possession, dear one," Adamophelin said. It sounded like it was smiling. "It only works if you let it. If you want it. Some people would say it's freeing, to be relieved of the need to make choices."

Eloise fired. One, two, three bullets. Melinda peeked around the bend to see Adamophelin standing like a half-human, half bovine creature, grinning as Eloise emptied her rounds into its thick folds of flesh. The bullets passed through the monster harmlessly.

Damn. At least Adamophelin's attention was drawn. Melinda unhooked a canister with one hand, gripping the spear with the other. She had to get close enough to the web to collect the souls. She shimmied to the side of the rock to spot a narrow ledge by which she could creep up the side along the cliff to get to the web, and still be mostly blocked from Adamophelin's view by one of the blob-like boulders. A sheer drop next to the ledge disappeared into a sea of gray fog. No telling how high they were, but she was sure there was no coming back from a fall like that.

Before Melinda started along the ledge, she saw Eloise toss the pistols to the side and hurl a knife at Adamophelin. It passed through its body and hit the web behind it. The blade melted into a disc against the web and fell with a clatter.

"Now you've hurt my feelings," Adamophelin said, leering. It took a step forward, like a bull that had learned to walk on hind legs. It was both hideous and captivating to watch. Melinda couldn't tear her eyes away.

"Stop!" Harston jumped out. He grabbed the glowing purple chains, dusted with the gravel.

Melinda watched cautiously, as she inched along the ledge. Only a warped boulder stood between her and Adamophelin, but she could glimpse the scene between the rock's crystal arches. She was close to passing Adamophelin now, but it didn't notice her from its periphery.

They might just be able to pull it off.

"Dearest Harston. You just don't know when to quit with your pathetic magic, do you?" Adamophelin said.

Harston shouted and swung the amethyst chain toward Adamophelin. It hit the demon and seemed to meld into its chest. As its flesh rippled around the wound, Adamophelin swelled up and roared. Melinda grimaced at the sound. It was like a cross between a donkey's bellow and a crow's squawk, but amplified enough that she nearly clamped her hands over her ears. Where the chain touched, Adamophelin's skin started to split open, spilling shadows.

It was working.

"Throw the spear now!" Harston's voice cracked. He held on with both hands to his end of the chain, looking for all the world like he was lassoing in the world's biggest stallion.

Next to him, Eloise had scrambled backwards. She turned to run in the direction Melinda and Harston had come from, but Edglings gathered in a growing crowd to block her.

Melinda stepped out from the boulder and hoisted her spear. Whatever magic Harston had used made the knotted hair around it glow orange, like a thread of lava.

It follows your will, she reminded herself as she took aim. *So, I will you to find your mark.*

Before she could move, the glob of rock next to her shifted.

Earthquake. No—the rock ballooned out into her arm, sticky as translucent violet molasses. Trying, she realized, to absorb her and the spear into it. She struggled to pull away but more of the matter gooped around her arms.

"Dear Harston, you have no power here." Adamophelin's grin nearly split its bulging face, making Melinda think of a cross between a giant worm and flattened bison. "You're in my realm now. Do you think I didn't know the instant you arrived here? On my land, on my turf? You might as well be walking on my heart, my eyes. We've been a part of each other for so long. Can't you feel me in you still?"

"You can't use me anymore," Harston snarled and yanked the chain. "I know your games."

The chain held fast, burning a deep purple into Adamophelin's flesh and sending more shadows streaming out of its chest.

"I can't even use your pitiful soul for my doorway," Adamophelin mused. "But maybe your soul matter could be food for my little ones."

Melinda squinted, something catching her eye as she tried to pull herself out of the sticky boulder. "Behind you!"

A stampede of Edglings flowed up the cliff. Eloise scrambled up a rock before the Edglings leapt like monkeys.

Harston wasn't as lucky.

The Edglings swarmed him, plunging their fingers into his stomach and face like blades made of shadows. Harston screamed and flailed backwards, the chain falling from his hands.

"Harston, watch—" Melinda started to shout. She cut off in horror as Harston toppled.

Right over the edge of the cliff.

"Poor, pathetic man," Adamophelin said sadly, letting the slack chain drop. It lifted its hands in the imitation of a shrug, its fingers long and bending like albino grass snakes. "So desperate for any semblance of true power. At least his insecurities make a delicious feast for my Edglings."

Melinda shoved against the sticky rock that folded around her shoulders and head now, but it was no use. It enveloped her completely in a globular cage. She was able to breath somehow, at least. She beat her hands against it, but a force burrowed into her from all sides, like she was trapped in the center of a tornado.

Through her purple cage, she glimpsed Adamophelin turn and her breath caught. Like amethyst jewels, its gaze was full of cold, reptilian calculation and greed. It grinned, and she realized with a sinking feeling that they had been played. They'd never had a chance.

"Dear Mellie," Adamophelin purred. "You will be utterly delightful as my human host. And as Abel's protégé, it's more than fitting."

"In your dreams." Melinda dug her heels in and tried with all her strength to drive the spear forward. The single strand of hair flared like fire and the barrier of the boulder started to give.

"Don't let him in," Eloise hollered nearby. The rock Eloise perched on started to sag, malleable, a second away from enveloping her as well. She jumped off, kicking a few Edglings along the way.

"Don't fret, Mellie. There are perks," Adamophelin continued. "Feel a sample for yourself."

The top of Melinda's rock entrapment opened to let red smoke funnel in, hitting her with a warm tingle that burned away all her fear and frustration. It felt like the buzz of alcohol, surge of coffee, and clarity of tobacco rolled into one but punched up. Her smile came on instinctively as the smoke coursed into her. She lowered the spear. She could hear every miniscule pebble fall, could sense the rush of blood coursing through Eloise's veins. It wasn't just her hearing that was heightened. Her eyesight felt like she was looking through a viewing glass. The warped boulders sparkled prismatically, the moons overhead rippled in texture. She could practically see the motes of this world's air floating, could taste the three-dimensional flavors of the atmosphere.

More importantly, she didn't feel afraid anymore. She didn't feel weak. No wonder Harston and Eloise had served Adamophelin. She was sure she could punch through a wall or stop the whole horde of the Edglings with a snap of her fingers.

"That's right," Adamophelin whispered. "Power. Yours for the taking. All I ask is that we are partners. Together."

But—she tried to ground herself through the surge. *This is wrong*, she told herself.

Why? The rest of her sang back. It felt too good to be wrong.

Because ... she struggled through the intoxication of power but then pinpointed it. *Adamophelin.* The demon hovered at the corners of her mind, watching. *Feeding* off her surge.

"I don't want it," Melinda gasped through the rush. "Take your power...back to hell."

"Shame," the monster said. "You would've been a fun vessel."

Adamophelin retracted. A small red whirlwind shot out of her and back into its fist.

She sank to her knees within the boulder. Empty. Weak. The grief that once consumed her, that she had managed to stuff into a tiny ball inside herself, came back tenfold, along with a swell of despair. A dry sob wracked her.

Focus, she told herself, her fingers tightening around the spear.

"Let's try something else," Adamophelin mused. "It can't hurt to have a little more reinforcement on my doorway. You want to join your friends? Sounds nice, doesn't it?"

She could feel Adamophelin in her head, digging like a rat for an insecurity to gain a foothold so it could undermine and upheave everything she knew. Like it had before with Harston and Eloise.

"Well," Adamophelin breathed, the words gurgling in her head. "This is interesting. You've only ever been with your beloved. Don't you worry that you'll bore him, your lack of expertise? Or that you're missing out?"

Adamophelin constructed a picture in her mind, of Lance embracing Candelaria, of him entwined with Topaz. Melinda ignored the vision and tried to shove the spear through the boulder.

The single hair flashed, and the boulder yielded a little more. The spear was almost halfway through. *Please work*, she thought.

"Or maybe you worry that, deep down, you're a killer?" Adamophelin showed her images of the carnage in the mines, the blown-apart bits of the scorpions and injured snow kraken, and all the other creatures they had destroyed.

"I did what I had to," Melinda shot back. The small hole in the boulder that the spear created grew, and she was almost able to shove her arm through. "And I'm going to stop you and your doorway."

"Dear Mellie, so naïve." It chuckled again, making her skin crawl. "We can make a beautiful symbiotic relationship."

Remember what you're doing, she told herself fiercely, though a wave of exhaustion that turned her limbs to jelly. *And why you're here.*

"You don't have to fight all the time, Mellie. You can take a break from your guilt and your incessant need to try to protect others. You don't have to help Abel, with all of his flaws, his secrets. He's just as tainted as me, you know."

She thought of Abel. Kind. Gentle. Offering her work and teaching her how to fight when she was aimless and reeling from her momma's death. Giving both her and Lance a sense of home, of belonging. Of purpose. "Nothing you say is gonna change my mind about him. He made a mistake. We all do."

"So, boundless devotion guides you," Adamophelin sneered. She thought she detected a hint of jealousy.

"Nope," she said. "Just my gut. And it's all I have. Whatever he had to do, whatever mistakes he made, that doesn't mean he's not worth saving."

"Your gut?" Adamophelin laughed. "Seems like it led you astray. Seeing as how you can't save anyone. Not even your beloved."

Melinda squeezed her eyes shut, trying not to picture Lance's drawn face, how his eyes had fluttered shut outside that decrepit barn.

I'm trying my best, she told herself. *That's all that anyone can do.*

"Maybe your best isn't enough, did you ever think of that?"

"No," she said aloud, hating the quake in her own voice.

"Death follows you wherever you go. You kill creatures without discrimination. Don't you ever consider they might have souls too?"

"Shut it."

"What about saving your family?"

A vision of her momma's face came to her, caved in on itself and rotting. Melinda knew the Edge infection wasn't her fault, knew there wasn't anything that could be done to save her. But that didn't make her feel any better.

She pressed forward once more with her spear and finally stumbled out of the sticky boulder. It hardened behind her. She lifted the spear, which felt like a thousand pounds. With the last of her strength, she threw it some thirty feet, directly at Adamophelin's chest.

She missed.

Adamophelin's laugh rolled over her. "Even with all your guns and toys and fists and words, you're so weak you can't save anyone. Not even yourself."

She had fallen to her knees without realizing it, Eloise's shouts distant. Adamophelin picked up the spear with fingers that looked like bleached meat casings. The strand of hair fused into the spear sparked again and made his fingers bubble. For a second, Melinda was sure the demon would drive the spear into her, ending it all, but Adamophelin growled and dropped it.

"Harston's magic. Inventive," Adamophelin said, glaring at the spear. The demon straightened, easily twice the size of her. From this angle, Melinda could see the rows and rings of triangular teeth that flashed in its pink mouth when it talked.

Adamophelin took several long strides toward her and draped purple chains over her neck like a garland. The chains ground into her skin sharp as shards of glass. They tightened around her, swaddling to the point of being crushing.

Adamophelin leaned down, bringing its jeweled eyes a few inches from Melinda. She tried to reach for her bag, a pistol, anything. But she couldn't move or speak. She could barely feel.

Adamophelin plucked one of the canisters from her belt.

No, Melinda tried to scream.

It flung the canister over the side of the cliff.

She couldn't move as Adamophelin continued to throw the canisters from her belt and bag.

Two. Three. Four. Five. Six.

All the canisters plummeted over the cliff into the gray gloom and with them, the rest of Melinda's hope.

Now she had no way to save the souls.

Sorry, Lance. Sorry, Abel.

A strange relief washed over her, reminding her of the relief she felt when her mother finally passed. Relief was the wrong word maybe. Giving up. Letting go of the heartache of trying. A little part of her looked forward to the end. It had been too hard, for too long. And she was so tired.

I tried and it wasn't good enough.

Them's the cards.

Adamophelin had won.

CHAPTER TWENTY-SIX

Getting her soul siphoned into a monster's web didn't feel nearly as bad as one might suspect.

How about that, Melinda thought drowsily as Adamophelin started to direct her soul onto the web. She rubbed her eyes, a Herculean effort. It felt like she had traveled for days without sleep. Emotions were muted, confused. She could feel her body still, though every inch of her skin was numb as sparks of light floated from her toward the web.

A scream stirred her from her thoughts. Distant, like it was miles away.

"Melinda!"

She turned, squinted. It was a figure, standing at the edge of the cliff. Melinda's vision cleared a fraction and her hands twitched, touching the purple chains heavy around her neck.

It was Eloise, urgent and bloodied. "The spear!" she yelled as she hurled rocks at the onslaught of taunting Edglings. Melinda's gaze fell to the spear, forgotten and dark by her boots, until Adamophelin's voice distracted her.

"You can be with your beloved forever, entwined, for all eternity," Adamophelin whispered. "Death can't promise you that. Life can't promise you that. Only I can promise that. See for yourself."

Melinda turned back to the crimson web in front of her. The lattice of souls formed a doorway that was slowly expanding. Through it, she spotted rivers and streams, mountains and roofs.

She felt like she was on a bird soaring high, glimpsing towns and roaming cattle, fir forests and iced lakes, snowy plains and running deer.

"No one will bother the two of you."

Orbs of the souls buzzed brighter than balls of lightning, restricted by Adamophelin's red web of magic. They reverberated, lit, hypnotic.

Like starlight, she thought. The web was too mesmerizing to turn away from, even as more of the same light flittered from her arms and hands onto the web.

"The doorway will be fully open in a moment or two." Adamophelin sounded immensely pleased. From the corner of Melinda's eye, she saw the demon turn to walk toward Eloise, who still hurled stones from the top of a rock surrounded by Edglings. "Your turn, sweet Eloise. Your delicious soul can speed up the process."

Eloise didn't bother with a response but laughed bitterly—almost hysterically—instead.

"Dear one," the demon went on. "You can follow Harston to an unfortunate demise or be at peace on my web."

"Gunslinger, snap out of it!" Eloise hollered.

"She's too far gone," Adamophelin said smugly and the chains around Melinda's neck grew heavier. As they tightened, her hands bumped her waist, touching a patch of heat.

Her fingers brushed the inside of her pocket, feeling the wooden talisman Lance had given her, the only warm thing in this place. Though her fingers seemed like they were made of wet clay, she managed to pull it out. The figurine stared back at her from between her fingers, bruised and stained with blood.

Lance.

Warmth prickled her fingers as visions came to her. In a split second she saw the flash of Lance's smile, crooked, lit by a desert sunrise or a warm campfire or the flicker of candles. The people they saved. Aunt B's good-natured tsking. Abel's eyes crinkling as he told a joke. Chili and golden brandy. Fresh strawberries and flower stalks. Her momma's face, before she got sick.

Lance, with his sunny way of looking at the world, despite its darkness.

One orb hummed insistently from the web, and Melinda focused on it. The orb buzzed again, angry and bumping against its restraint.

Lance.

Another orb pulsated in unison. The one in the center, glowing brighter than the rest.

And Abel.

They were there, ready to help her. She concentrated on the two throbbing orbs.

"Mellie! You can fight this." Lance's voice came to her, faint like a thought.

"I tried Lance, I did. But it's all over. I got nothing left. And even if we break his doorway I lose the souls—I got no way to get you back home. I can't save you, I can't save anyone."

"You're not done yet, love."

"I can't stop the demon. I'm trapped and I got nothing to fight with."

Abel's voice bubbled up, fainter still. "That's not true."

"Abel!" Melinda's heart twisted at the sound of his familiar voice, though he sounded so weak, and a thousand times fainter than Lance. She strained to hear him.

"You have us … others … me. Use the spear. On me. Break the web."

Melinda's eyes drifted down to the darkened spear by her feet but shook her head. "Abel, I can't. I don't have a canister to save anyone. If I break the web, you're good as gone." A sob wracked her. It was all hopeless. Out of the corner of her eye, Eloise screamed as Adamophelin placed new purple chains around her.

"It's the only way to stop Adamophelin." Abel's voice hung heavy. "I wish I had time to tell you more. I wish you didn't have to pay for my mistakes. You have to …"

"There's got to be another way!" she cried. But the sadness emitting from Abel told her there was no other way.

Lance's voice floated to her, before fading: "You've got to do this, Mellie."

They were right. Even if she couldn't retrieve the souls on the web, she had to try to close Adamophelin's doorway to save the countless others the Edglings would attack if they made it through.

New resolution flowed into her along with a resigned dread. Lance and Abel's soul orbs flickered with increasing speed on the swelling web. Slowly—whether by her will or with the help of Lance and Abel—the sparks of light drifting off her reversed, slamming back into her skin with increasing speed.

Melinda's eyes refocused and she tore off the purple chains, now as brittle as dried parchment. Adamophelin hadn't noticed yet even though it stood a few feet away with its eyes closed.

Eloise slumped weakly against a rock in the violet chains that bound her, with the crowd of Edglings nearly blocking her from view.

Adamophelin's white-yellow fingers rested on the soul web, bubbling and burning bright, like the end of a cigarette. It would funnel its own power into the web to kickstart the process of growing the doorway, Harston had said. And it was working—the doorway was bigger than a wagon wheel now. One Edgling, then another, squeezed through the doorway toward a view of a snow-capped forest.

"Dammit, Adamophelin," she muttered to herself. "It's going to take more than mind games to stop me. To stop us." She felt on the ground for the spear and staggered to her feet.

"You're just as stubborn as Abel," Adamophelin said irritably without opening its eyes. "You would have been a lovely addition. I had hoped for a better fate for you than fodder but ah well."

The Edglings surrounding Eloise turned toward Melinda, faster than a waterfall after a thunderstorm, following Adamophelin's will as instantly as a thought.

Melinda pointed the spear at Adamophelin, preparing to lunge.

But Harston said it wouldn't kill Adamophelin, just slow it down. Abel's words came back to her, and she looked at the web instead.

Abel's soul reverberated at its center like a prized gem.

Tears pricked at Melinda's eyes. She tried not to think about how she'd never feel Lance's embrace again, never hear his drawling voice. She wasn't ready to say good-bye to either of them. And she never would be.

She threw the spear at Abel's soul in the center of the web as the Edglings descended. This time, she didn't miss.

CHAPTER TWENTY-SEVEN

When the spear hit its mark, Abel's orb exploded outwards.

The force of the impact sent Melinda flying backwards. The ground scraped beneath her, then, nothing. She grabbed a rock just in time as she slipped from the cliff's edge. She kicked her feet at the gray cloud yawning below her, searching for a foot hole. Above her, the blast had sent Eloise tumbling and disintegrated her purple chains.

"*No!*" Adamophelin bellowed in fury, doubling over for a split second. It straightened to yank the spear out of the web and throw it to the side.

The splintered lines of the web, without a center, began to fall and the doorway shrunk rapidly. Adamophelin grabbed the orbs of souls and shoved them back into place, frantically trying to rebuild the web. Ignoring both her and Eloise, the Edglings scrambled to squeeze through the doorway, now the size of a pie.

Melinda tried desperately to find a foothold, anything that would let her hoist back onto the cliff. But the rock was smooth against her boots and her grip was sliding.

Eloise had picked herself up, her hair in disarray, fringed jacket shredded from the blast. Not far from her, the spear rested on the ground, pulsating a grayish white—the same color as the soul orbs. Maybe, Melinda suspected, some of Abel's power had fused with it.

"Eloise," Melinda shouted. "Try the spear again!"

Eloise's eyes narrowed and she grabbed the weapon. Adamophelin turned. Its flattened nostrils flared as it rose its free hand, summoning a blob of rock to bend toward her. Eloise ran faster than Melinda thought was possible.

"Eat this, dog meat!" Eloise screamed and threw the spear into Adamophelin's throat.

Adamophelin roared. The gray light from the spear exploded into the monster's center. Adamophelin locked stares with Melinda one last time in an expression she couldn't read as its purple orbs dilated.

"*Abel*—" it hissed.

Melinda closed her eyes as Adamophelin blew up. Flaps of white chunks rained around them and down over the cliff into the gray. A stench like month-old fish wrapped in manure nearly made her retch. Not that she had to worry about that much longer, since her fingers had gone numb from grasping the rock. She was a second or two from plunging into the nothingness below.

No way out now, but at least we stopped Adamophelin, Melinda thought. Aunt B would be safe. And so would everyone in Five Peaks, everyone she had ever met. She'd join up with Lance and Abel's souls now, she hoped. She closed her eyes, preparing for the fall.

Before her last finger slipped, a hand cuffed her wrist. Eloise huffed over her and yanked her up. With the lift, Melinda found a toehold to get herself over the side and stumbled next to Eloise.

"Close one, gunslinger," Eloise wiped the sweat off her face. "We gotta get out—"

Melinda ignored Eloise and raced to the crumbling soul web. Behind it, the doorway to their world was a pinpoint. The Edglings stood nearby, watching.

"Lance!" Melinda hollered. "Wait!"

"You're going the wrong way!" Eloise shouted.

The web was an indistinct mass now, a reddish cloud that reminded Melinda of the first time she had seen Harston, way back when at Abel's. One by one, the souls flew off. They soared like dandelion seeds on the wind off the side of the cliff before disappearing into the gray mist. Melinda's hand dashed to her pocket. It was a fool's idea maybe. But she had to try. She pulled out the wooden carving that Lance had made and swung open its head where some dried bits of tobacco remained.

"They're just containers infused with its intentions," Harston had said. *"We infuse objects with sentiment and power all the time."*

She held up the wooden carving to the collapsing web, where only two souls remained, ready to fly off. "I got no idea if this will work but please, Lance if you're there, c'mon over."

She reached out to the pair of souls, one of which buzzed a feeling of familiarity. Like home. She lifted the figurine to it. It shook and separated from the web as the other soul detached and dissipated. Lance's soul started to float away like the others but moved toward Melinda's hand instead. The wooden figure flared. The web disintegrated entirely, and the doorway to their world winked out.

"Damn gunslinger." Eloise approached Melinda as the ground rattled. She spat at the spot where the web had been. "How're we getting out of here now?"

"The Edglings ..." Melinda glanced warily at the watchful figures. Some perched on boulders, looking down at them. Others stood in a loose circle.

"We don't have to worry about them none. When that ... *thing* possessed me, I could feel the Edglings under its control," Eloise said. "Now that their pappa demon's gone, they're free."

The ground shook again, a warning. The double moons had moved down to the horizon now.

"Let's get out of here," Melinda said.

"The way we came?"

Melinda shook her head. "Harston knew a magic spell to open the membrane and get us home. Without a way to break that barrier, we're stuck ..." She trailed off when she noticed the Edglings around them scurried backwards when she looked at them. Almost like they were scared. Of her.

"I'm not going to hurt you," Melinda told them, hardly believing what she was saying. "As long as you leave us alone. This is your home. We just want to leave."

Eloise narrowed her eyes at them and gave a joyless chuckle. "Since the demon is gone, looks like they're looking to us as their new mommas."

"Great. We just want to leave." Melinda threw up her hands in exasperation. "What are they doing now?"

The Edglings had lifted the spear and moved it closer to her. She examined it. The purple stone was now translucent. It still glowed a gray-white, like Abel's soul orb had. Maybe a little part of him was infused in it. She didn't dare hope that he was in there somehow, but in any case, she had a feeling it might work against the membrane.

"I think they're trying to tell us this will help get us back home," Melinda said. She nodded a thanks to the Edglings and turned to Eloise. "But we got one stop to make first."

As they ran down the cliff, the wooden figurine bumping warm against her pocket, Melinda told herself again what she could scarcely believe.

Adamophelin—and its doorway—were destroyed.

CHAPTER TWENTY-EIGHT

Melinda leaned over Lance's snoozing body, nearly jumping out of her skin.

"Give the man some room, Miss Melinda," Gene said, entering the Edge Riders' tent. Behind him, the glow from the sunrise permeated through the flapping entrance, warming Lance's face.

"How does this work?" She gripped the wooden statue, a part of her afraid to let it go. What if she went through all of that just for his soul to dissipate into the ether, like the others? The Edge Riders had drenched the room in a heavy incense, promising the soul transfer would be safe, but doubts still crowded her mind.

Gene gently took the wooden statue, eyes bright as grass in the sunlight. He held it to Lance's mouth and opened it. The tiniest whiff puffed up.

Melinda shifted. "What's happening? Is it working?"

"Sure is, I can see the soul particles going back," Gene said. "It'll take a minute or two."

She gripped Lance's hand and waited.

A throat cleared in the flapping entrance of the tent. Eloise hovered, her face and clothes as dirty as Melinda's. She glanced at the bed next to Lance's where Angelo lay unconscious, not quite dead but not quite alive either.

"You think your friends can fix him?" Eloise's voice was tired, not barbed as it usually was.

"Maybe," Melinda said. "These Edge Riders have seen a lot of monster sicknesses. If he wakes, I'll make sure to let him know you helped carry him out of the Edge, saving his life."

"Least she could do," Gene murmured. Melinda shot him a look.

"I have no qualms about killing to survive." Eloise drew up her chest, a tiny flicker of defensiveness in her voice. "It's a shame his lover ended the way he did, but if the cost of my freedom is a bullet, so be it."

"Don't know if we see eye to eye on that, but you saved my life back there and I won't forget it," Melinda said. "I'll tell Sheriff Mathings to have your name cleared. You want a fresh start, I know a place that would be more welcome than most."

"You can go off, gunslinger," Eloise said, thorny as a cactus. "I don't need your help or your pity."

"Offer stands, if you ever change your mind."

"I got other plans. Our debt is settled. Hope not to see y'all around." Eloise strode out.

"Good riddance," Gene said quietly to her receding back.

A current seemed to run through Melinda's fingers as Lance's hand flexed.

His eyes opened.

Dark blue, like a stormy ocean. Blinking. But clear, taking in the inside of the tent and Angelo's sleeping figure next to him. Lance's forehead furrowed at the sight, until his gaze landed on her. His forehead smoothed. He smiled.

She bent down and hugged him, words failing her.

"Mellie." Lance winced and touched his chest. "Last thing I remember was the barn."

"Not the soul web? The demon?"

He shook his head. "Just the barn, everyone shouting. It was like being underwater. You were ..." he looked troubled. "In the fire."

"Take it easy," she managed, trying not to bawl her eyes out from relief. "Your soul's restored. That's got to feel good."

"Think I aged a hundred years, but I'm all right." Color flooded back into his face. He sat up, grabbing her hand.

"Thought I'd never see you again," she said. She watched him read her gaze and sense the weight of what she—they all—had gone through, and his grip tightened. They kissed. She drank in the warmth of his skin that felt like rolling up in her favorite blanket, his taste that made her feel like she could sink forever into a sweet oblivion. He was solid, real. Alive.

Gene cleared his throat and took off his bowler hat, beaming.

Lance pulled back. "Abel?"

"I tried. I couldn't ... I'm sorry." Her grief slammed back into place and his face fell.

Sorrow folded into the spaces around his cheeks, and he looked steadily down at the woven blanket on his knees.

"The other souls were lost too," she said quietly. "But the demon—and its doorway—are gone for good."

After a long moment, Lance nodded, rubbing his temples.

"Condolences for your loss," Gene said timidly. "If it's any consolation, Miss Aine always says the dead continue on, one way or another. And it sounds like your friend's soul was a bright one."

"He was. I couldn't have asked for anyone better to help me along in life. Not much more we can do now, except head home." The sound of Lance's voice cracking and hollow, as though he was trying not to break down entirely, made Melinda's eyes mist up.

"Five Peaks isn't going to feel much like home anymore. Not without Abel," Melinda couldn't help but say as Lance climbed out of the cot, looking stronger by the second. Their eyes met, solemn.

"You could always join the Edge Riders," Gene offered. "They said they'd be happy for the help. A few of them are going in the direction of High Hawk next week and offered to take me home. I'd figure I'll learn what I can from them until then. Nothing more valuable than knowledge, after all."

Topaz burst into the tent, beelining for Angelo's sleeping form. "Any change?"

"Not yet," Gene said. "They're mixing up something to dispel the shadows that settled into his soul. But they said he needs to fight."

"Well, my hon's nothing if not a fighter. I know he'll come out of it." Topaz sighed and spotted Lance. She broke into a smile. "Glad one of you is up, at least. That gives me hope."

Someone passed at the opening, and Melinda glimpsed Bina's curls and her wave. Topaz nodded to her and—Melinda couldn't believe it—blushed.

"You thinking of sticking around?" Melinda said.

"Yeah. The Riders are ... interesting. Can't go anywhere until this geezer wakes up anyhow." Topaz gave Angelo's shoulder a gentle squeeze. "I promised the Edge Riders we'd help them track their more elusive swarms once he's up and about."

"So, you're getting into the monster-hunting business," Lance mused. "Good thing we're retired or I'd say we have some competition. I already feel bad for those critters."

"Could be they don't all need to be hunted," Melinda piped up. The Edglings, at least, had shown that they didn't mean harm, not necessarily. Maybe some of the creatures could be left alone, if they weren't hurting anyone.

Lance cast her a curious look. "Take a hit to the head, lately?"

Topaz grinned at both of them. "Don't be strangers."

"Give Angelo our thanks," Melinda said as Topaz threw her arms around her and planted a kiss on her cheek.

"Appreciate your help keeping me alive," Gene said to them. "Never thought I'd see as much as I did. And survive it."

"You did good." Melinda said as Gene embraced her and then Lance.

Melinda snoozed on the cot while Lance prepped the horses and supplies for the long ride home. They ate a quick meal and said the rest of their goodbyes. She had hoped to see Tsen, but they had gone off to monitor the foothills and make sure Melinda's trip to the Edge hadn't provoked any new critters. She watched Lance scratch Mud's nose and hoist up, savoring the sight of him moving with ease. He reached into his pocket to pull out his pouch of tobacco. "What?"

"Can't get enough of seeing you," she said, strapping the stone spear from the Edge on Pepper's bag. The spear had stopped glowing, so she thought any chance of Abel's power remaining there was small to zilch.

"What is that, a souvenir?"

"Maybe something. Maybe nothing," she replied.

She mounted, the exhaustion hitting her like a wall despite her nap. Aunt B and the town that waited for them—and the new house and farm they'd settle into—felt so far away, so different than the reunion she'd pictured. She glanced at Lance and saw the same pain in him, mirroring her own. He tried to smile at her, but it was a new kind of smile with a sadness mixed in that might never go away.

"You ready?" she asked.

He nodded, solemn. "Always. With you."

Pepper and Mud started up their easy walk, their backs to the rising sun as they headed home.

ABOUT THE AUTHOR

KC Grifant is a Southern Californian author who writes internationally published horror, fantasy, science fiction and weird west stories for podcasts, anthologies and magazines. Her writings have appeared in *Andromeda Spaceways Magazine*, *Unnerving Magazine*, *Cosmic Horror Monthly*, *Tales to Terrify*, the *Lovecraft eZine*, Siren's Call Publications and many others. She's also contributed to dozens of anthologies, including: *Chromophobia*; *Musings of the Muse*; *Dancing in the Shadows - A Tribute to Anne Rice*; *Field Notes from a Nightmare*; *The One That Got Away - Women of Horror Vol 3*; *Six Guns Straight From Hell*; *Trembling with Fear Year 1*; *Shadowy Natures - Tales of Psychological Horror*; *Beyond the Infinite - Tales from the Outer Reaches*; and the Stoker-nominated *Fright Mare: Women Write Horror*. A member of SFWA and a co-founder of the San Diego HWA chapter, she enjoys chasing a wild toddler and wandering through beachside carnivals. For details, visit www.kcgrifant.com or @kcgrifant on the social networks.

Website: www.KCGrifant.com
Social media: Instagram, Twitter, Facebook, TikTok: @kcgrifant
Newsletter: https://scifiwri.com/contact/

ACKNOWLEDGEMENTS

This debut novel would not have been possible without the support and kindness of many, and I am deeply thankful for them.

Heather, Steve and the rest of the team at Brigids Gate Press gave this story a home, for which I will be forever grateful; Michelle's eagle eye spotted excellent edits; and Luke at Carrion House created a truly stunning cover that turned out better than I had ever hoped.

I was lucky enough to have English teachers (way back when) who appreciated imaginative fiction and facilitated spaces for experimental writing. Thank you Ms. Swope; Mrs. Luckoff; Mrs. Leonard-Peace; Mr. Smith; Mrs. Rosenthal and many others—your enthusiasm meant the world.

The fantastic indie horror writing community, both online and in-person, as well as the Horror Writers Association, became what felt like my first writerly "home." I have met many friends through HWA, including the entire San Diego chapter; the Obsidian Flash group (thank you, Donna!); mentors and instructors Greg, Moaner; and so many others.

It's especially helpful to receive initial enthusiasm for a debut novel while persevering through inevitable rejections. Kate Jonez was an early believer in this story, giving me confidence that there might be readers interested a Weird West feminist adventure; Anna La Voice gave great feedback and edits; and Eugen Bacon and Elyssa Berger were fans of previous short stories featuring these characters.

Finally, there can never be words enough to thank my close circle of "cheerleaders." All my gratitude goes to them:

To Paul and Irene, for providing enthusiastic feedback on drafts of the book and generally supporting me – thank you!

To Jason, for sharing an interest in the fantastical and signing us up for Doomtown card game competitions, which inspired my intrigue in the Weird West. The many evenings and weekends you spent watching a wild toddler while I wrote helped me immensely. You are my "density!"

To my daughter, even though she's a while from being able to read this, thank you for helping me see things in a new light, including my writing.

Lastly, the book simply would not have been possible without Vivian, who worked tirelessly on many rounds of edits and brainstorms, and who loves the characters as much, if not more, than me. I can't capture how much I appreciate your amazing edits, invaluable feedback and relentless support. A million thanks, more than I can ever say.

MORE FROM BRIGIDS GATE PRESS

Paperback ISBN: 978-1-957537-05-4

Arthur, whose life was devastated by the brutal murder of his wife, must come to terms with his diagnosis of dementia. He moves into a new home at retirement community, and shortly after, has his life turned upside down again when his wife's ghost visits him and sends him on a quest to find her killer so her spirit can move on. With his family and his doctor concerned that his dementia is advancing, will he be able to solve the murder before his independence is permanently restricted?

A Man in Winter examines the horrors of isolation, dementia, loss, and the ghosts that come back to haunt us.

Paperback ISBN: 978-1-957537-10-8

During the Spring Equinox underneath London, four people enter the caves, but only one will survive. Each trespasser must battle their own demons before facing the White Lady who rises each year to feed on human flesh.

Paperback ISBN: 978-1-957537-21-4

Welcome to the Weald.
The Five Turns of the Wheel has begun.
With each Turn, blood will be spilled,
and sacrifices will be made.
Pacts will be made ... and broken.
Will you join the Dance?

In the Weald, the time has come for The Five Turns of the Wheel.
Tommy, Betty and Fiddler, the sons of Hweol, Lord of Umbra,
have arrived to oversee the sacred rituals ... rituals brimming with
sacrifice and dripping with blood.
Megan Wheelborn, daughter of Tommy, hatches a desperate plan
to free the people of the Weald from the bloody and cruel grip of
Umbra, and put an end to its murderous rituals. But success will
require sacrifice and blood as well. Will Megan be able to pay the
price?

Paperback ISBN: 978-1-957537-31-3

Stewartville. A town living in the shadow of the prisons that drive its economy. Haunted by the ghosts of its past. Cursed by the dark secrets hidden beneath. A town so entwined with the prisons waiting outside the city limits that it's impossible to imagine one without the other, or to ever imagine escaping either.

When a teenage boy digs into the history of the town, he discovers a tunnel system beneath Stewartville, passageways filled with dark secrets. Secrets leaning not to freedom but to unrelenting terror.

Stewartville. Where the convicts aren't the only prisoners.

Visit our website at: www.brigidsgatepress.com

Printed in the USA
CPSIA information can be obtained
at www.ICGtesting.com
LVHW040459051223
765560LV00003B/331